I0818601

An Uncommon Affair

A Novel of Regency Romance

Teresa Sweeney

Courting Romance Publishing
California

An Uncommon Affair is a work of fiction. Names, characters, places, and incidents are the products of the author's imagination or are used fictitiously. Any resemblance to actual events, locales, or persons, living or dead, is entirely coincidental.

Published in the United States by Courting Romance Publishing

ISBN 978-1-940319-02-5

First Edition

Cover Photography by Christina & Jason Brusaca

By Teresa Sweeney

Always Rebecca

A Love Match, Indeed!

An Uncommon Affair

To my parents. Loving, supportive, generous.
Thank you, Mama Dee and Papa Ern.

An Uncommon Affair

Chapter One

The Duke of Aubry's daughter, Lady Catherine Brentwood, wiggled herself into the soft red velveteen squabs, shifting this way and that on her seat, trying to find a comfortable position. Normally, with some engaging discourse, the carriage ride from London to her great-uncle's estate, Beaumont Manor, was considered a short duration compared to traveling to Aubry, her home in the north country. She had journeyed home enough times to consider an hour's ride in a well-sprung carriage easy to tolerate. However, after enduring the overwrought concerns of her companion, Miss Rachel Morgan, she was ready to change her opinion on what she considered easy. The short trip had become tedious and taxed her patience. She was more than ready to reach her destination and remove herself from Rachel's singular company.

Her traveling companion was a distant cousin on her mother's side with little to recommend her in terms of title or fortune. The Duchess of Aubry had agreed to sponsor Rachel and help make her fashionable. Unfortunately for Catherine, the duchess believed her daughter was the means to make that happen. The duchess ordered her daughter to keep Rachel attached to her at all times, hoping Catherine's popularity would rub off on the shy young girl.

Catherine was the only daughter and the youngest child of the Duke and Duchess of Aubry. She had made her *come-out* two years ago and was considered one of the *ton's* jewels. Her beauty and wit instantly marked her a *diamond of the first water* among the aristocracy. She exuded a confidence that no debutante was known to own and before long, Lady Catherine had a host of admirers vying for her favor. After her first Season, she earned the reputation of one whose hand was impossible to capture in marriage, the *on dit* was that her father, the duke, found no suitor exceptional enough to wed his daughter.

The real truth was that Catherine was not inclined towards any of her admirers. Although they were eager to please her, professing openly of their ardor, she knew they secretly coveted her because of her connections and substantial dowry. She had yet to feel that any of them were genuine in their addresses and she found herself little affected by the lot. The attributes that made her extremely eligible, also placed her in the rare position of being able to select her choice of husband.

Catherine, like all children of the aristocracy, spent her nursery days under the supervision of her nannies and governesses. Aside from the occasional summons where she was commanded to present herself to her parents, her interaction with them was minimal, so she was not overly pressured to marry during her first or second Season. She knew as long as her reputation was above reproach, she had at least two to three years to do as she pleased, before she drew speculation from the *ton* about her unmarried state. The duke would then intervene and contract a marriage for her. She expected her parents loved her, for they had never raised a harsh word or hand, but their pride would never allow their daughter to become a spinster, nor would they relinquish using her to make a strategic alliance through marriage. It was the way of the *ton*, after all. Marriage was the most effective method to keep the aristocratic bloodlines pure and its wealth both intact and increasing.

The most stable influence in her life had always been her grandmother, the Dowager Duchess of Aubry. She seemed to appreciate Catherine's strong will and caliber of wit. Her grandmother had often commented that Catherine reminded her of herself during her heyday: a young girl not easily cajoled, intelligent of mind, and overconfident. A picture of her grandmother painted after her marriage to the duke was a constant reminder of just how much Catherine resembled her. In their youth, both owned glorious golden locks, a smooth complexion, luminous blue eyes, a straight nose and heart shaped lips, all packaged in a shapely body.

Catherine's two older brothers cared little for having her around when she was a child and disliked her cousin, Edward, even more, for whose bidding she was presently engaged. Catherine's and Edward's fathers were brothers. Catherine's father as the eldest inherited the dukedom, while Edward's father as a third son was expected to follow tradition and earn his living as a clergyman. The Duke of Aubry most assuredly planned to secure a parish for his third son, until that son had the audacity to fall in love and marry beneath his station. Adding to the insult, he married a commoner and had the effrontery to engage in trade. Edward suffered the most from the marriage that cast the third son of a duke and his family from polite society. Catherine's brothers and cousins teased and bullied Edward to distraction for being below them in stature. Catherine, a mere child when Edward made his majority, was aware of his mistreatment, but she never pitied him. It seemed he had grown stronger and smarter for every abuse her brothers directed at him. She admired the way his courage never wavered and over the years her affection for him increased.

She spent many hours in Edward's company for he had grown an attachment to her in her infancy. More times than not, she sided with Edward against her arrogant and discriminative brothers. Both Catherine and Edward were particular favorites of their grandmother and paid her the most attention. She possessed many cherished memories of the time they spent together and over the years, a sincere affection developed between them. The dowager enjoyed her audacious granddaughter and favored Edward who reminded her so much of her third son. She doted on them and did her best to guide and help them. She supported Catherine in her quest to choose her own suitor and did everything in her power to aid Edward's entrée into the *bon ton*. She knew the aristocracy was prejudiced against the merchant class who, with their newfound wealth, tried to break into the upper echelons of society by marrying off their daughters to destitute lords.

However, Edward was a Brentwood descended from a line of dukes and the dowager saw no reason for her peers to abjure his company. Unfortunately, when Edward was a child he engaged in fisticuffs with the current Duke of Aubry's eldest son and bested him. The duke never forgot the affront and took pleasure in forswearing his nephew when he tried to engage the *ton*. It was the duke's abjuration more than Edward's connection to trade that placed him at the fringes of Society. However, no one ever gave Edward the *cut-direct*, the dowager more so than her ducal son, held too much influence to offend.

Nevertheless, Edward felt the *ton's* censure, exceedingly so, when he lost his parents in an awful carriage accident. Edward had just made his majority and the death of his parents made him feel unsure of his place in the world. The dowager wasted no time in settling her vulnerable grandson's doubts about his position in Society. She reminded Edward of his noble blood and character. Then, she secured the aid of her good friend, the Duke of

Hartford, to mentor and champion her grief-stricken grandson into the *ton*.

Even with the Duke of Hartford's support, Edward learned his business association with the merchant class placed him *beyond the pale*. He found himself rebuffed at balls and galas by noble parents who had no desire to marry their daughter to someone that would remove her from the sphere from which she was born. Eventually, he turned his attentions to the company of widows and paramours. These experienced women welcomed him cheerfully and regaled him a most proper and considerate lover. Eventually, he was discussed widely enough in parlours for a reputation to be born that preceded him wherever he went. Mothers began to fear he would ravish their daughters, while *Corinthians* and *dandies* worshipped him for his conquests.

Now, thanks to the dowager's brother, the Marquis of Beaumont, Edward was receiving the respect he craved all his life. The unmarried and aging marquis named Edward heir to his title and fortune, bestowing on him the honorary title of Lord Felton. As soon as the Prince Regent acknowledged Edward as the marquis's heir, the *marriage mart mamas* marked him highly eligible and the *bon ton* thrust invitation after invitation upon him, conveniently forgetting his ties to trade and his reputation as a rake.

Catherine knew his reputation was all a humbug. Over the years, she had spent enough time with him to know that he was far from sinister. He was a true gentleman and she trusted him completely. She held

Edward in the highest esteem, owning a strong affection for him, so when he summoned her to Beaumont Manor she came without question.

It was rumored that Edward was hosting a party and that one lady in particular was invited as a possible contender for him to wed. Her uncle, the Marquis of Beaumont, was pressuring Edward to marry and produce an heir. It appeared Edward was getting cold feet for she knew no other reason for why he urgently requested her presence. Catherine supposed he knew she would come regardless of the reason. However, Edward did not know that Miss Rachel Morgan would be accompanying her. Their grandmother had suggested that Rachel might be thrown into the mix as a candidate. Miss Morgan was a sweet biddable girl and if nothing else had a pretty face to recommend her. Catherine silently laughed thinking if Rachel knew why she was being dragged along to Beaumont Manor, she would go into hysterics. Miss Morgan was a meek girl and the thought of accompanying Catherine without a proper invitation to herself had nearly put her into a swoon. Catherine knew Edward would not fancy her, his tastes ran similar to her own. Like Catherine, Edward would desire someone to challenge and inspire him, not someone to abide him.

Catherine was in no mood to wait for the footman to lower the carriage step when they finally arrived at Beaumont Manor. Weary and anxious to see who made up

Edward's house party, she practically jumped out of the traveling coach when it came to a stop. Her rash exit alarmed Rachel into choking on the air she gasped.

Catherine turned to look at her coughing cousin through the carriage door and asked, "Rachel, Are you all right?"

Rachel, seeing that Catherine did not injure her person upon her indecorous departure, managed to calm herself and respond, "Yes, my lady, though you did put the fear in me. Why did you not wait for the footman to lower the footstep?"

Catherine rolled her eyes, quelling her frustration over having Rachel for a companion. She found her cousin tiresome. Rachel's countenance was far opposite from her own. Catherine loved excitement and activity, where Rachel preferred the quiet and calm. Catherine was fearless and looked for adventure, while Rachel was shy and leaned towards solace. The past weeks spent introducing Rachel into polite society had become dreary for Catherine who discovered she had to hold, figuratively speaking, Rachel's hand throughout the Season's ball and fetes. It was not enough that she introduced Rachel to her friends or included Rachel in her entertainments. She learned that Rachel was too timorous to engage in any type of conversation or enjoyment. Catherine found herself with a burdening shadow instead of a lively companion. Her tolerance was more than tested. She was hopeful the small sojourn at Beaumont Manor would place Rachel into a comfortable enough situation that she could take a break from her wearisome company. It was not that she disliked the girl. Catherine actually thought her quite charming and intelligent when she was not intimidated by her superior society, but unless Catherine could get others to see her at her best, the chances of her attracting a suitor were becoming excessively slim. To add injury to her meekness, the *bon ton* were speaking maliciously of her, saying that Miss Morgan had nothing to recommend her, not even a personality. *The on dit* was moving through the grapevine faster than Catherine could curtail it.

Catherine waited while the footman turned down the carriage steps for Rachel to exit. She watched her cousin cautiously disembark and then stop when she reached the portico steps. Catherine knew Rachel balked because she feared she would be barred from entrance. Her patience exhausted, Catherine grabbed Rachel's hand and yanked her forward admonishing, "Do not start again, Rachel. You are my guest and you will see that his lordship will bid you welcome."

Catherine turned when Beaumont's butler greeted her. She pulled Rachel across the threshold and proceeded to the drawing room where she expected everyone had convened. She called over her shoulder to the butler, "I know my way and do not wish to be announced. Have our bags taken to our rooms and see to stabling my cattle and feeding my footmen. I know I need not ask, but I shall not be accused of failing to care for my property and servants."

Catherine entered the drawing room, towing Rachel along. She was surprised not to see Edward in the parlour, but was pleased nonetheless to see her great-uncle, the Marquis of Beaumont. Dropping Rachel's hand, she walked briskly towards him leaving Rachel unattended in her wake. She exclaimed, "Uncle! You are looking exceptionally well. I hope my cousin has been of service to you and is proving himself worthy to be your heir."

Beaumont laughed and replied, "My dear Catherine, I am glad you have come to join our small party. You need not concern yourself on how Edward manages, for a more proficient and attentive heir I could not have wished. Who have you brought with you?"

Before Catherine could answer, she heard a familiar voice and upon seeing Lord Westfield, she cried, "Maw-ree. I did not know you would be here."

Lord Jonathan Shelby, the Earl of Westfield admonished in a cheerful fashion, "Catherine! You must desist with calling me 'Mari.' It was a childish endearment that should have been forgotten eons ago. You put my wife in distemper with every exaltation that you make to me."

Catherine gasped. It had never occurred to her that a childhood nickname could cause anyone an offense. Catherine's father, the Duke of Aubry, and Jonathan's father, the then Earl of Westfield, were hunting partners and friends. Jonathan used to accompany his father when he visited the duke's ancestral home to hunt in his parks. Jonathan was too young at the time, barely six years old to join in the excursion, so he spent his days with Catherine, two years his junior in the nursery. On one of these days, Catherine had managed to talk Jonathan into playing the groom in a marriage ceremony. Later, when their fathers commanded their appearance before dinner for an interview, Catherine was quick to inform her father that she was married and planned to return to the Westfield ancestral home with her husband upon his departure. The duke was livid while his lordship, the Earl of Westfield, laughed. A further interview with the young aristocrats enlightened the worried parents that Catherine's announcement was the result of a mock marriage ceremony. Needless to say, Catherine and the heir to the Westfield earldom were properly chaperoned in the future. A year later, Jonathan left the nursery and quickly forgot the episode; however, Catherine treasured the memory and quickly made him into the gallant she knew him to be. Their society diminished when Jonathan joined his father in the hunt and Catherine's interest took her company in other directions.

Not until last year when Edward invited Catherine to a small sojourn at her own family estate did she come across Jonathan again. At the time, her cousin Edward was actively pursuing Lady Elinor, the current Lady Westfield. Edward had high hopes of breaking what he thought to be a jejune ardor between Jonathan and Elinor. He invited Catherine hoping her beauty and past history with the earl, would distract him enough from Elinor to cause discontent between them. His plan was unknown to Catherine, but she unwittingly aided his cause when she called Jonathan *Mari*, the French word meaning husband. The childhood misnomer caused Elinor to doubt

Jonathan's love for her. Edward found he cared too much for Elinor to see her in pain and in hindrance to his own wishes, he explained the history behind Lord Westfield and his cousin, Catherine. Though Edward lost Elinor to Jonathan, he felt amply rewarded in gaining the Earl and Countess of Westfield as his most cherished and trusted friends.

Catherine found herself speechless after being reprimanded by Jonathan, a first for those who knew her. Jonathan started laughing, before Catherine offered, "I am sorry, Jonathan. I did not know."

He took both her hands in his and said, "Do not become sullen. I know you meant no harm, but you must refrain from further use of the endearment and place the cherished memory away as I have done."

At that moment, Elinor walked into the parlour escorted by Lord Felton. Upon seeing her husband holding Catherine's hands in his, Elinor balked and raised an eyebrow, glaring at her husband. Catherine, along with the others in the room, found the situation too humorous to hold back their chuckles. Jonathan with a smirk on his own face, quickly dropped Catherine's hands and briskly walked towards his wife to beg her pardon.

Edward was intuitive enough to realize that Elinor had become the brunt of his cousin's folly and to distract his guests from laughing at Elinor, he exclaimed, "Cousin!

I thought you had changed your mind and chose not to attend."

"No, not at all," replied Catherine who checked her own mirth and regained her composure. Pulling her shoulders back and raising her chin up, she presented a regal posture to her cousin. "You know that I would at least allow you to try to amuse me, Edward. I was detained because mama had visitors."

She added, "Allow me to introduce you to Miss Rachel Morgan. She is a distant cousin of ours. I have discovered that mama is her godmother. She sponsored her *come-out* and I have decided to take her under my wing."

Edward thought the young girl common but pretty. She had an oval face with large brown eyes, a small nondescript nose and brown hair to match. She was a petite girl, rather shy, not unusual for a young debutant. He bowed to her and said, "It is a pleasure to meet you, Miss Morgan. I am glad you have arrived in time to enjoy our Spring Festival."

Rachel blushed and replied, "Thank you, my lord, for receiving me; however, I do feel that I am intruding upon your festivities."

Catherine barked, "Oh, do not start that again Rachel!" She looked at Edward. "It took me a day and a half to convince her that you would welcome her. In fact, I told her that you would offer her the first set of dances at your country-ball in honor of her *come-out*. Do not make me a liar, Edward."

Edward checked his temper. He had wanted to ask Lady Anne, the woman whom he hoped to pay his addresses for the opening set, but he would now only embarrass everyone if he refused to offer for Miss Morgan. With a tight smile, Edward looked at Miss Morgan and said, "I do hope you will do me the honor and save the first set of dances for me, Miss Morgan."

Rachel blushed, bowed her head before replying, "Of course, my lord. The honor is mine."

Edward introduced Rachel to his uncle, the Marquis of Beaumont, and then to the rest of his party: the Duke of Hartford, the Earl and Countess of Westfield, Mrs. Tate and her daughter, Bell, Lady Anne, and Mr. Lawrence Cowper. They managed a short discourse regarding the condition of the roads for travel and the weather before they were summoned in to supper. Too distracted with his own thoughts to banter, Edward spent the whole meal strategizing how best to explain to Anne that it was she, not Miss Morgan that he wanted to secure the first set of dances. He wanted her to know that she was first in his affection without sounding like a besotted fool. He spent the entire dinner in quiet reflection, thoughtlessly ignoring his dining partners, of which, one was Miss Rachel Morgan.

Without a mistress of the manor, the duty of hostess lay with Elinor as the most senior lady of the peerage, to lead the ladies to the parlour once Beaumont gave her his nod. Rachel begged her excuses to retire to her room the minute Elinor rose from her chair. She claimed she was weary from traveling, but Edward surmised that Rachel felt awkward among the esteemed titled. Once the ladies made their exit, he led the men to his study for their after dinner port.

He did not think he was alone in wanting to rejoin the females, especially when he saw how quickly the gentlemen finished their sweet fortified wine with no inclination for discourse. Edward's own mind was preoccupied with speaking to Anne for he wished to secure the second set of dances at the ball with her. Unfortunately, it seemed his plans to engage in a tête-à-tête with Anne would take precedence to the whirlwind he knew as Catherine. He anxiously entered the parlour, but before he could make his way to Anne who sat with Mrs. Tate, Catherine exclaimed to him, "You must help me, Edward, or Rachel will never make an advantageous connection. She is too meek in Society. She is quite likable once she is comfortable and able to be herself. Grandmama approves of her, in fact, she told me she thought she would do well for you."

Edward flushed and curtly replied, "Catherine, mind what you say!"

She replied, "Do not be so harsh, Edward. We are among family, aside from the Tates, and I know that their aspirations lay in another direction. Where is Riverdale anyway?"

Edward knew that Catherine, like everyone else in the *ton*, kept apprised of the latest scandal. Mrs. Tate and her daughter, Annabelle, had caused the most recent fodder for speculation. Mrs. Tate's deceased husband was a merchant, yet her daughter was quite genteel and in the possession of a significant dowry. The Patronesses of Almack's forgave Annabelle her sin of having a father who was engaged in trade, mostly because they believed she had the good sense to estrange herself from the man and his influence her whole life.

The Patronesses were a governing body that was made up of the *ton's* most powerful and titled ladies. During the Season, Almack's Assembly Hall was the premiere marketplace for introducing debutantes to eligible suitors and these formidable ladies alone determined who received vouchers to attend the Wednesday night assemblies. Remarkably, the patronesses found Bell's devotion to her mama and her charming manners without fault and made a rare exception when they approved vouchers for the merchant daughter and her mother to attend the assemblies. Admittedly, the overwhelming number of gentlemen who were interested in meeting the angelic looking debutante helped to persuade them. While Annabelle's pretty face drew many admirers, it was the determined Lord Riverdale that had secured her interest.

Normally, Edward enjoyed Catherine's candor, but tonight he found her remarks rude. He responded, "Riverdale has not arrived and I am afraid you have failed to notice Lady Anne."

"Oh, yes," remarked Catherine, "the chaperone."

Edward calmed himself before retorting, "No, Catherine, not the chaperone. Lady Anne is my guest." While it was true that Anne hired herself out as a chaperone during the Season to supplement her living, it bothered Edward that the woman he admired was looked upon as a servant. Rationally, he knew that Catherine could not know that Anne was the object of his affection; regardless, he took offense to her slight.

The room became uncomfortable. Before Edward and Catherine could volley any more remarks, Elinor excused herself and asked Anne to accompany her to the nursery to check on her son. The Tates followed suit retiring for the evening, while the remaining males joined Beaumont in his study.

Edward growled at Catherine who said, "What?!?"

In a controlled, but far from calm voice, Edward explained to Catherine that he was not interested in pursuing Miss Morgan. He repeated himself until he was sure she understood that his interest lay elsewhere. When he finished his diatribe, Catherine asked, "Where?" Edward retorted it was none of her business before sending her off to her room.

Chapter Two

Catherine stretched her arms over her head and her legs deep into the folds of her warm bed sheets while struggling to open her eyes. She had a long evening after everyone else had retired to their rooms and was still feeling quite weary from staying up so late. Her body felt lethargic. All she wanted to do was snuggle into her bed's warm cocoon, return to sleep and try not to remember Edward's late night scold. Her cousin was livid for her frank remarks regarding Rachel and had taken her to task for it.

She had retired to her room when Edward ordered and was actually grateful to him for it. Her body had grown weary by the second after the long day of travel and socializing. Her abigail had helped her dress for bed and then heated her bed sheets with the warming pan. No sooner did she remove the pan from the mattress, than Catherine dismissed her and climbed into the enticing sheets, laying her head on her crisp starched pillow. Sleep was about to overcome her when she heard a discriminate tattoo on her bedroom door. She recognized the special knock that was known only to Edward and herself, and made her way to open her door to him. She knew immediately that he was still angry with her. She read the grimace on his face easily and she feared if she uttered one word that he would lose the fury he was holding in check. His outburst would most likely arouse everyone in the household, bringing them all to her door to witness her public chastisement and humiliation. She did not attempt to ameliorate him, but capitulated to his demands. She donned her robe and slippers and followed him to his study. Edward walked so fast that Catherine had to quicken her steps to try and keep up with him. Not one word was muttered and she knew better than to speak. She used the time to gather her wits and prepared herself for the reprimand she knew she was about to receive.

She really could not help being forthright. Her grandmother applauded her whenever she cut to the chase and the behavior was easy to engage when she was among family. Her rank gave her certain privileges and one of them was to be an *Original,* if she so chose. Catherine abhorred acting like a coy debutante, though she could play the role as good as any lady of quality.

Catherine watched Edward take his seat behind his mahogany writing desk. She obeyed him when he signaled her, with a wave of his hand, to sit in the winged chair that faced him. With a stiff posture that she usually assumed when in an interview with her father, the duke, she inquired, "May I ask, my lord, what was so important that it took me away from my warm bed?"

Edward glared at Catherine for her sarcasm. She knew very well he would demand an audience with her for her less than decorous arrival. Though he wanted to yell at her, he checked his temper knowing he needed her for an ally. He decided berating Catherine would not serve his purpose, so he softened his voice and queried, "Catherine, I thought you came to aid me in my quest to secure a wife, not to sabotage it?"

"Edward, I know not what you mean. How have I sabotaged your efforts?"

His patience broke and he bellowed, "By bringing Miss Morgan and causing injury to Lady Anne!"

She responded, "You are not serious, Edward."

"Absolutely," he replied.

"But she is in service, Edward," she continued. "I thought you were tired of living at the fringes of Society and were looking to make an advantageous match that would elevate your stature."

Edward smirked, thinking, "*Indeed I was*," and then without hesitation answered, "Indeed I am, though the advantage is to my heart and happiness. Lady Anne is in service only because her gaming father pilfered her dowry and left her penniless. To me, she is all that is desirable, coming from a bloodline more pure than my own. Even if that was not the case, my wishes to betroth myself to one that has touched my heart outweighs everything else."

"You are sure, Edward?"

"Yes."

"Then, I am all felicitation for you, but why if your mind is made up, did you beckon me to come?"

He confessed, "Doubts, perhaps. I asked myself the same questions that you just posed, but I finally realized that I value a 'love match' more than I do the *bon ton*. I always craved to be part of that inner circle and now that I am, I find it lacking without someone to love, support, and partner with me. I do not just want someone that will add to my consequence with prestige and coffers. Though honestly, Lady Anne's consent to my addresses would definitely add to my prestige, for she is a formidable and compassionate woman."

Catherine asked, "You know her well, Edward? How is that? When I am more in Society than you?"

"She is a dear friend of the Duke of Hartford and the Westfields," he answered. "We have met on a number of occasions and volleyed wit more often than conviviality. She reads me like a book except in the area of my ardor, which she does not trust to be genuine. I fear she believes all the *on dits* regarding my amorous escapades and thinks I merely wish to seduce her. I hope to convince her differently. Your entry with Miss Morgan did not help my pursuit."

"I am sorry, Edward," she apologized. "Rachel has no designs on you. She would probably be as mortified as yourself by my candor if she knew of it. She will not cause injury in your quest for Lady Anne's hand. I regret that I secured the first set of dances for her with you for your ball."

Edward had planned a Spring Festival and Ball to mark and celebrate the end of the sheep-shearing season. He wanted to reward his guests, tenants, and servants. He hoped to offer for Anne at his ball. It had been years since a festival was celebrated at Beaumont Manor and Edward had planned an extravagant event. He held to tradition and planned to participate in the sheep-shearing contest himself. He was to partner with Mr. Lawrence Cowper, a young man recently come to live and work at the manor. Mr. Cowper, Catherine learned, was the grandson of her great-uncle's first and only love. Upon the death of Mr. Cowper's mother, he traveled to Beaumont Manor to learn if Beaumont was his grandfather, for his grandmother had always spoken endearingly of him. He was disappointed to learn he was not, but happy to accept the friendship and hospitality of her grandmother's one time admirer.

Both Edward and Lawrence had been practicing for over a week perfecting their fleecing skills. They both hoped to put on a worthy show for they knew their exhibition would draw a crowd of commoners looking to see the lord of the manor compete with their own. Plus, they knew the spectacle of seeing their lordship shirtless, working with his hands and sweating, would greatly amuse them.

Edward and Catherine talked at length and rose to retire to their suites when they heard their voices had become thin from exhaustion. Edward hugged Catherine and told her he was glad she had come. He then escorted her to her room where Catherine wasted no time to slip under her bed covers and fluff her pillow. While making herself comfortable for slumber, she recalled Edward's ardent declaration of love. The thought made her smile. She was happy for him. *"Now, if only I could find love for myself."*

Catherine sat at her toilette table looking at her image reflected back to her from the gilt wood mirror that graced the wall above her console. Her abigail was pinning her shako hat on her golden coif, complimenting her newest riding habit made of pale blue merino cloth. Mary smiled at her and said, "There. You look the *pink of fashion,* milady."

Catherine replied dryly, "Do I?" Mary's smile straightened and Catherine admonished, "Oh, do not fret. It is not you that I find lacking, but my own idle life. Tell me, Mary, was your journey comfortable and did you bring my whole London wardrobe as you always do?"

Mary had traveled later in the day in a separate carriage in order to pack all of her mistress's belongings. She hated to leave anything behind, for even though they were expected to return within a sev'night, she knew her fickle mistress could easily change her mind. Catherine had an impetuous spirit driven by her restless nature, which was why she felt out of sorts.

Yesterday had tired her. First, at being closeted away with Rachel in the carriage and then, at having Edward berate her into the long evening hours. The day had only just begun and already she felt poorly. She needed to exert some energy to lift her spirits and she thought a spirited jaunt would shake off the weariness that was already creeping upon her.

She tried to focus on Edward's happiness, hoping to ward off the dreariness that was weighing upon her. It pleased her that Edward had found his love match and she wondered if she was looking for her special person in the wrong places. The idea of looking for love among the common class made her laugh, imagining what the duke would say should she bring home a solicitor or, "Ha! A man of business." No, Catherine concluded, she could never marry a man who worked for a living. Unlike her cousin, she was not free to choose anyone other than what society dictated was her due in consequence.

Catherine turned around to look at Mary and asked, "Where is everyone, Mary? Do you know?"

She answered, "The ladies, milady, are on the west lawn near the hedge grove playing with the infant, Viscount Shelby. I do not know where are his lordships."

Catherine rose. She did not think any of the other ladies would be in the mood for a late ride. She hoped Edward was not engaged and would relish the invitation.

If nothing else, he would command a groom to accompany her. She left her room to search him out.

Catherine knocked on the door to Edward's study. She did not recognize the voice that bid her "enter," so she slowly pushed the door ajar to peer inside before entering the room. She did not want to interrupt her cousin if he was in conference.

Her gaze alighted on the man sitting at Edward's desk with his head dropped to read a ledger. She waited for that head of light brown hair, streaked with blond highlights, to lift and greet her.

When the intruder did not announce himself, Mr. Alistair Chapman raised his head to see who had entered. He pushed his wire rim glasses that had slid down his nose, back into place and felt his mouth twinge in a grin. He saw a beautiful blond woman attired in the Season's newest mode of fashion. Her blue riding habit matched her eyes and he thought her quite lovely. He watched her smooth her skirt under his scrutiny, indicating that his assessing gaze made her uncomfortable. For some reason, the idea pleased him.

His grin grew wider, enjoying her befuddled state and he asked with a touch of arrogance to his voice, "May I be of assistance, my lady?"

Catherine did not like the smug look on the man that held her attention. She was used to being admired for her beauty, but this man looked more amused than besotted. She thought he was grinning at her expense. His gaze made her tremble and she did not like the idea that he knew he had discomposed her. Catherine expected since he was in Edward's study, that he must be his man of business, but his fine crafted coat and linen were too superior for one in service. His short crop hair was also indicative that he was a man of fashion, not a dandy, but surely a man used to superior society. Catherine realized she had yet to respond and saw that he had risen and was making his way towards her. He said, "Allow me to introduce myself. I am Lord Felton's man of business, Mr. Alistair Chapman. I expect you are Lady Catherine. Your features, especially your blue eyes and regal nose mark you a Brentwood. You are Lord Felton's cousin, are you not?"

Catherine was surprised at the man's confidence in addressing her. She noted he had none of the obsequious nature she expected from servants. He had a commanding presence and a sort of charm that was out of place for a man of his class. She watched him come to stand before her. He looked into her eyes and asked, "Are you ill or are you a mute?"

Catherine opened her eyes wide and bellowed a guffaw before covering her outburst with her hands. She realized that she, again, had failed to respond to his question. Had she not laughed, she would have played the mute, but her response gave her away for the jejune girl she felt like. She quickly pulled her countenance together and replied in her most aristocratic voice, "Mr. Chapman, I was expecting to see Lord Felton."

"I surmised, " he retorted. "Perhaps, you will allow me to come to your aid. His lordship is either still on the home farm or in route on his return."

Catherine remembered that Edward had said he planned to visit the home farm this morning to practice his fleecing skills with Mr. Cowper. Edward was to partake in tomorrow's Spring Festival Sheep Shearing Contest. Catherine smiled and recalled, "Oh, I forgot. Lord Felton is fleecing his sheep. Is he not?"

Alistair returned Catherine's smile and replied, "Indeed, he is. I am, you know, his trusty servant. Are you sure that I cannot act in his stead?"

"I suppose you must since his lordship is absent. I am in great need of exercise. I wanted to borrow a mount and a groom for an escort, since my cousin is unavailable to accompany me. Can you see to my needs, Mr. Chapman?"

Alistair could not help but be amused at Catherine's condescending manner. He had grown accustomed to being the recipient of the snide and lowering barbs of the privileged class, especially the tone the titled used in addressing those they considered inferior to them because of their station in life. He took no offense and replied, "Certainly, my lady. Perhaps, you would allow me to be your escort. I need to stop by the home farm first to check on the preparations for tomorrow's festival. If you do not mind the short detour, I would be happy to accompany you on a brisk ride over his lordship's property."

"I do not mind visiting the home farm," replied Catherine. "I would like to see the preparations myself and I am certainly intrigued with what contemplates a brisk ride. Am I to understand that you will not check me should I give my mount his legs?"

Alistair found himself grinning, again. He thought Catherine's eyes sparkled, instead of that lazy glare so prominent in the idle rich. He disapproved of those noblemen who strove only to seek their own pleasure and failed in their duty to their properties. He knew many estates that fell to ruin through neglect and gaming, even worse, tenants that suffered from lack of attention. He was glad that Lord Felton did not fall into that category for he enjoyed working for him. He assessed his employer's pretty cousin and liked what he saw in her. She owned a boldness and desire for activity that intrigued him. *"No,"* he thought, *"She is not one to be languorous."* He responded to her question, "I would not think to check a rider if their proficiency is evident."

Catherine smiled and retorted, "Your response is quite diplomatic, sir. I see why Edward keeps you in service."

"Indeed," he replied. "Perhaps, you would like to inform your uncle of your travels, while I see to our mounts."

Catherine recalled her grandmother's wishes and said, "You have put me to mind of a service I am charged to complete for my grandmama. She has asked that I visit a childhood friend. I have a letter to discharge. Instead of a tour of Beaumont's property, will you escort me to her cottage after we visit the home farm?"

Alistair smiled, bowed, and said, "It would be my pleasure, my lady."

Catherine found herself captivated by his alighted eyes and smiled. She felt herself warm and her cheeks blush crimson. It embarrassed her to think that a simple man of business had achieved what no man of title in the last two years had ever done. Excite her.

Chapter Three

Catherine was used to having her wants met with expediency, so it surprised her that she did not mind waiting for Alistair to complete his business at the home farm. She followed him in his wake, trying to match her own gait with his long stride while he strode from one point of business to another, speaking with various farmers, stewards, and servants. Her blue woolen skirt brushed her legs and kicked up the dirt from the hard packed ground each time she stepped to keep up with him. She was amazed at the number of booths that were being set up for tomorrow's Spring Festival and even more impressed with the manor farm. She knew Beaumont Manor received its food from the industry of this farm. There were penned cows, chickens, and pigs; plots of vegetable gardens; buildings used specifically for the purpose of making dairy products and processing meat. There were also the barns and other buildings used for storage and to house the overflow of horses from the stables located closer to the manor.

She did not know if the home farm had gone through a transformation for the festival, but the property was pristine: free of debris, tidy, and organized. Catherine wondered if Alistair's management was responsible for the farm's success. For a time, her curiosity kept her occupied while he ordered the servants to do his bidding and resolved issues that were brought to him.

She followed Alistair from one section of the farm to another and soon grew weary of the monotony of walking to and fro, until she began to change up her pace. To amuse herself she timed her steps to the cadence of the sheeps' jarring baas and imagined she was a soldier marching to the drum. Before long, her arms were pumping in rhythm. She had to stifle laughing out loud for acting so childishly, until she realized that such antics witnessed and discussed, could bring scandal to her name. The idea so frightened her that she looked about to see if anyone had spied her hoyden behavior. When she saw no one that could betray her solecism, she released a trill of giggles in relief.

Alistair stopped and turned to look at her. He raised an eyebrow, and asked, “What, pray tell, is so amusing, my lady?”

Catherine smirked, liking that the man who had seemed to have forgotten her was indeed not indifferent, for why else did his temper appear riled. *"He must of thought I was laughing at him."* Unable to reveal her thoughts, she replied, "I fear if you do not slow your pace, Mr. Chapman, that I shall swoon from exhaustion. Then, may I ask, how will you carry me home?"

Alistair grinned at the girl's sassy query. Did the minx really think her jejune actions were unknown to him? He would have to been blind not to see her shadow marching right along beside him. Her stomping as if on parade had amused him until he heard her laugh. It was in that moment he decided to end her exhibition before it could be remarked upon. *How would he carry her home?* He answered, "Very easily, my lady."

Catherine's face blushed when his retort had her imagining him lifting her up into his arms. She realized, looking at him, that Alistair looked more like a rogue than a gentleman with his penetrating gaze. It surprised her that she felt more intrigue than fear from his provocative knowing look. His eyes held her spellbound and she was not even sure she was breathing, her mind enthralled with the sensations coursing through her body. Not until Alistair made his apologies, did the mesmerizing hold he had on her diminish.

"Forgive me, my lady. I did not think how taxing this must be for you. It is just that I was trying to quickly finish my business, so as not to delay your errand."

Regaining her wits, Catherine replied, "Nonsense. I do not have to follow you about, Mr. Chapman. My own interests, or I should say curiosity keeps me at your side, even more precisely in your wake. I was only jesting when I said I would swoon. Please finish your tasks. I will wait for you inside the main house, where perhaps I can find something cool to drink."

"As you wish, my lady," he replied before snapping his fingers to beckon the nearby lackey who waited upon him. The boy listened to his orders and then preceded Catherine into the house, where she expected he would provide her with something refreshing to quench her thirst.

She drank in solitude, for no one of her station was present to keep her company. Those tenants and servants who worked the farm would never dare speak to a better unless they were addressed first. Servants were the invisible class. They went about their duty trained not to draw attention to themselves, whereas, tenants respected the sphere unto which the lord placed them and would not trespass into a higher society unless invited.

Catherine took a sip of her lemonade and let the cool drink revive her while she considered her plans. She had little choice. She would attend Edward's ball and then depart the next day for London, where she would return Rachel to her family. She supposed she would then join the rest of the *ton* attending the social events that marked the Season. The idea did not excite her. In fact, she found the galas were becoming dull with the same people, playing the same flirtatious games. She had tired of the insincerity of it all, but knew there was little else for her to do, other than to continue to hope she could find a titled gentleman who would love her more than the immense dowry attached to her. She was in the middle of contemplating her bleak future when Alistair interrupted her thoughts.

"All done," he said. "Are you ready to travel or are you wearied and wish to return to the manor?"

Catherine smirked at the man's ill judgment of her. She replied, "My, what a low opinion you have of my fortitude, if you think a little walking and sitting taxes my strength. Or, have you changed your mind and do not wish to escort me to visit my grandmama's friend? Perhaps, it is you, sir, that wishes to return to the manor."

Catherine's challenging rebuke surprised Alistair and he raised his brow in response. He thought she was a bold miss and could not help but laugh out loud at her haughty retort, before answering, "I am dutifully and agreeably at your service, my lady." To show he was in earnest, he proffered his arm in escort. Catherine rose from her chair, smoothed out her skirt before lightly resting her hand on his forearm. She was stiff, displaying the proud and regal manner of a duke's daughter, until Alistair took her hand, threaded it through his arm to bring her body closer to his. The action discomfited her and once again, the nearness of his body made her stomach flutter. She barely heard him murmur, "I am glad you are no simpering miss, my lady."

Catherine lost her ability to conjure up a proper response. She was beginning to think her uncle's estate had placed some sort of spell on her, for never before had she been unable to return a witticism. Before she could rally herself, Alistair escorted her through the front door and led her to her mare. He pushed aside the mounting block with his foot and lifted Catherine by the waist up unto her side saddle. Catherine was so captivated by his admiring look, that she did not scold him for handling her so intimately. Instead, she steeled her eyes at him to discern what, if any, were his intentions. She realized she did not know anything about his character, other than he was strong, self-assured, and handsome in a bookish sort of way, especially when he wore his glasses. He was an enigma. She knew he was of common stock, but her intuition told her that he was her equal in everything else, for surely no inferior person could be as bold as he.

For a while, they rode quietly side by side, maneuvering their cattle around the potholes and ruts that marked the weary and well-traveled lane used to carry carted goods to and from the home farm. The crossroads at the end of the lane opened into the public road that was widely used by local tenants and travelers making their way to London. Catherine breathed in the fresh air and took in the colorful landscape before her. The pastures were lush and green with bright colors of wildflowers blooming. The sky was clear and the sun visible, promising a warm day, exceptional for a country known for its inclement weather. Catherine saw the end of the lane approaching and hated to leave the peaceful pasture that enveloped them.

Although they had not spoken, the traffic that they were sure to encounter once they entered the public road would most likely make it difficult for them to engage in any conversation, especially a private one unto themselves. She saw Alistair smile out of the corner of her eye and turned her head to question him on what he found amusing. Before she could query him, he asked her, "Do you jump, my lady?"

Catherine asked, "Excuse me, Mr. Chapman. Do I jump what?"

Alistair pulled on his reins to halt his horse. Catherine followed suit to await his answer. He did not hesitate to respond. "These roads are terribly rough and the public lane is even more broken, making us keep our pace slow to ensure we do not injure our mounts. I was thinking that since it has not rained in over a week, that the pasture would be firm and make a more pleasant ride. However, there is no access to the public road should we venture across the grass, aside from jumping the yew hedges that eloquently mark the border of Beaumont's property. If you are capable of making the jump, I suggest we enjoy the brisk ride I mentioned earlier. The hedges are not tall, but I would not recommend the attempt if you had never spurred your heels to the task before."

Catherine laughed and rebuked playfully, "This is not the first time that you have underestimated me, Mr. Chapman. I am a proficient rider and have more than once participated in the hunt, jumping both hedges and streams, though I admit to leaving the grisly finale of the fox to others. I am most agreeable to giving our horses' their heads."

Catherine pulled her reins to turn her mare into the verdant grazing land before Alistair could respond. She bent over her horse's mane and offered a word of encouragement before spurring her into a gallop.

Alistair released a hearty chuckle and felt his competitive nature spark when he saw Catherine's mare kick up clods of sod to take the lead. He quickly gave a quick heel and slap of his reins to race after her. "By golly," he exclaimed, "she can ride." He bent forward reveling in the chase, feeling the wind speed over his head and the strength of his stallion galloping beneath him. He laughed again when he saw Catherine inadvertently tug on her reins when she looked back over her shoulder to locate him. Her tug had signaled her horse to slow down which allowed Alistair to gain and pass her. He heard her bellow a curse, but knew better than to glance back. He encouraged his horse into greater speed and did not slow down until he reached the end of the pasture where he brought his horse to a stop. He turned his mount around in time to see Catherine race towards him with her hair escaping her hat and her skirts bellowing in the wind. He learned she was not a graceful loser when she shouted, "You, sir, have the better horse." To that Alistair replied, "Most definitely." And then he laughed.

When Catherine and Alistair approached the white washed cottage bordered with evergreen yew box hedges, Catherine explained that Mrs. Margaret Howard was the daughter of the late Marquis of Beaumont's steward. Maggie, as she was known to the Dowager Duchess of Aubry, was a childhood friend and over the years, Catherine's grandmother, maintained the connection through missives and visits. Margaret Howard was one of the few who visited the dowager at her cottage for an extended stay, especially after losing her husband three years previous. She lived now in the home that the current Marquis of Beaumont retired upon her and her husband, Mr. Howard, the man who had replaced Margaret's father as steward.

Alistair informed Catherine that he knew Mrs. Howard well, because Lord Felton had recommended him for Mr. Howard's position five years ago, when the man's health started to decline. Catherine was surprised Alistair had worked at Beaumont Manor for that long. She asked him if he had always been in Edward's service, even before he became Lord Felton.

He replied, "Not until this last year when Beaumont named him his heir. Lord Felton and I had a previous connection that I imposed upon five years ago when I was seeking employment. Both Lord Felton and I found the timing of my inquiry providential. I will confess that I have been quite happy at Beaumont Manor and like to think I have served your uncle well."

"There is no doubt, Mr. Chapman," she replied. "My uncle's estate is well managed and appears very profitable based on what I have seen."

"Thank you," he said.

Margaret Howard opened the door and was surprised to see the granddaughter of her dear friend, the Dowager Duchess of Aubry. Maggie had met Lady Catherine at the dowager cottage on more than one occasion and knew she was the dowager's particular favorite. Mr. Chapman, she knew, was Beaumont's steward, for he had been a frequent visitor after Mr. Howard relinquished his role to him. Maggie thought Mr. Chapman a kind man to have set aside time to visit her husband after he retired. Mr. Howard struggled with what he felt was a forced retirement pressed upon him because of his failing health. Maggie appreciated Mr. Chapman's visits because they distracted her husband from melancholia. Her husband had once been a robust man and his weakened constitution had eaten away at his pride, making him feel useless. Maggie knew that Mr. Chapman's visits to seek her husband's advice on estate management, were simply a ruse to boost his self-esteem. She would always be grateful to him for the compassion and friendship he had bestowed on her husband.

Maggie greeted cheerfully, "Lady Catherine! Mr. Chapman! Now this is a delightful surprise. Please come in."

Both Catherine and Alistair entered the cottage and followed Mrs. Howard into her small sitting room that was warmed by a crackling amber fire. The room was the picture of coziness with a flower patterned chintz sofa and matching curtains, an embroidered fire screen, a throw rug, and end tables decorated with laced doilies. Catherine wasted no time in delivering her grandmother's missive to Mrs. Howard. She smiled, saying, "Grandmama is well. She sends in her own words what news, if any, there is to tell. She probably invites you to sojourn with her, which is hardly necessary, since I believe you have an open invitation to come at will."

Maggie returned Catherine's smile and replied, "She is too generous and kind to me." She looked at Mr. Chapman and queried, "And how do you fare, sir, with two lordships to command your business?"

Alistair laughed and answered, "I am very well, Maggie. You are too hard on Beaumont and Felton. They are more than generous and easy to serve. Tell me, how are you managing and do you have someone to bring you to tomorrow's festival? I will not hear that you stayed away because you had no transport."

Maggie laughed and said that he need not concern himself. Her neighbors took good care of her and she was traveling with them to the fete. Catherine watched Mrs. Howard and Alistair converse. She was impressed with his commanding and caring countenance. It was clear that if Maggie did not have a means to travel to the festival that he would have arranged a conveyance to take her. It was also obvious that this common man was very uncommon in his manner to those who should be his equal. He flaunted an authoritative demeanor as though he held a position of power and consequence. Catherine could tell that Mrs. Howard held Alistair in high esteem.

Mrs. Howard was disappointed she could not convince her visitors to stay for supper. Alistair argued that they had already visited longer than they should have for the sun was ready to set. He reminded her that traveling the uneven roads to Beaumont Manor was difficult enough without losing daylight. Mrs. Howard agreed and saw her guests to their horses. She watched them take their leave, returning their waves of goodbye as they made their way down the lane.

An empty and quiet road greeted the travelers. Only the slap of their cattle's steps on the hard ground pierced the solitude until Alistair spoke, "I am afraid you will miss supper at the manor, my lady. I hope your uncle does not worry because of your absence."

Catherine turned her head to reply to a concerned Alistair, "Not at all, Mr. Chapman. My uncle will assume I am too tired to attend tonight's meal and activities, since I left instructions for a tray to be made up and placed in my room."

Alistair pulled on his reins to check his steed. Catherine followed suit and asked, "What is wrong?"

He answered tersely, "I do not think your action was wise, my lady. You left yourself at risk. An alarm for your well-being would not be raised until tomorrow, for Beaumont will be under the assumption that you are retired safely in your room."

Surprised, Catherine remarked, "Are you telling me, sir, that I am not safe in your company?"

Alistair noted that their mounts were becoming restless, standing idle, so he pressed his heels into his steed to start him forward. Catherine again followed suit, but did not release Alistair from her inquiry. She prodded, "Well, sir, I demand that you answer me. Are you a threat to my safety?"

Alistair smirked and said, "Hardly." He continued, "You misinterpret my meaning. The point is that Beaumont believes you are at the manor. What if a highwayman attacked us and we were left injured on the road? We would not be missed until tomorrow, instead of tonight, because you misled your uncle."

Catherine retorted, "Are you telling me that you are incapable of dealing with a highwayman?"

Alistair laughed and was speechless at the girl's audacity. He found it incredulous that she managed to change the focus to him, rather than take responsibility for her own reckless behavior. He had no wish to engage in a conversation that might give her personal insight about him, so he said nothing regarding her inquiry to his abilities.

It perturbed Catherine when Alistair did not answer her question. She was used to gentlemen championing her, gentlemen who were more than eager to take up a gallant role to impress her. It bothered her that Alistair was not prepared to save her from a highwayman, or any other peril that might come their way. In her anger, she said, "I would not be afraid, Mr. Chapman. I do not think there are any known incidents of bandits on this stretch of road. Poor tenant farmers mostly populate this area and most highwaymen look for the traveled roads of the aristocrats." She then spurred her horse into a gallop, hoping to leave Alistair in her dust. To her chagrin, her mount no sooner found its legs than Catherine felt herself flying off her saddle, hitting the hard-packed rutted dirt with a painful thud. She had the wind knocked out of her and was so stunned that she kept her eyes closed until she knew that she had not killed herself. She was so focused on catching her breath and subduing her rapid heartbeat, that she did not see Alistair approach her, though she did hear his panicked voice when he asked her if she was all right.

When she did not answer, she felt him touch her. The pressure of his hands moving down her arms was comforting until her senses returned and she realized the impropriety of those roaming hands. Embarrassed, she quickly slapped them away. She explained that she was not injured and only needed a moment to come to rights.

Alistair accepted Catherine at her word and left her to check on her mare. He became angry to see that the horse had injured one of its fore legs, probably from placing it and then twisting its hoof in a deep pothole. He did his best to calm the agitated horse, stroking its mane while he held its bridle to speak to the young filly in a soothing voice. He slowly walked the hobbling mare onto the smoother side of the road where it was less traveled.

By now, Catherine had righted herself, hugging her hip to try to squelch the shooting pain that pulsed through her. She watched in wonder while Alistair took care of her mount. He was remarkably patient, calming her mare and then, when it seemed that the horse was no longer skittish, she watched him take both his hands and stroke its foreleg. She could tell he was checking for a break and he wasted no time to administer aid. He took off his cravat from his neck, ripped it lengthwise and then bound her mare's leg. She watched her horse tentatively place its hoof on the ground. Alistair patted the mare's shoulder, consoling her with soft words. Catherine walked over to him and immediately noticed his anger. Before he could scold her, she remarked, "You need not say it. I know my negligence in spurring my mare on this weathered lane is responsible for her injury. I feel terrible for my foolishness. Tell me, Mr. Chapman, is her leg broken?"

Surprised by her remorse, he said, "No, I believe it is merely a strain, but I will not press her into further injury by having you ride." He then asked, "How do you fare?"

Catherine blushed, "I am more embarrassed than injured, but will probably own a bruise or two to show for my folly. If I am not to ride, will you walk with me and keep me company?"

"Of course," he answered "We will walk for a while to make sure your muscles do not stiffen up from your fall. Then, we will double up on my steed. Otherwise, it will be a remarkably long and tiresome walk back to the manor."

With reins in hand, Alistair and Catherine led their horses down the public lane. The sun was beginning to set and Catherine grew concerned.

She asked, "It will be dark soon. Will you be able to find our way back to the manor?"

Alistair could hear the fear in her voice and in a reassuring voice answered, "Yes, I know these roads well having traveled them often, even at night. Do not be concerned. We will have a full moon this evening to light our way back."

Catherine smiled, then relaxed. She said, "I am glad. I must confess that I am used to my coachman conveying me about in the evening hours. I find the night enveloping me on a land absent of anyone but us, disconcerting."

It amazed Alistair how much joy he felt seeing the worry leave Catherine's brow. He wanted to offer her even more comfort, so he took hold of her free hand with his own and squeezed it. Then, he confessed, "I am more than capable, my lady, of dealing with a highwayman."

Catherine could not help but smile at the man who offered her the words she needed to completely assuage her concerns. Looking at his strong physique, she had no doubt that he could deal with any reprobate that approached them. She felt her heart begin to race when Alistair returned her smile and realized she could not name another gentleman that had ever made her heart flutter. The sky began to darken and Catherine's eyes turned to the disappearing horizon. She gasped at the loveliness she saw. A blend of fiery reds, oranges, and yellows pressed down into the earth leaving only a fading blue light to warn travelers that night was upon them. Catherine remarked, “I do not believe I have ever seen a more beautiful sunset.”

Alistair felt Catherine move her hand and thought she was going to disengage herself from him. He was surprised when he felt her entwine her slender fingers with his own rugged ones. The intimate act touched off a series of tremors inside him. He could not remember the last time he had engaged in such romantic folly. He knew he should release her hand, but he convinced himself that there was no harm in indulging in a chaste romantic interlude. They walked quietly for a while, hand in hand, until he noticed that Catherine's steps were beginning to falter. He stopped and turned to look at her. He remarked, “You are tired.”

“My legs, yes,” she admitted, "but, my mind is quite active, full of wonder for this alien world I find myself. I do not think I have ever walked down a public lane in the dark. My ears and eyes are on alert, waiting. If I was alone, I think I would have swooned by now, but with your company I feel the moment exhilarating. There is no place I would rather be.”

Amazed, Alistair challenged, “I am sure you would rather be in Town at one of the many balls you frequent than to be here with me, my lady?”

She answered, “Surprisingly, no, Mr. Chapman.”

Alistair's mouth gaped at her forthright answer. He released her hand and then turned to grasp both of her shoulders. He looked deep into her eyes to discern if she was sincere and noticed his manner did not frighten her. If anything, she stared right back at him. Then, she surprised him by standing on her tiptoes to bring her lips over his. She asked, "Are you going to kiss me, or not?"

Alistair gained his senses in time to check his behavior. Tersely, he replied, "Not." Then, he took a very discombobulated ladyship and lifted her up unto his saddle. He quickly mounted behind her and noticed her stiff posture. He could tell he had embarrassed her and decided it best to explain.

He said, "Do not take offense, my lady. I will confess that it takes all my willpower not to kiss you. However, you are entrusted to my care and in respect to my employers, I will not trespass on their trust in me. I will remind you that you are the daughter of a duke and would likely have regretted a dalliance with a steward upon tomorrow's reflection. I only hope that you see my refusal, not as a slight, but as the compliment it is meant to be."

Alistair felt Catherine relax. He guessed that his confession appeased her pride. Then, she leaned back into his body. He felt her softness and he silently cursed, "*Heaven help me*." He thought he saw her smile.

Chapter Four

Catherine woke when she heard her abigail enter her room. Under her droopy eyelids, she watched Mary set down a breakfast tray on her mahogany bed table and then walk over to pull back the heavy damask curtains, to tie them into place with their tasseled golden cords. Bright morning light filled her room, chasing away the darkness that had recently enveloped Catherine, rousing her from slumber. She stretched out her arms and legs, then took a cleansing breath before scooting herself into a sitting position. She chuckled when Mary turned and saw she was propped up in bed. Her maid opened her eyes wide in surprise and exclaimed, "Ah! You are awake, milady, and here I thought you might sleep through the festival."

Astonished, Catherine started to bolt from her bed. She asked as she threw back her coverlet, "What time is it, Mary?"

"It is past one o'clock, milady," she answered.

Catherine chided, “Why did you not wake me earlier, Mary. I have probably missed the sheep shearing contest.”

Mary felt her mistress's reprimand keenly and stiffly offered in her defense, “You have given me standing orders, milady, to never wake you from a sound sleep. You have always argued that nothing is more important than one’s rest. I am sorry if I erred.”

Catherine realized the blame was hers and said, “No, Mary. The fault is mine. Tell me, has everyone left?”

She replied, "Aye, but that nice Mr. Chapman returned, concerned for your health, he was, especially when he noticed your continued absence. It was he whom ordered your breakfast tray and told me to inquire about your well-being.”

Catherine's sorrowful face turned cheerful. She asked, “Did he?”

“Aye, he did,” answered Mary with a knowing grin. “And he said I am not to dawdle. I must report back immediately to inform him about your health.”

Catherine laughed, saying, “Well, what are you waiting for, Mary. Report to Mr. Chapman that I am well and will be down in half past the hour. Be sure to tell him that I expect him to escort me to the festival and then hurry back to help me dress.”

Mary took off to do her ladyship’s bidding and Catherine bounced out of her feather bed and began her morning ablutions.

Alistair was pleased to hear that Catherine was in good health and would be down in a half hour to attend the festival. He had mixed feelings regarding his escort of her. He thought Catherine was as bold as she was beautiful. He earnestly enjoyed her company, even when she behaved childishly. He found her competitive and combative nature, more charming than annoying. It was obvious to him that she had been pampered since childbirth, her every want and whim met, but he noticed the attention did not leave her self-absorbed or without character. She intrigued him and when in her company, he felt genuinely cheerful. He knew nothing good could come from spending time with her, for it was futile to encourage an alliance between a duke's daughter and a man of business. His head told him to desist, but something encouraged him to proceed.

He sent word for a buggy to be made ready thinking if Catherine's hip was bruised, then a chaise would be the most comfortable ride for her. He was especially glad he had ordered the conveyance when he saw her pause with each step she took. She looked beautiful wearing a sprig muslin walking dress that opened in the front to reveal a matching underskirt. It was a light and airy dress that complimented her piquant essence. She wore a jonquil spencer with a heart shaped bodice that he guessed matched the top of her dress, for he could see the eyelet trim peeking over her jacket's collar. A pomona satin ribbon wound under her bosom and more sea green ribbons wrapped around her puffy sleeves tying into crisp decorative bows. She carried a matching jonquil parasol in one hand and tapped it on each step as she descended the staircase. Her hair was plated and threaded with matching satin ribbons to form a crown atop her head. Her loveliness brought a smile to his face and he hoped, that perhaps, she dressed to impress him.

Catherine's heart was racing so fast that she thought she might swoon. She hadn't felt so overcome since she made her curtsey to the Queen upon her *come-out*. She was glad she had her parasol in hand to balance herself while she descended the staircase. The tattoo made by the parasol when it hit each step calmed her nerves like the sound rain makes when it hits the windowpane. She was pleased she took the time to fuss over her wardrobe for when she saw Alistair, she knew without a doubt that he admired her.

She liked what she saw as well. Catherine's first impression of Alistair was that he was a lean bookish sort of fellow and most probably owned nothing to recommend him. Yesterday's excursion had proven her wrong. She thought him quite compelling. His self-assurance and strength emanated from him like a fey animal. She found herself drawn to him and noted that today he was far from bookish. He wore a superfine dark blue double-breasted coat with buff pantaloons. His cravat was made of fine linen and tied, to her amusement, in a mathematical fold. She smirked thinking it a pun on his academic mind. She also noted his Hessian boots were polished to a brilliant sheen. She concluded he was the picture of an aristocrat and wondered, *"Who is this man?"*

Alistair was the first to break the silence. "You look stunning, my lady. I am glad that yesterday's fall does not keep you from today's festivities. How did you sleep?"

Catherine replied, "I am well and in your debt, Mr. Chapman. I would have been much disappointed to miss my uncle's festival. As it is, I think I have missed the sheep shearing contest?"

"I am sorry to confirm your assertion, my lady," he answered. "The contest is indeed over."

She queried, "And pray, how did my cousin, Edward, do?"

Alistair laughed, "His lordship did not put himself up to ridicule I am happy to report. I believe his tenants are in admiration of him and Mr. Cowper."

Catherine exclaimed, "Oh! Well done!"

He proffered his arm and commanded, "Come, I have ordered the chaise buggy to transport you to the home farm if you are able to travel."

Catherine smiled and replied, "Thank you, Mr. Chapman, I am quite able."

"Indeed," he retorted, raising a brow at her in admiration to which Catherine blushed.

Catherine had spent more than one afternoon in the company of an admirer anxious to show off their driving expertise. She knew a whip when she saw one and

Alistair's dexterity was clear from the moment he took the reins into his hands. He had a light hand and with a flick of his wrist, he had his cattle responding to his command. If Catherine did not know better, she would have thought that Alistair was a member of the "Four-in-Hand," the men's club that extended invitations to only the finest drivers. Its members wore blue with yellow striped waistcoats and Catherine wondered if Alistair owned such an article.

Her curiosity was getting the better of her for she could not make out the enigma that sat beside her. Her mind was guessing at all types of circumstances to explain his dress and manner. She thought perhaps Alistair was an impoverished aristocrat. The idea made more sense to her than him being of common blood. He had the markings and air of a nobleman, and none of the invisible, obsequious, and accommodating manners attributed to the serving class. Catherine understood the traits that described the common class were as generalized as thinking that all aristocrats were idle, uncaring, and self-indulgent, yet many were measured by their air of distinction. A common person had to mimic their betters if they hoped to improve their lot in life. *Could Alistair had once been a footman whose master had given him an education?* Her curiosity peaked with every conjecture.

She remarked, "My cousin must pay you well for your attire is of the first class, Mr. Chapman. I say, you outshine many of my acquaintances."

Alistair smirked and replied, "I do not know for what you truly wish to know, my lady, but I will confirm that I am well paid; and I shall take your remark on my attire as a compliment, rather than a slur on the company you keep."

Catherine choked, "I did not mean to slander my friends, Mr. Chapman."

He retorted, "Then, what was your intent, Lady Catherine?"

Catherine was never one to walk away from a challenge and she was far from being subtle. If anything, she was direct, often to the chagrin of her family. She decided she would not let this man of business discomfit her into acting like a coy debutante from which she was far from. She gritted her teeth and confessed, "You peak my curiosity, sir. I am not sure that you are what you present yourself to be. Are you perhaps, an impoverished aristocrat?"

Alistair laughed, "No, my lady. I am not an impoverished aristocrat, nor am I like you, a member of the idle rich. I am and I must say, most content to being his lordship's man of business. Before Catherine could continue her line of questioning, Alistair slapped the reins against his cattle's flanks to start them into a trot which jostled Catherine abruptly. She quickly clutched the side of the buggy when the jolt almost shook her from her seat. Alistair noted from a side-glance that Catherine was not happy with his brusque maneuver.

They continued on in silence, Catherine's temper simmering until they reached the home farm. Alistair made his way around the carriage to assist Catherine with her descent. Her stiff body and tight lips clearly spoke of her discontent. He left the attending ostler to care for his conveyance while he saw to calming his companion.

Rigid with fury, Catherine was ready to take her leave of Alistair. She started to turn when he stopped her by saying, "Come, let us not quarrel. There are only a couple of hours left to the festival before everyone retreats and prepares for the supper-dance. Allow me to escort you among the booths and show off our talented community."

Catherine's pride did not want to relent, but her traitorous body responded to his solicitous words and she found herself looking up into his eyes. She saw an earnest plea to stay with him and she realized she had no wish to leave his company. He offered his arm in escort and she acquiesced by placing her hand on his arm.

He escorted her to a row of booths where various colored woolen spools of yarn and textile samples were being displayed. Alistair stopped at the first booth to greet a young girl of about six years of age and a matron who overlooked her play.

Alistair hailed, "Good day, Mrs. Johnson. How goes the demonstrations? Are the wee ones learning their ancestral art?"

"An art indeed, Mr. Chapman, but I fear a lost one," she replied.

Catherine watched the young girl whose keen concentration peeked her own interest. She noticed that while the girl held a stick in her left hand, she was gently pulling a wad of wool fiber with her right hand, thinning the raw fiber into a long thread. Once she reached a certain length, she saw the girl flick the stick to make it whirl rapidly in motion. The girl's eyes alighted and she beckoned the matron, "Mrs. Johnson. Come see. I am doing it. Look at how the fibers are twisting."

Catherine asked, "What is all the excitement? What is she doing?"

Both Alistair and Mrs. Johnson turned to look at Catherine. Alistair asked her, "Have you never seen a drop spindle, my lady?"

Catherine blushed and then with all her regal countenance, she lifted her chin to respond, "No, Mr. Chapman. I have not. Is there a reason, the daughter of a duke, should know about such things?"

Alistair laughed at Catherine's haughtiness and knew her question was in pure defense to disguise her embarrassment. He responded, "I apologize, my lady. Of course, your expertise would not be in spinning of wool, but in the embroidery of it, as tutored to all ladies of quality. Perhaps, however, your curiosity encourages you to try your hand at the spindle?"

Catherine was indeed tempted and Alistair's grin baited her into trying her luck. Mrs. Johnson handed her a spindle and explained that the wooden whorl, a spherical piece of wood, provided the weight that causes the spindle to turn. She further explained that the purpose of the spindle was to twist the woolen fiber to make it strong. Fiber is the raw wool shorn and cleaned from the sheep. Spinning turns the fiber into yarn that is then turned into textiles. Mrs. Johnson frowned, complaining, "hand spinning is becoming a lost art form, turning honest working families into paupers."

Catherine thought Mrs. Johnson was going to exhale a diatribe, but instead the matron took some fiber and pulled some of the hairs loose, twisting them while she continued to pull. She told her ladyship that she was creating a leader of yarn to start her off. Catherine watched Mrs. Johnson tie the leader to the spindle and then showed her ladyship how to continue.

"You see, milady, you tug out a little of the hairs. Then you flick the spindle and as it spins, it twists the fibers into yarn. 'Tis easy, once you get started," said the matron.

Catherine gently took hold of the spindle. She followed Mrs. Johnson's instructions, flicking the spindle as she had seen the matron do, but she failed to keep the leader taut. Catherine watched the yarn kink. Then, the spindle changed direction. Within moments, the fiber broke and the spindle fell to the ground. Alistair could not keep himself from chuckling at Catherine's disappointed expression. Before anyone else could laugh at her expense, he hurried her off to the next booth exclaiming, "I would stick to embroidery."

She replied, "You would not say that if you saw my samplers, full of loose and uneven stitching." Her own laughter bubbled up when Alistair opened his mouth to reply and realized he had nothing to say.

They walked together and he showed Catherine each of the booths exhibiting the rudiments of the textile business. She saw all kinds of demonstrations: the sorting; the cleaning and dying of wool; the carding and combing of wool; and the various inventions that spun wool. After trying her hand at the drop spindle, she tried her hand at a spinning wheel, before she resigned herself from further participation. She agreed with Alistair that spinning was an art form and best left to the hands of artisans.

From the textile booths, they moved on to the refreshment tables and Catherine was happy to take a repast of lemonade and pigeon pie with Alistair. She heard her stomach rumble when he handed her her meal and laughed when she realized she was not the only one who heard it roar.

They found a dry patch of lawn near an ancient oak tree that shaded them from the sun that had bathed them in warmth throughout the day. Alistair dropped the woolen blanket he had borrowed from one of the textile booths and unrolled it on the lawn. Catherine watched him smooth the blanket out for their use. She handed him her food, so that she could graciously drop to sit on the blanket. She straightened her skirt and then reached out her hands to retake her food from him. She admired his gallantry and like a person hypnotized, she watched him lower himself to take his seat next to her on the blanket with puppy-eyed wonder. She continued to gawk at him while he ate his meat pie. When he finished, he remarked, "I thought your hunger would have ravaged that tart by now."

Catherine realized that she had been mesmerized the whole time and had he not spoken, she would still be staring at him like a lovesick fool. She rallied herself and smiled mischievously at him. Alistair thought she looked like someone ready to engage in a prank and wondered what she had on her mind. He had to check his laughter when he saw her open her mouth wide and take a large bite of her pie. With cheeks full of pastry, she began to make "mmm" sounds to demonstrate just how delicious the tart tasted. It was quite a gauche display. He would not have thought a duke's daughter could act so outrageously and he had to admit the unladylike exhibition delighted him. He remarked, "I see that you have decided to punish me for eating my pie so quickly. Watching you, I wish I had enjoyed it with the same relish you are displaying."

She grinned; her cheeks puffed out. She chewed and savored her meal, until she found Alistair watching her lips too intently. Feeling flushed, she quickly swallowed her food and wiped her lips with her serviette. She turned her attention to the landscape, hoping that Alistair would follow suit. The verdant meadow stretched forever. The yew hedges and evergreen trees framed the property and Catherine thought it was a perfect view for a painting. She kept her eyes on the panoramic landscape and listened to the distant baying of sheep, not realizing she was gently being lulled into slumber. Not until Alistair braced his body, by placing his hands on the ground behind him, did she realize she had being leaning on him. She shot to a sitting position and was about to beg his forgiveness, when she saw that he had risen and was extending his hands to help her up.

"Come," he said. "Let us take a walk before lethargy sets in."

She was pleased that he did not take liberties with her or embarrassed her for her lack of decorum. She placed her hands in his and felt herself tremble. Alistair pulled her to her feet. He watched her straighten her skirt and smooth her hair. She took his arm in escort and realized she found Alistair's company more inviting than any other man of her acquaintance.

She asked, "What did Mrs. Johnson mean when she said that spinning was a lost art form, turning hard working families into paupers. Surely she jests?"

"Not at all," he replied. "You realize that the industrial age is upon us. We are gradually moving from a domestic system: where families get paid to produce textiles in their homes, to a factory system: where one machine can replace the work of five people. The work in a factory is dirty, dangerous, and the wages meager."

He continued, "From a business perspective, the factories create a consistent look and feel to the wool that is desirable to buyers. The machines can produce textiles at a faster rate than hand spinning or weaving, thereby ensuring a greater profit. However, from a national perspective, without regulation to monitor this new industry, our commonwealth are being forced to leave their farms. They cannot afford to keep them without the extra income they had made from producing textiles in their homes."

"I have been to these factories," he added. "I am appalled at their filth and the long hours that women and children are expected to work." He pondered a moment before remarking, "You know, there was a time when a craftsman was responsible for the welfare of their apprentices and workers, but these factory owners care not for their employees. They seem to think their only responsibility is to pay a wage and a poor wage at that! I fear our commoners will uprise, if parliament does not intervene soon with regulation to protect them."

Catherine asked, "Does Beaumont know?"

"I have not worried him, but Felton and I have had serious discussions. We are working to help our own tenants. It would be foolish to ignore the new inventions, but we are looking to establish our own factory nearby, so our tenants do not need to leave their lands to work in them. We will not profit much from the venture other than to keep our community healthy and intact. We are not even sure if the project is feasible because for our factory to succeed it must be competitive. We are trying to determine how to do that and still offer a compensating wage. Parliamentary regulation is our only hope for success."

She inquired, "Who champions you in the House of Lords? Felton has yet to inherit his seat."

"Felton has Westfield's support and the Duke of Hartford's ear," he replied sounding rather defeated.

"And you will soon have the Duke of Aubry making inquiries," chimed Catherine. "For I will make sure he is aware of these factory atrocities."

Alistair smiled at her enthusiasm for championing such an unladylike cause. Before he could comment, they both turned their heads to the sound of a laughing child and a lamb baying in earnest. They saw a small boy lunge at a fleeing sheep and the sight of it brought them both to laughter.

Chapter Five

Catherine sat on a gilded satin chair, before a full length cheval glass mirror, watching the reflection of her abigail press a golden curl into place. She bit her bottom lip in frustration. She was about to admonish Mary again for taking her sweet time in finishing her coiffure, when her maid shook her head at her impatient mistress. Mary assured her that she could not move any faster. She reminded Catherine that she had to apply the same amount of time with the heating tongs to each curl, to produce a head of ringlets that matched in length. "Nothing, milady," Mary reproved, "looks worse on a young lady than a drooping curl."

Catherine had no choice but to agree and resigned herself to Mary's ministrations. It seemed that the task took forever, but in the end she was pleased with her overall appearance. She was anxious to see if Alistair's appraisal would agree with her own. She wore a white gauze high-waist dress over a pale-blue slip. Puckered lace trimmed the square of her low cut bodice and her capped sleeves, while a fancy border of puckered light-blue satin and white gauze trimmed the hem of her gown. The sapphire teardrop necklace that hung from her slender neck brought attention to her blue eyes and her décolletage, reminding gentlemen that she was a woman grown.

Catherine felt she looked her best. She hoped Alistair would ask her to dance and not let convention rule his conduct. After all, the Spring Festival was the only type of acceptable forum that approved of the classes mixing. Her station alone kept the common at bay, so she realized if Alistair did beg her for the favor of a dance, then it would be the first time she ever danced with a man in service. Her chaperones always frowned when an untitled gentleman approached her at a dance, so she could not imagine them condoning a man of business or a tradesman seeking her favor. These thoughts distracted her until Mary's voice broke her reverie, "Your cousin, milady, was asking for you earlier, She was wondering where you have been and if it is still your desire to depart tomorrow."

Catherine heard the censure in Mary's voice. It was obvious that her maid knew she had abandoned Rachel. She confessed, "Yes, I know I have been negligent in my duty towards Rachel, but she is in good company and I desperately needed a break from her."

Mary nodded her head, saying in support of her mistress, "Aye, that one needs a lot of encouragement, though she does not seem worse from your neglect. Shall I pack for tomorrow's departure or does milady have other plans?"

Catherine smiled and replied, "I will let you know tomorrow, Mary. Let us see how the evening goes, shall we?"

Catherine skipped the receiving line where her uncle and her cousin, Edward, were welcoming their guests. She went straight to the ballroom and scanned the room looking for Alistair. She was disappointed to find him absent and was ready to search him out in her uncle's study when she felt his presence behind her. She did not know how she knew it was him, but she trusted her body's response and froze.

Alistair knew better than to pay court to a duke's daughter. He had considered not coming to the dance, but when he approached the manor still arguing with himself, he knew his thoughts had been in vain. He circumvented the receiving line and went directly to the ballroom to immediately look for Catherine. He saw her head moving side to side scanning the crowd. His ego led him to believe she searched for him. He reminded himself again there was no future between a duke's daughter and a man in service, but he admitted he was determined to spend an evening with her, regardless of the futility of an alliance. He hoped she felt the same way. He had enjoyed her company and had to admit an attraction to her. He could not remember the last time he had felt so cheerful, almost hopeful for what the future might bring. Even with their sparring, the day had proven to be more enjoyable than he had expected with Lady Catherine making him smile more often than not. He was drawn to both the ease and excitement he felt in her company. Plus, he thought she understood him in a way no one had before. His cheery disposition faltered knowing such thoughts could bring nothing but grief for him and for Catherine. He knew to engage in a flirtation with a duke's daughter was pure foolishness and could only cost him his position in Felton's service. Before he could convince himself to leave, he found himself standing close enough to Catherine to smell her floral scent. He recognized the fragrance of roses and guessed she must have bathed in perfumed water. He knew he should walk away before she turned around and saw him. He reminded himself he was trespassing into a sphere he had no wish to join. The space between them pulsed. He was close enough to her to see the fine hairs at the nape of her neck bristle. When he saw her muscles tense, he knew it was too late to walk away. Catherine knew he was here.

Catherine's heart raced. She began to feel lightheaded, so she tried to convince herself that it was not Alistair standing behind her, but only her nerves getting the better of her. She feared if she did not reduce her rapid heartbeat, that she would soon make a spectacle of herself when she fell to the ground in distress. She almost fainted when he addressed her.

"Good evening, my lady," he greeted.

Catherine took a cleansing breath and drew from years of training to regain control of her nerves. She slowly turned around to give her accelerated heart rate time to slow down. She was surprised to find Alistair standing so close that she had to look up to see his face. She gasped when she saw how much he admired her.

Alistair heard Catherine's rasping breath when their eyes met and he realized that he too had failed to exhale. He had never seen a more beautiful woman and the sight of her in a ball gown that accentuated her figure with delicate golden curls framing her face had him forgetting to breathe.

Catherine had never felt shy in her life, nor did she ever feel it necessary to seek someone's good opinion of her. Living her life in the highest echelons of society, with the exception of royalty, she owned a self-confidence that came from being admired from suitors and debutantes alike. The only time she had ever felt unsure of herself was the day she met Alistair in Edward's study and every other time she was in his company. She knew it was because she admired him and wanted him to reciprocate her feelings.

Finally finding her voice, she returned his greeting, "Good evening, Mr. Chapman." She silently admonished herself for sounding like a green girl at her first social affair. She did not recognize the timid soft voice that left her lips, but she was very familiar with her fluttering heartbeat. She could not seem to control the errant muscle, especially after seeing Alistair eloquently dressed, sporting the formal black dress of a gentleman.

He was amazingly fit and handsome. Catherine was immensely attracted to him, especially his self-assurance that gave him an air that commanded respect from those around him. She responded to this man of mystery. He stirred her emotions and affected her like no other man had before.

Alistair inquired, "If you are not otherwise engaged, my lady, I hope you will give me the honor of the opening set?"

Catherine forgot every coquettish ploy she was taught to manage suitors and answered with complete honesty, "I am not engaged, sir. I would very much like to dance with you."

She was not sure whether it was her forthright answer or the beaming grin that Alistair returned that made her blush and become uncharacteristically shy. He proffered his arm in escort and when he saw her hesitate to take it, with undue patience, he waited and watched. Catherine had balked at taking Alistair's arm because the reality of the situation hit her. She was not just accepting a dance, but a man her parents would find completely ineligible. Their keeping company would be remarked upon and she questioned if she was ready to have her name aligned with his. She looked up and saw his knowing eyes. She thought he meant to communicate his understanding, but instead, his look only challenged her. Without further thought, she placed her hand on his arm and felt immediate pleasure when he covered it with his own and gave her a magnificent smile. Alistair promenaded her over to where the couples were starting to form their groups for the quadrille.

Alistair had seen Catherine balk and was pleased when she followed through with her acceptance. He had wanted to spend the evening with her, but now wondered the wisdom of it, feeling the intense energy that pulsed between them. He could feel her racing heartbeat from where her hand rested on his arm and was fairly sure it matched his own. He knew they each needed to check their emotions before either of them did anything foolish and was glad for the complicated quadrille for which they were about to engage. He thought, *"We will each be thinking of making our figures and be apart more often than together. There is no harm indulging in one dance. Then, we will bid each other good evening and goodbye."*

Catherine admonished herself again, when she felt her heart start to beat erratically. She was so overwhelmed with excitement, she was afraid that she would forget her steps. *"Don't be a fool. You have danced the quadrille a hundred times and have nothing to fear."*

She heard the music and noted the other guests that made up their set. Without thought, she stepped and promenaded through the dance, feeling more like an observer than a participant. Her attention was on Alistair and nothing else. On those occasions when they came together and their hands touched or their bodies brushed, her feelings heightened. She could tell that Alistair was experiencing as much emotion as herself.

She was glad her uncle had retired early and her cousin, Edward, was too distracted with his own affairs of the heart to see the spectacle she was making of herself. Without a proper guardian or the society matrons to check her manner, she expressed her *joie de vivre*. She was sure everyone knew that she admired her partner. When the quadrille ended, she encouraged Alistair to keep her company. He did not seem to mind, so they spent the whole evening together. He seemed to know that propriety never allowed a debutante to engage in more than two dances with the same gentleman, unless that man was her husband or fiancée, so they settled in out-of-site locations, like an alcove or balcony, to be discreet. The evening ended too quickly and Catherine was sorely disappointed to take her leave of Alistair, especially without some token of affection. She desired a kiss, but he had already told her that he would not abuse the trust that Felton had placed on him. She retired, hoping that on the morrow, Alistair would confess his feelings to her. Only then, would she consider her father's displeasure over wanting to marry a man of business.

Catherine's maid had no idea what occupied her mistress's mind when she uncharacteristically acquiesced without complaint to every tug and pull she made in disrobing her for bed. She did not know that Catherine was absorbed in recalling every detail of the evening, remembering Alistair's touch, voice and manner. If Mary had known what engaged her mistress's thoughts then she might have reminded her of what the duke might think about it all. Instead, Catherine's emotions were not checked and she was allowed to crawl under her bed covers to dream of a future with a man that had captured her heart.

Catherine awoke refreshed and full of energy. She was excited to see Alistair and to talk to him. Last night had been magical and though no confessions of ardor were spoken between them, she was positive he wanted to further an intimacy with her. She was sure they could come up with a viable solution that would enable them to explore their feelings. Perhaps, she could stay on at the manor for an extended sojourn. She could ask Edward for his support. Had she not dropped everything to come to his aid in his pursuit of love? She pondered, *"Does not my situation equate with his? Lady Anne, after all, is in service and yet his offer to her is acceptable. Why should I not be given the same consideration?"*

Catherine had high hopes of Edward supporting an alliance with Alistair. While she had no idea what a future looked like with him, she was sure with his intelligence, her dowry and her father's connections, that something could be arranged. She had already accepted in her mind Alistair's proposal of marriage by the time she knocked on the door to Edward's study. She recognized Alistair's voice immediately when he bid "enter." She knew he was alone, for if Edward was present, he would have been the one to answer her tattoo. She rushed in, shutting the door behind her before he could comment.

She greeted him cheerfully. "Oh, Alistair, I am glad I have found you alone. I have so much to say."

Alistair felt a frisson of happiness the minute he saw Catherine enter, until he realized why she was so enthusiastically seeking him out. Her face betrayed her intentions, bursting forth with so much giddy emotion. He knew she was going to confess her feelings for him and he had to stop her before any damage could be done.

"My lady," he answered. "I am afraid you have caught me at an inopportune time. His lordship has given me multiple tasks and I must ask you to leave me to my business. I will be sure to let Felton know that you were looking for him."

"But I am not looking for Edward," she chided. "I want to speak with you."

Alistair felt like a beast for crushing her spirit, but he knew it was for the best. He replied sternly, "I am afraid I have no time to give you today."

"But," she pleaded. "I must speak with you. We have much to discuss."

Alistair stood and berated, "My lady, are you so used to getting your way that you are unable to accept rejection? I have done my best to be of service to you, as I would to any of his lordship's guests, but I cannot placate you today and must ask you to leave. I am sure that you understand that Felton's desires usurp your own. Unlike yourself, who only seeks amusement, I must work for a living."

Catherine did not hear her *congé* or even wonder at the audacity of the man to dismiss a duke's daughter. Instead, her pride focused on those words that slandered her character. She instinctively retorted, "Perhaps, sir, there is a task that I may complete for you, that will prove I am capable of more than just amusing myself."

At first, Alistair wanted to smile at the bold minx that stood in front of him. He thought it admirable that her first instincts were to defend herself, rather than weep from his outright rejection of her. He felt wretched that he had to treat her so cruelly, but he knew no other way to protect her than to offend her, "No, my lady. I do not think you are capable of assisting me."

Alistair's harsh words shocked Catherine to the core. She thought she might cry, so before her body reacted in a way that could only embarrass her, she turned and exited, almost colliding into Edward when she rushed through the door to make her way back to her private suite.

Surprised to see Catherine bolt from his study, Edward watched her until she disappeared from his sight. He could tell that she was upset and entered his study to see what might have happened. He raised his eyebrow at Alistair when he realized that Catherine had been alone in the room with him. He scolded, "This will not do, Alistair. What were you thinking having my cousin without a chaperone in your company?"

He answered, "She entered of her own accord, my lord, and shut the door herself. I immediately made her leave."

Edward asked, "What did she want with you?"

"I am sorry, my lord," he replied. "But your cousin has distracted me from my work. In a moment of frustration, I told her I was busy and had no time for someone who only sought amusement." She did not respond well," Alistair chuckled, "to my criticism."

"And yet," remarked Edward, "she still seeks you out."

Alistair replied, "I think she is bored, my lord, and looking for purpose to prove me wrong. She asked that I assign her a task to show me that she is capable of industry. When I refused, she left abruptly."

"This does not sound like my cousin. She cares not what others think. There is more to this than you are telling me," he stated. "I noticed you partnered with her in the quadrille. Exactly, how many dances did she favor you?"

Alistair stalled in his answer, so Edward remarked, "Never mind, I retract the question. I have a feeling I do not want to know." He walked over to his uncle's desk where Alistair had been reviewing some account books. Alistair quickly relinquished his seat to his employer and waited for his direction. Edward sat down and instructed his man of business to take the seat across from him. Edward placed his elbows on the desk and clasped his hands to rest his chin on them. He leaned forward, steeled his eyes at Alistair and said, “I have not pursued your private business, Alistair, because it is precisely that, private. But, you must know that an alliance between a duke’s daughter and my employee, even one that is a gentleman is insupportable.”

Before Edward could finish, Alistair remarked, “Yes, I know. I made an error in judgment by showing particular attention to Lady Catherine. I have tried to rectify the mistake by making myself disagreeable.”

“My cousin is too intelligent to fall for such a ruse,” he remarked. "You have no plans to resolve your issues with your family?”

Alistair bellowed a resounding, “No!”

“Then,” replied Edward, “since I cannot evict my cousin, I shall send you to take care of some business at my other estate that I have neglected. You may return, once Catherine has left. Does this meet with your satisfaction?”

“Since when do you ask the consent of one of your employees, Felton?” asked Alistair.

Lord Felton laughed, “That is the first slip you have made since you came to seek me out for a position, Alistair. And to answer your question, I have never commanded my friends, whom I consider you one.”

Catherine replayed Alistair’s harsh words over and over again in her mind. Something did not ring true. She chided herself for her feminine sensibility and took a deep breath. “Nothing,” she determined, “will be resolved unless I can clear my mind and act rationally.”

She raised her head off her bed pillow, where she had lain prostrate in sobs ever since returning to her room and slamming the door behind her. She conjured Alistair’s face and remembered how pleased he looked when she had first entered Edward's study. It was not until she declared that she had much to say to him that a marked change occurred. She realized, *“He wanted to abuse me, so I would take him in dislike and leave without revealing my feelings for him. Foolish man. Does he think me that fickle, that unsure of my feelings, that a simple “by-your-leave,” will halt my pursuit?”* Catherine laughed, acknowledging, *“I am the pursuer. My goodness! Is that not a flip of the coin?”*

She rose and brought herself to rights, refreshing her face with cool water. She repinned some strands of hair that had come loose from her coiffure and smoothed out the wrinkles on her dress to make herself presentable. She collected her wits and strode to Edward’s study to battle with Alistair. She was determined to make him see reason and convince him that he was more than an acceptable suitor. After all, she would explain, she should know.

However, to her chagrin, Edward’s study was empty and she became worried. Her intuition told her that Alistair was gone. She remembered Edward's shocked and displeased face when he saw her leave his study. He probably learned that she had been alone with Alistair and removed him from the manor. He was a decisive man and would not hesitate to take action if he thought she needed to be protected. She sought him out immediately and found him in the library with Lady Elinor, the Countess of Westfield. She tried to check her anger, but her voice revealed her fiery emotion. "What have you done, Edward? Where did you send him?"

Elinor gave Edward a sympathetic look and without saying a word left the two cousins to battle out their differences.

Arrogantly, he asked, "My dear cousin, you take me unawares. Whom exactly do you speak?"

"You know exactly that I am referring to Alistair," she replied. "I want to know where you sent him."

Edward scolded, "You forget yourself, Catherine! It is improper of you to address my man of business on such intimate terms and furthermore, my business affairs or the whereabouts of my staff is none of your concern."

Catherine balked and instead of pursuing a line of questions she knew would not be answered, she left. She returned to her room and pulled the bell cord to summon her abigail. Before long, Mary entered and queried, "Yes, milady?"

"Oh, Mary! Good, you are here," she exclaimed. "I want to leave immediately. Please pack our bags and inform Rachel that we must depart, post haste."

"Is anything wrong, milady?" her maid asked. "You seem as though the devil is chasing you."

Catherine took a moment to calm her anger. After a few moments, she felt her body relax and responded, "I am fine, Mary. In fact, I am more than fine, since it appears that my cousin may have saved me from making a fool of myself."

Chapter Six

Catherine's guilt washed over her when Lord Bellows brusquely helped her to descend from his racing curricle. His tight mouth and furrowed brow prominently displayed the temper he was keeping in check. No doubt the anger that coursed through him would be released in a series of oaths the moment Catherine left his company. Last night, at the Anthworpe Ball, she had received his advances with the sweetest of dispositions. She had danced with him twice, had promenaded the length of the ballroom with him, laughed and smiled as though no other man existed. She accepted with alacrity his invitation to drive with him through Hyde Park on the following day. Like those that preceded him, his lordship had every expectation to believe she earnestly welcomed his attentions. The realization that he was wrong hurt his pride excessively.

The moment Catherine returned from Beaumont Manor, she had energetically thrown herself into the social scene, acting like an enthusiastic debutante. She sent easy to read signals: a demure smile, a flutter of eyelashes, a playful swat with her fan to a hopeful admirer, that she was ready and open to be wooed. Much like the governing Prince George, who gives no thought to how his extravagant spending affects the National Treasury, Catherine too, behaved recklessly, dallying with her suitors without consideration for the broken hearts she left in her wake. Well, perhaps not hearts, but a number of egos were bruised and the slighted gentlemen did not keep the injury they felt to themselves. Before long, Catherine's name was bantered about in clubs and parlours for being a tease. The *gossipmongers* were happy to spread the *on dits* of how she encouraged and rejected an inordinate amount of eligible gentlemen.

Catherine had enjoyed keeping company with Lord Bellows at the Anthworpe Ball. She had accepted his invitation to ride with him through Hyde Park the next day, because she was not indifferent to the handsome gentleman owning a healthy head of auburn hair and matching golden-brown eyes. She admired his athletic build. She caught herself a number of times observing him under her lowered eyelashes and had no reason to believe that he augmented his shoulders or legs with padding to enhance his physique. She enjoyed conversing with him. His lively wit made Catherine break into a smile on more than one occasion. Not once during the evening did she think of Alistair, so she hoped as she made ready for bed, that Lord Bellows might be the one to usurp Alistair Chapman from her heart and mind.

Unfortunately for the earnest gentleman, who had hopes to show himself to advantage with his driving skill, their ride through Hyde Park corresponded with the Four-in-Hand's flamboyant jaunt to Chalk Hill and back. Members of the Four-in-Hand Club were superb whips who paraded their yellow-bodied barouches in a single file. They made a splendid spectacle, dressed in blue and yellow striped waistcoats under their long drab coats garnished with mother of pearl buttons the size of a five-shilling piece. His talent paled in comparison to the superb handling of the Four-in-Hand Club members, who owned a self-assurance that, unluckily for Lord Bellows, reminded Catherine of Alistair.

The exhibition recalled for Catherine how easily she fell for Alistair's charm and the memory embarrassed her. Her mood quickly changed from an agreeable lady to a quiet and sullen companion. Her thoughts of Alistair had relentlessly plagued her days and the idea that he had trifled with her for his own amusements had depressed her. She shuttered when she thought what she may have allowed, if he had decided to do more than just toy with her inexperience. Regardless, the man had touched her heart and set a standard for which she compared all other suitors. For until she met Alistair, she had never experienced the type of emotions that made her feel exuberant, nor had she ever met a man that she admired above all others. Alistair challenged her mind and body;

she was determined that when she married she would settle for nothing less.

Lord Bellows gave up trying to engage Catherine in conversation or to even understand why she suddenly lost interest in him. He thought it quite ungracious of her to not at least pretend that she enjoyed his company. He had lost all civility by the time they concluded their circuit and he returned her to her town home. He wished only to take his leave of her and wasted no time escorting her to her threshold, where he made his curt bow and left the minute the butler opened the door. Catherine knew that like the others, he would not return for she had abused him dreadfully. She concluded that it was time to remove herself from London, until she could rid her fascination for a man that did not want her, yet had captured her esteem.

Catherine was surprised to see their family butler, Frenton, in service. When the duke opened his town home for the Season, Frenton usually remained at Aubry to watch over the dowager. She waited until Frenton helped her to remove her pelisse and hat, before asking, "Did the dowager send you?"

He replied, "In a way. I am part of her entourage. My Lord Felton brought her in his carriage this past half hour. She is in the large parlour with his and her grace."

"Edward was at Aubry to collect grandmama?" The question was rhetorical. Catherine did not expect an answer, for though servants knew what went on in their master's residences, they would never admit to it. Holding confidences was highly valued with the aristocracy and any servant wanting to remain employed, knew better than to gossip or speculate about their betters.

Catherine was pleased that her grandmother was in London and made her way to the parlour to greet her. She hoped her arrival did not bring ill news and was glad to see her family in a happy exchange when she entered.

She greeted her grandmother with open arms and welcomed her warm embrace. "Grandmama! How good it is to see you."

The dowager hugged her granddaughter and then stepped back to look deeply into her eyes. She thought Catherine's cheery salutation a little too forced and worried that something troubled her. She replied, "It is good to see you as well, Catherine. I understand that Lord Bellows had your favor today. You did not invite him in?"

Catherine turned to look to her parents and laughed. She knew they were hopeful that she would settle upon one of the many offers that were presented to the duke. She shook her head and said, "No, I am afraid we do not suit and it would be unkind of me to give him false hope." She asked, "What brings you to Town, Grandmama?"

The dowager replied, "Edward brought me. He is quite serious in offering for Lady Anne and insists that I attend the wedding. He even requested Beaumont and Viscount Atwood to delay their Grand Tour, so they would be present."

Catherine queried, "Lady Anne has accepted? I have seen no announcement in the papers."

The dowager replied, "He plans to offer at the DeRos Ball that is being held in honor of Lord Riverdale's engagement to Miss Tate. He is most confident."

"I am glad for him," she responded.

The Duke and Duchess of Aubry had been listening attentively. Their nephew had created quite a stir with his recent assistance to help Mr. Cowper gain his viscountcy. The title had been dormant for years waiting for a blood male heir. It was in that which drew their interest.

The duke asked, "I understand that Mr. Cowper's, excuse me, Viscount Atwood's property is not far from my own estate."

"Yes," responded the dowager. "It is really quite a sad story. Atwood's grandmother, Alana, was cast from her family when she married her husband. Her father thought the man beneath them. I understand he was a military man with only an impressive service record to recommend him. He was reported dead, so Alana relocated when she found she was with child. I am told she feared her father would steal and rid her of her baby. It was believed the viscount thought he could contract a more advantageous and profitable marriage for the Atwood coffers if Alana was without child. She fled her father's protection when she heard he was negotiating a new marriage for her. Apparently, he felt so betrayed that when the very alive Captain Poole came looking for his wife, the viscount told him Alana had died in childbirth. They never learned of each other's existence. Mr. Cowper called upon my brother because his grandmother had always spoken fondly of him. Thanks to him and Edward, Mr. Cowper learned he is not without family. Alana's sister and family lives and they just discovered that Captain Poole is also alive. Mr. Cowper, the new Viscount Atwood, and Beaumont are to make their way to Southwick, the coastal town where Captain Poole lives, for a visit. You know Alana settled in the seaside resort of Worthing. Only a few miles separated them and they never knew it."

The duke added, "I understand his aunt, Baroness Litford, verifies his lineage and that Prinny has validated his claim."

"Yes, as I was informed. Edward told me that Atwood's properties have been sorrowfully neglected. He has sent his man of business to set all to rights, so that Atwood can take ownership at the end of his Grand Tour. He has given his man *carte blanche*."

The duke replied, "Edward must trust his man impeccably to empower him with unlimited authority."

"My brother does as well," she replied. "He has been a godsend, managing his affairs at Beaumont Manor, ever since he lost good old Mr. Howard."

"His previous steward, I believe. His wife was your playmate if I remember the stories correctly," remarked the duke.

She offered, "Yes, she is still a dear friend whom I hope to bring to visit in the near future."

Catherine's mind raced while her parents and her grandmother reminisced. Alistair was at the Atwood

Home, not far from her family estate. Catherine decided it was time to go home.

Catherine's parents refused her request to return to Aubry without a family member to escort her, plus they did not think it proper for her to miss Edward's upcoming wedding. The dowager claimed Edward was determined to win the hand of Lady Anne and would marry her with due haste.

"No," her parents decreed. Catherine was to remain in London until her grandmother returned home and it appeared that would not happen until after Edward's wedding.

On more than one occasion, the dowager tried to speak to Catherine privately to learn what bothered her. She thought Catherine's spark was missing. Her daughter-in-law, the duchess, proclaimed that she was missing the company of Miss Morgan whom, after a timid and unsuccessful entry into the *ton*, chose to return to her home in the country. The dowager knew that was not the cause, for if anything, Rachel had taxed Catherine's patience. Something was amiss and she was determined to get to the bottom of it. She knew it was unlike Catherine to prefer her home when the Season was still in full swing with balls and fetes to attend. She decided she would watch Catherine tonight at the DeRos Ball to see if someone was behind her granddaughter's depressing manner.

Catherine's disappointment in having to wait to seek out Alistair added to her already sullen mood. Her abigail, Mary, was quick to notice her lackluster personality when she dressed her for the DeRos Ball. Never before had she ever seen her mistress not interested in attending what would be the notable crush of the Season.

Everyone had been talking about Lord Riverdale's betrothal to Miss Annabelle Tate, the daughter of a deceased merchant. If not for the approval of the Almack's Patronesses, many believed even Bell's substantial dowry would not have bought her entry into London's crème of society.

To her credit, Lady Anne (Miss Tate's hired chaperone and more importantly strategist) created so much interest among the *bon ton* that before anyone discovered Miss Tate's dowry came from trade; they were already charmed by her and did not care. Of course, the fact that her father's demise broke her connection to the merchant class helped to recommend her. The *bon ton* may abjure the society from which new wealth is burgeoning; but the wealth itself is not an affront. Besides, Lord Riverdale was not in line to inherit his father's title, so there was no need for the upper echelons of society to create a ruckus. It was becoming quite the fashion for third sons and penniless aristocrats to increase their coffers by marrying daughters of the new wealth. The aristocrats in these alliances gained the funds they so desperately needed and the rich merchants bought the titles they coveted for their daughters, hoping to increase their own prestige.

Catherine fumed at another example of a match made between the separate classes in society. She regressed in her thoughts, for truly, she was happy for her cousin Edward and Lord Riverdale. Her complaint was that she also wanted happiness and was not sure that fate would allow it.

The DeRos Ball was indeed a crush. Everyone who was anyone came to see the engagement of Lord Riverdale to Miss Annabelle Tate. In addition, their attendance provided them with a special attraction in witnessing Lord Felton's romantic overture to Lady Anne. In the middle of the ballroom, with couples gliding around their perimeter, Edward bent down on one knee and recited a piece of Shelley poetry. He then rose, offered for Anne and placed a diamond and gem encrusted bracelet on her wrist. The act reminded Catherine of Rossini's Italian opera *La Cenerentola,* where Prince Ramiro is reunited with Angelina and returns her lost bracelet. To the glee of Edward's audience, Lady Anne accepted his offer and congratulations abounded. Catherine silently cheered, *"Good for you, Edward!"* She then realized that she would soon be able to return home and confront Alistair regarding his feelings for her.

Catherine scanned the ballroom for her parents and hoped they would be ready to leave soon. She went in search of them and found her father first. He was deep in conversation with someone she did not know. She was prepared to circumvent him in search of her mother when she saw him acknowledge her and beckon her to present herself. She dutifully obeyed and made her proper curtsey upon greeting them.

The duke said, "Daughter, I would like you to meet the Marquis of Gracemoor. His son, Lord Mercer, is a friend of Riverdale's and he was looking to find him. I thought you might know him, since recently you were both guests at Beaumont Manor.

Catherine, curtsied again and replied, "My lord, I am pleased to meet you. I am afraid I am not honored with your son's acquaintance and therefore, I am unable to point him out to you. I wish you good fortune in your quest."

His lordship smiled and said to the duke, "She is a beauty, Duke. She and my son would make a fine match. What do you say?"

Catherine's jaw dropped. She looked at her father for permission to leave. The duke wanted to laugh at his daughter's discomfiture. He could tell she was taken aback at Lord Gracemoor's crassness, but he was used to it. His daughter was a prize that was continuously sought after. He would be happy when she was settled. He had a *tendress* for her, though he rarely remarked upon it. She reminded him of his own mother, the dowager, whose spirit always held his admiration. He wanted a match for his daughter where her husband would cherish her spirit instead of crush it. His tendency was to let Catherine have her way as long as her actions led her towards a suitable match. He felt he had time before he had to intervene. He said to his daughter, "Go, see if the duchess is ready to depart, Catherine. I will meet up with you soon."

Catherine hurried off.

Lord Gracemoor continued, "Well, Duke. Do you think I jest with you? My son is at the age where he should be starting his nursery. An alliance between our families would be advantageous to us both."

The duke simply replied, "Catherine is young. I am allowing her to enjoy a couple of Seasons. If your son has an interest to promote, he may do so. Until then, I suggest we leave any talk of alliances to them."

Catherine had always known that one day her father would contract a marriage for her, but even though this was her third season, she still thought she had time to promote her own wishes regarding her betrothal. Her parents had yet to harangue her, so she never thought her father was seriously considering offers for her hand. Lord Gracemoor frightened her. What if he convinced her father that his son offered her the most advantageous alliance? Would her father force her to wed? Catherine shuddered. She wanted to go home to the safety of her ancestral home. She would leave tonight if she could, but alas, she had to wait upon Edward's marriage.

In respect to Lady Anne's wishes, a small number of friends and family gathered at St. James Church. No banns were read. Edward had secured a special license. He felt he had waited long enough to make Anne his wife and was not interested in waiting the three weeks that were required to have the banns read in church. Catherine liked the intimate affair and thought something similar would be to her liking; however, she realized her position as the daughter of a duke made it impossible. She expected her wedding would be full of the pomp and circumstance due her station. She had sat in the front row along with her parents, the dowager, and Beaumont, so they were the first row to exit after the ceremony, behind the bride and groom.

Catherine felt she was being watched, which of course, she usually was, being a duke's daughter who always wore the first stare of fashion. She kept her eyes forward, not wanting to connect with her admirer's eyes, but his intense gaze chilled her. It was almost as though someone beckoned her. When she reached the church's threshold, her curiosity got the best of her, so just before her pupils shrank from walking into the daylight, she turned and searched out the area from where she was sure her admirer stood. When she found no one, she chided herself for her ridiculous notion. She accepted it was her frazzled nerves that were responsible for her unease and knew at that moment that it was time to go home. She needed repose. She needed to see Alistair and put this infatuation of hers to rest.

Chapter Seven

Catherine followed her grandmother into her father's ducal carriage and did her best to check her rising frustration over the sluggish pace that oversaw their departure. She had hoped to be already home at Aubry and it angered her that her journey home was only just beginning. It had been over a week since she saw Edward wed and now, seeing the servants move at a snail's pace to load their own conveyance with her trunk, she began to wonder how far they would be able to travel before sunset. She watched the footman assist her grandmother into the carriage and then followed to help settle her into her seat by placing and tucking a lap blanket over her legs. Catherine then situated herself into her own red velveteen squab before looking out the window to wave goodbye to her father. The duke had remained vigilant, watching their baggage loaded, their persons boarded and now, standing stiff and proud, overseeing their departure. When the carriage rambled away, she waved to her ever watchful father, while her absent mother, no doubt, was still abed, even though the sun was near its zenith.

Her grandmother's entourage followed behind them. She expected to see their transport pass them as soon as they left the city. The servants would travel ahead to greet them at each of their posting inns and eventually, open the Aubry home to await their arrival.

As Catherine looked out her window, the thought crossed her mind that she could walk faster than the vehicle traveled, but she soon checked her unkind thoughts when the carriage jolted from hitting a pothole and she saw her grandmother grimace. She tended to forget, unlike her coachman, that her grandmother required a sedate pace for her fragile bones.

The days of travel were exhausting, so Catherine was not surprised when they finally arrived home that her grandmother immediately retired to her room. It was not uncommon for the dowager to seclude herself for days to rest her wearied body after a long trip. Catherine was glad she would not be under her grandmother's watchful eyes, for the lady would never allow her to ride without a chaperone or visit a gentleman in private. She planned to visit Alistair on the following day and without another person with authority over her in residence, she knew there was no one to stop her from doing as she pleased.

She barely slept, waiting for the morning to come. Her nerves bristled with anxiousness. She rung the bell cord to summon her abigail the moment eight bells struck the hour on the long case clock. She was sure her maid would think that she owned a brain fever if she was called to serve her mistress any earlier. She was glad she had a reputation for morning jaunts or else Mary might very well seek out the dowager with concerns about her health.

The moment Mary entered her suite, Catherine instructed her maid to dress her in her favorite blue merino riding habit. She liked the way the jacket pinched her waist to show off her curves and was partial to the decorative braiding and epaulettes that were so much the rage, ever since England had warred with France. The style complimented her figure and she wanted to look her best should she come upon Alistair when she visited the Atwood Home. With the dowager sound asleep and no one else (aside from Frenton raising a brow in disapproval) to prevent her singular departure, she mounted her mare and crossed over her father's lands to the Atwood Home. She planned to confront the man who had occupied her mind since she first met him.

For weeks, Catherine recalled every word and action she shared with Alistair, her emotions churning inside herself until they erupted in a furious and self-incriminating diatribe. When all was said and done, the one thing that raised her ire the most was feeling that Alistair had likened her admiration of him to a moonstruck calf. It embarrassed her to know that he did not desire her, but tolerated her because she was Edward's cousin.

She concluded that in order to settle her bruised ego and erase the man from her thoughts, she needed to set the record straight with him. She would show him that she was indifferent to him and definitely was not pining away for him. She had made up her mind to shun and ignore him. That was how she treated any gentleman whose arrogance affronted her, and then she realized the churlishness of her strategy. How could she abjure him if she sought him out? She could not act surprised to see him because the Atwood Home, though a small property in comparison to the Aubry Estate, was only accessed cross-country or through a private lane.

Catherine pulled on her mare's reins to check her progress just as she crested the grassy knoll that overlooked the Atwood Home. From her vantage point, she could see a flurry of activity laboring on the property. She saw many workers and what appeared to be a single gentleman giving orders. She guessed it was Alistair. She thought she saw him pause and scan the landscape. She quickly pulled the reins to turn her mare's head, dug her left heel into the horse's flank and with her crop, slapped her horse to race away before Alistair could spy her. She embarrassingly realized that she was indeed a moonstruck calf.

The next morning after a restless night, Catherine rose with a weary body and spirit. She could easily sleep the day away, but she dragged herself out of bed, determined to rally herself from her woebegone thoughts. She was not sure if it was her pride that made her face the day or fear that her abigail would inform her grandmother that she was ill. She felt humiliated after yesterday's exhibition. She understood that nothing good could have come from confronting Alistair, other than more embarrassment. She decided to chalk up her mortification as one of life's lessons. In the future, she would tread carefully in any affair of the heart. She was sure she was not the first or only young debutante to believe that when a person fell in love, the feeling was automatically reciprocated. She would learn from her experience, but she feared that she would never be able to trust her instincts again, for they had proven false.

Yesterday, she was so afraid of Alistair seeing her that she raced away. At first, all she felt was the pounding of her beating heart, then as she settled into a rhythm riding her horse, she began to feel the power that carried her and drew comfort from her mare's strength. She knew in that moment that while she could not control her life, she could command her horse and that feeling lifted her spirit. She rode until she felt renewed in body and mind. By the time she finally brought her horse to a walk, her outlook was greatly improved. She told herself that she just needed to be careful not to ride in the direction of the Atwood Home or place herself in a vicinity where she could run into Alistair. She would travel northwest to enjoy the hills and vales of her father's property and forget about the man who rejected her.

Catherine rose early the next day for another morning ride. Again, without a guardian to check her behavior, Catherine mounted her side saddle, kicked her heel into her mare's flank and using her crop, urged her horse into a run. She leaned into the galloping stride and with the cool breeze brushing her face, felt reinvigorated. She soon forgot the woes that had revisited her in her sleep. The passing landscape raced by her and she enjoyed seeing nature's kaleidoscope of shapes and colors. She pressed her mare, riding hard, kicking up clods of sod until she reached the top of a grassy slope. She was completely unaware that someone watched her. Strands of her golden hair had escaped her well-secured blue shako hat and while she rested her mare, she brushed them away from her heated cheeks. She felt excited from her vigorous ride and smiled joyfully. *"Finally,"* she thought, *"I feel happy."*

Catherine leaned forward to stroke and pat her horse's neck, rewarding her for a magnificent gallop. She cooed sweet words of praise and then confessed to her trusty steed how happy she felt. She decided in that moment to keep up her morning riding regimen. She was confident that before long, the cobwebs that muddled her mind, otherwise known as the rakish Mr. Chapman, would be cleared away. She was still leaning forward when a male's voice startled her into dropping her reins, her crop, and heeling her mare's flank. The horse recognized and obeyed the signal, sprinting off. Catherine instinctively grabbed the pommel before she lost her seat and held hard, while earnestly shouting, "Whoa!"

Her heart raced with fear. First she imagined her mare would trip over the loose reins and then she saw the forest that lurked in front of her. She was sure without having her leather ribbons to guide her mare that she would mistake her horse's direction, lose her seat and be hurled head first into a trunk. Riding side saddle was dangerous enough without losing control of her mount. Unlike men who rode astride and could guide a well trained horse with the pressure of their legs, a woman sat perilously on her side saddle. She had to keep her hips and shoulders parallel to her horse's ears, in order to have her weight equally distributed, or else she risked falling off when her weight shifted to one side. Catherine closed her eyes, hoping her body would become one with the horse and intuitively respond to its movements. Instead of letting her sight sway her judgment, she prayed her other senses would help her to keep her seat. She was preparing herself for the worst of all scenarios when she was lifted from her mare and placed across the lap of----Catherine opened her eyes and exclaimed, "Mr. Chapman!"

"Yes, my lady," answered Alistair through gritted teeth. "As you would have realized had you had your eyes open when I called to you. I shall inform his grace that your horse master should be duly whipped for teaching you to ride with your eyes closed."

She berated, "You will do no such thing, Mr. Chapman! Without reins in hand, I was using my instincts, rather than my vision to secure my safety."

Alistair looked amused at Catherine's response, for it had sound reason behind it. When he pulled on his steed's reins to bring his horse to a stop, she tersely added, "If you would put me down, I shall look for my mare."

"I see you offer me no thanks for rescuing you," he retorted.

Catherine, who was still embraced in his body and could not help but look into his eyes, replied, "I have more decorum than that, Mr. Chapman. I do indeed thank you; however, I cannot wonder if you are not the one who spooked my horse in the first place."

In defense, Alistair retorted, "A proficient rider, which you claimed to be, my lady, would have his ribbons firm in hand. Had I known that you exaggerated your ability, I would have approached you with caution and ample warning."

Catherine fumed, clenching her fists and digging them into her skirt. She countered, "Any experienced rider can be caught unawares, especially when they believe they are alone. You are a bully to chastise me for no other reason than meanness."

Alistair dropped his mouth at Catherine's childish rant and saw her eyes become teary. He feared she was about to break her composure when he felt her body tremble. A sob burst forth from her mouth, for she now began to understand the peril in which she had been. Alistair hugged her, feeling guilty for having upbraided her and breaking her brave front. He apologized, "I am sorry, Catherine. I am indeed a bully."

His apology pacified her and she was able to stop her emotions from getting out of hand. She thought him sincere and she believed that in using her Christian name he revealed a modicum of affection for her. The idea made her nervous and very much aware of him. She felt her heart flutter again and remembered her resolve to be chary.

Alistair, with Catherine still in his arms, nudged his steed towards the copse of trees and said, "Let us look for your mare. She should not be far off, now that she is unburdened."

Catherine's mare was nipping at some tall lush grass in a small clearing among the slender silver birch trees. Alistair gently slid Catherine off his lap to the ground and then adeptly dismounted. He pulled the reins over his horse's head, brought the horse over to where Catherine's mare fed, and dropped the reins into the lawn. Most horses (unless spooked) would not wander far with reins pulling at their bit.

Catherine stood where Alistair placed her and watched as he set his horse to graze. She saw him retrieve a bota bag and a small parcel from his riding satchel. Then, he took a small blanket that was rolled up and tied behind his saddle and carried the goods over to a soft spot of lawn shaded by an ancient oak tree. He rolled out the blanket, placed the bota bag and package on it, before taking his seat. He beckoned Catherine to come over and join him. Catherine blinked, then paled. She was not sure of Alistair's intentions. As much as she had desired a romantic tryst with him, she knew she would never recover from such a trifling. Her heart was too engaged.

Alistair thought Catherine was still suffering from her runaway mare debacle when he saw her skin's pallor and her eyes open wide with fear. He encouragingly beckoned her forward again and was surprised to hear her gasp. He thought perhaps there was something behind him that scared her and immediately turned around to search out the threat. When he saw nothing to worry him, he returned his gaze to her and finally understood why Catherine looked petrified. He had called her to come to him while patting the blanket. Even with all her admirers, it pleased him to know that Catherine was an innocent. The revelation bubbled out of him with a resounding guffaw that broke Catherine's frightened trance. He explained, "I thought you might like a small repast to calm your nerves before you return home. Baroness Litford sent me off with some bread, cheese, ham, and wine. Would you like to eat before your return home?"

"A picnic?" she queried.

"Of sorts," he offered, hoping his easy manner appeared non-threatening.

Catherine looked at her mare grazing contently nearby. His laughter had relieved her momentary fright. She felt silly, remembering how even when encouraged Alistair would not kiss her. She took a moment to regain her composure by smoothing her riding habit, securing her loose strands of blond hair under her hat, and tugging on her blue kid gloves. Alistair watched her *gird her loins*, as though she prepared for battle, but then she marched in a very graceful sway towards him. He thought if she wanted to look severe she would need to check the alluring manner in which she moved her hips.

Catherine dropped gracefully to a spot where the repast provided a barrier from Alistair's body. The moment she took her seat, he started to tear off a piece of bread from the loaf Baroness Litford had given him and handed it to Catherine. He took a small knife from an inside pocket of his coat and used it to slice a piece of the cheese and ham. Then, he handed the victuals over to Catherine to place on her bread to eat. He said, "I am sorry, my lady. I do not have a cup. Can you drink from my bota bag?"

Catherine had never drunk from one before, but said, "I do not know. I have never tried, but am quite willing."

He replied, "If you will allow me, I will squirt the vintage into your mouth. These things can be tricky and I would hate for you to ruin your riding jacket."

Catherine nodded and watched while Alistair raised the inverted bota bag to squeeze a sampling into her mouth. She swallowed and laughed, before reaching for the bag that Alistair had placed on the blanket. She exclaimed, "Oh! Do let me try."

He handed her the wine bag and watched while Catherine wrestled with the contraption until she successfully reaped her reward.

"I am sure that this is most unladylike, but a great deal of fun," she stated. "Thank you for not letting the rules for what befits a lady keep you from accommodating me."

He smiled, bent his head in a mock bow and said, "Your servant, my lady." His voice sobered when he looked into her eyes. He beseeched, "I hope, my lady, that you will forgive my rudeness from when we last saw one another. My only excuse is that I was distracted by my work. At the time, you mentioned you had a lot to say to me. No doubt, a rebuke for monopolizing your time at the festival and ball."

Alistair saw Catherine's eyes widen and then her mouth turned up into a grin. She responded, "I accept your apology, Mr. Chapman. I do not take umbrage to your directness, only to your assumption that my single purpose in life is amusing myself with entertainments. I hope to prove you wrong."

At long last, Catherine felt a modicum of relief from the mortification that burdened her since Alistair's rejection of her at Beaumont Manor. She realized she had unconsciously feared that he had spoken to others of her infatuation of him and made jest of it, but now she understood that his brusque manner was because he wished to spare her from embarrassment. Her body relaxed knowing she had nothing to fear from him. She finally accepted what he had always known, that a connection between her and a man in service was insupportable. He was an admirable man, and just perhaps, they could find enjoyment in mutual friendship. Surely, no harm could come of an amenable acquaintance.

She asked, "If you do not mind my asking, why were you visiting Baroness Litford?"

Alistair grinned at her noted relaxed candor. It had been a risk to mention their last meeting, but he could tell his apology assured her that he would never reveal to anyone that she admired him. His declaration seemed to dissolve the awkwardness between them. He was glad because he liked Catherine more than he ought and now that she was once again comfortable with him, he wished to enjoy her company. He was sure he could keep his emotions in check for the short time he was at the Atwood Home. Once he returned to Beaumont Manor, more than likely, their future paths would never cross.

He responded, "Baroness Litford is Atwood's aunt. Are you acquainted with the Litfords?"

"No," answered Catherine. "Although they are our neighbors and of the aristocracy, their rank is near the bottom of our order. I am sorry to say the duke has not cultivated a relationship with them."

"A pity," he replied. "They are an exceptional family and one I am happy to acknowledge. I was at her home today because I promised the baroness that I would keep her apprised of the work being done at the Atwood Home."

"Oh!" she exclaimed. "Are you tending to the viscount's business?" Catherine acted ignorant. She did not want him to think she kept apprised of him.

He answered, "Felton has charged me with the management of Atwood's properties and the renovation of his home. Baroness Litford has many of the family heirlooms, paintings, and furniture. She wanted me to see them, so I was aware of the inventory and use them as I see fit."

She remarked, "I would like to see what you have managed to accomplish."

"And so you shall," he replied. "Perhaps, instead of venturing north, you could exercise your mare south and visit me in the next day or two. I would be happy to show you the progress."

Catherine responded, "I should be coy and say, perhaps I will, but I have never been timid, Mr. Chapman. I would very much like to see the property and renovations, so be warned, sir, you may expect me tomorrow."

Alistair laughed, offering, "I am not in admiration of a coy debutante, my lady. I look forward to seeing you tomorrow. Shall we collect our mounts and find our way back?"

Catherine felt her stomach flutter from Alistair's compliment. She wondered if it was possible that Alistair genuinely liked her, not in the way of her other admirers, who esteemed her beauty and wealth, but as someone who approved of her character, her mettle, and her mind. The idea thrilled her and she chimed her response with alacrity, "yes."

Catherine rose early again the next morning to take her ride, but this time with a clear destination. She had Mary secure extra hair pins to hold her coiffure together, but ended up laughing when she felt the pins slide out of her hair while she galloped towards the Atwood Home. Mary probably did not own enough pins to keep Catherine's hair in check.

Before long, Catherine rested on the same slope she ventured that first day to see Alistair. She guided her mare down the grassy hill towards the Atwood Home. Just like her first visit, she spied a flurry of activity. She was pleased she had an invitation to take her all the way to the house. She was too curious to simply return home after a distant glimpse. Catherine drew many a look from the laborers when she cantered up to the front of the house. She looked to and fro, hoping she did not arrive at a time when Alistair was absent. One of the laborers took off his hat and said, "Begging your pardon, milady, but might I be doing something for ye?"

She responded, "Yes, thank you. I am looking for Mr. Chapman. Can you inform me of his location?"

The young laborer bowed and said, "He is inside, milady, but I do not think it a proper place for ye to enter. If ye wait here, I will look for him and tell him yer noble self awaits."

Catherine looked about and saw a mounting block. She replied, "That is not necessary, sir, but if you will watch my horse, I will announce myself. I am expected, you see, to inspect the properties."

"Very good, milady," the young man replied. Catherine nudged her horse over to the mounting block and allowed the laborer to assist her dismount. He was awkward and timorous in aiding such a fine lady, but his look showed he found his task an honor. Catherine tried to give him a shilling and was surprised when he refused. As she walked away, she saw a number of the other workers smile and pat him on the back. She wondered if something improper had transpired, but decided the man had acted nobly and she guessed his peers simply acknowledged his deed of gallantry.

She entered the home and found it rather decrepit and musty. The sunlight crossed the door's threshold and spotlighted the dust particles that floated in the air. It saddened Catherine to see a grand home in such disrepair. Once her eyes became accustomed to the darkened interior, she noticed upon further inspection that a large quantity of work had already occurred. Wallpaper was stripped, walls repaired and washed, the chair rail was in the process of being refurbished and a carpenter was working on rebuilding the staircase. Catherine carefully watched her footing with each step that took her deeper into the house. She entered the library and gasped from the stench of mildewed books. Someone had started removing the collection from the wall cases and was making multiple stacks of them. She went over to where the books were stacked and picked up a few of the volumes from the various towers. She realized that not all of the books were ruined. They were being sorted and it pleased her to learn that many could be repaired. Startled, she jumped back when she heard a scurry of feet and realized some vermin still wandered the floors. She nearly fell over some refuse before a strong set of hands caught and righted her. She knew it was Alistair, even before he spoke. His strength calmed her fears and she felt safe.

He remarked, “You are a brave lady to venture in this chaos without a guide. I wish you would have waited for me to escort you, but I expect you have not yet learned to be chary.”

Catherine turned to face him. She retorted, “There you are wrong, sir. I tread very carefully; however, I do not let fear govern me.”

He asked, "Where is your attendant, my lady? I cannot imagine the duke approves of your riding alone off his property."

She answered, "My grandmama, knowing I am a proficient rider, Mr. Chapman, gives me the freedom to ride without companion when I am at Aubry."

"As you say," remarked Alistair who highly doubted the young debutante. He continued with a wave of his arm to encompass his surroundings, “You must think that our progress is slow based on this room, my lady, but I am happy to reveal we have accomplished much. Aside from the roof, where the damage was beyond repair, the house is very sound.”

“I am glad to hear that, Mr. Chapman,” she responded. “I do prefer refurbishment to demolishment of our ancestral homes. I believe, they each tell a story and I hate to see so much of our history lost."

"There is a lot of charm to this house," he added. "And with all the conveniences we are installing, Mr. Cowper will find himself in the pink of comfort."

"Oh, do tell," she queried. "What have you done?"

"Well," he replied. "I don't mean to be indelicate, but we have installed multiple water closets and have laid out piping for indoor plumbing. I have also placed a special order for a Franklin kitchen range. I am sure Atwood's new cook will be most impressed. Has his grace installed one at Aubry?"

"I cannot say, Mr. Chapman. I have never been to the kitchen, nor spoken with our cook about one," she stated. "I believe our housekeeper handles that part of the household affairs."

Alistair laughed.

Catherine looked curious and asked, "What?"

"I expect," he said. "That your housekeeper handles all the household's affairs."

Catherine joined his mirth, adding, "Indeed, she does."

"Come," he said. "Let me show you the private suites on the upper floors. They are already completed and since you like to see history in a house, you will probably enjoy the ornate wall moldings and frescoes we refurbished.

Alistair listened to Catherine's enthusiastic remarks while he escorted her through each of the private suites. She was pleased with the wall colorings and complimented the new mahogany flooring that Alistair had installed. What a difference from the first floor where evidence of neglect was still prominent. Light penetrated through the new panes of glass and made the new brass wall sconces gleam. Catherine rattled on about how she would decorate each room, speaking of particular rugs, curtains, furniture, and artwork. Her excitement took over her body as she waved her arms pointing to where a perfect spot would be for an escritoire or a chaise lounge. "Lighting is everything," she explained. "Whether writing at a desk or reading on a sofa, it is beneficial for the eyes to have the best light."

Alistair laughed and remarked, "You have a talent, my lady. If you were not a duke's daughter, I think you would have hired yourself out as a purveyor of fine decorating. Perhaps, you will allow me to call on you for assistance when the time comes to fill and arrange these rooms."

By the time Catherine and Alistair exited the Atwood Home they were both in high spirits. Catherine watched Alistair command one of the laborers to collect her mare. Without invitation, she watched him grab her by the waist and hoist her up unto her side saddle. She instinctively grabbed his shoulders to steady herself and felt a frisson of excitement pulse through her. She wondered as she settled unto her seat if he noticed the spark that vibrated between them and what his intentions, if any, would be towards her if propriety did not censure him as ineligible. She could not deny that she enjoyed his touch and the intimacy of being held by him. She wanted to spend another day with him and could not refrain herself from asking, "May I come again, tomorrow?"

Alistair frowned. He feared he had once again erred, showing an admiration that he had no right to display. He was definitely attracted to Catherine and felt a strong meeting of the minds between them. He enjoyed her company and he could not deny that he wanted to spend more time with her; however, he also knew his position as a man of business made it impossible to encourage a liaison.

He responded using a softer voice than the one he used to discourage her at Beaumont Manor, "My lady, I have too much work and cannot properly host your visit. I fear I must refuse and beg you to find your amusements elsewhere." Alistair saw by the change in her face that he had affronted her. He added, "I am sorry to disappoint you."

Catherine smiled and replied, "May I not come as a 'purveyor of fine decorating.' You; yourself, qualified my talent. Might I come tomorrow and offer my assistance."

Alistair wanted to laugh at the lady's perseverance. He answered, "My lady. We are not at that stage where your talent may be utilized. You saw that the construction is still in progress. I thank you for your generosity, but must decline. I know of nothing that you could assist."

Catherine pondered for a moment, tapping her chin in consideration, before asking, "I could help you sort the books in the library and make an inventory of them. Please say, yes, Mr. Chapman. I am too idle at home and need a distraction."

Alistair had to bite his bottom lip, so as not to bellow out a guffaw at seeing her pouty mouth. When he spied her own lips begin to tremble, as though she feared rejection, he found he could not refuse her. Against his better judgment, he said, "Very well, my lady. If it pleases you to do so, you may come tomorrow and work in the library. I warn you, it is filthy work. The books need to be wiped of dust, grease, and checked for damage. You may find dead insects among the weathered pages or even a dead mouse on the bookshelves. Do you still wish to volunteer to such a task?"

"Yes!" she exclaimed. "You have described a thrilling adventure, more exciting than reading a Radcliffe mystery. Let us hope I do not find a dead body among the refuse."

"Let us hope not," he replied, laughing at the grisly idea. Then, he patted Catherine's mount on its rear to set her on her way. He kept watch over her with a grin on his face until she left his sight. He returned to the day's tasks and realized, when he began to bark out orders to his laborers, that he was still smiling.

Chapter Eight

Last night, Catherine's mind was too full of pictures of her and Alistair smiling at one another to fall asleep. She was so giddy that she kept tossing and turning on her mattress. She tangled herself in her bed covers and twisted her cotton lace-trimmed nightgown around her body more than once. Frustrated and physically tired from wrestling with her linen, she finally plopped herself on her back, lifted her derriere to pull and straighten her gown, and tried to relax. With eyes wide awake, she stared into the sober darkness, anxious for the day to come. She eventually fell asleep, but not before the long case clock chimed four bells. In spite of the few hours she slept, she awoke feeling thoroughly rested and energized.

She only had to blink a couple of times and stretch out her limbs to fully awaken her sleepy head and body. She kicked off her bed covers as though she had overslept and was late for an appointment. The frigid air chilled her thinly attired body, provoking her to move with expediency. She bounced from her downy mattress, scurried across the icy floor to tug the bell cord that rang for her maid, and then raced back to the comfort of her warm bed. Excited, she pulled the covers back over her legs, drew them up and hugged them with her arms. Resting her chin on her knees, she waited in anticipation for Mary to help her dress.

She could not remember the last time she had ever been enthusiastic to greet a new day, especially one where industry and grime awaited her. The more she thought about it, she realized there probably was never a time, for servants were the only ones that cleaned in the duke's household.

Catherine smiled seeing Mary enter carrying a pitcher of warm water for her morning ablutions. Her maid grumbled when she saw her excited mistress and admonished. "I do not know what has come over you, milady. Each day you rise earlier and earlier. What happened to nothing being more important than one's rest?"

Catherine retorted, "That was the old me, Mary. The new one professes industry is the balm to boredom. Help me dress, as I am expected at the Atwood Home to work in the library."

Mary replied, "I do not think his grace would approve of such an activity for you, milady."

"Oh, Mary," begged Catherine. "Please do not chastise me. No one will know and I am in no danger of causing a scandal by sorting through some books."

She tsked, "Everyone will know, milady. There is already talk among the lower servants that you ride without a chaperone. The dowager will learn soon enough of your riding alone."

Mary poured the warm water into the porcelain bowl on Catherine's toilette table, setting fresh towels and rose-scented soap on the side for her use. Then, she assisted Catherine with her slippers and robe.

Catherine looked at Mary, mischievously smiling at her loyal servant, before prodding, "But, dear Mary, you will not tell, will you?"

Mary frowned and cautioned, "It is not my place to speak with the dowager, milady, but you best put an end to this recklessness before she gets wind of it. You might think you have her wrapped around your little finger, but she is a tough old bird, and I, for one, wouldn't test her mettle."

Catherine ignored her maid's warning, proceeded with her morning ablutions and then pondered over her wardrobe. She could not make up her mind between vanity and practicality in choosing a riding habit to wear. She wanted to look nice for Alistair, but she did not want to ruin her best habit with the dust and grime she knew awaited her. She brooded until, Mary, plagued by her indecisiveness, sighed in frustration and chose for her an older garment of russet brown to wear. At first, Catherine balked at the dreary color, once the height of fashion, but then she relented into wearing the garment, knowing the color would mask dirt well. Mary convinced her that threading a coquelicot red silk ribbon through her hair, was all she needed to add to her looks. Then, she shook her head, adding, "as though you need anything to make you look pretty."

Alistair felt the hair on his neck bristle or perhaps his sixth sense called out to him. Whatever the reason, his thoughts were diverted from overseeing his laborers as he turned his attention to the nearby hill. He had no doubt that he would find Catherine there at its crest, for he always seemed to sense her presence. She looked glorious, sitting tall in her side saddle like a warrior queen. He saw her raise her face to the sun and just like a flower that opens its petals to the sun's rays, she also bathed in its warmth.

The sun illuminated her as she rested at the top of the hill. Alistair pictured her smiling and then he watched her as she slowly made her way down the verdant slope. She kept her posture straight on the precarious side saddle. Her grace marked her a true equestrian and it amazed him how a young lady with little life experience could continue to enthrall him. A resounding crash interrupted his reflection, returning his attention to the task at hand. He turned to address the fiasco.

Alistair was shouting at some of the laborers when Catherine reached the courtyard. She felt nervous arriving at such an awkward moment and her cheerful disposition wavered. She held her mare in check wondering what she should do and immediately relaxed when Alistair smiled up at her, his boyish grin ameliorating her.

He walked up to her mount, grabbed the bridle and then called to one of his men to take the reins, so that he could assist Catherine from her horse. She felt her body tremble in anticipation and became overwhelmed when he reached up to wrap his hands around her waist. Catherine's heart pounded so hard that she had to place her hands on his shoulders to steady herself. Then, she had to remind herself to breathe.

Alistair acutely felt the pulsating tension that always seemed to resonate between them. It was there the first day that she walked into Edward's study and it ignited each time they were together. Regardless, how compelling the emotions, he knew it was up to him, owning more experience in affairs of the heart than Catherine, to keep them from trespassing into territory that could only end in heartache. He carefully placed Catherine on the ground and immediately stepped back. With aplomb, he asked, “Are you ready to begin your task, my lady?”

She answered, “Yes, most eagerly.”

Alistair walked over to the portico where a number of barrels and crates were stacked in front of the house. He grabbed a piece of coarse fabric and returned to Catherine's side to hand it to her. He said, “I thought this might be of service to you.”

Upon further inspection, Catherine realized it was an apron. She grinned, saying, “Thank you, Mr. Chapman. This is most kind of you.”

Her affectionate gratitude made Alistair grin. *"Damn,"* he reflected, *"I cannot seem to do anything but smile when I am around her."*

He escorted her to the library, making sure she had enough rags and cleaning agents for her to complete her task. He informed her, "I will not be able to stay with you; however, if you need me, simply ask any of the laborers to inform me. If you are agreeable, I will return in two hours to share a small repast with you."

She replied, "Yes, thank you, Mr. Chapman. That would be very nice. Is there any particular way that you want me to sort the books?"

"I would like to weed out the damaged books, but you may approach the task any way you see fit. They need to be cleaned, inventoried and carted, so that we can remove them to refurbish this room. Do only as much as you like, my lady. Remember, you are here for your own enjoyment."

To Alistair's surprise, Catherine pouted and said, "It is indeed true that I volunteered to alleviate my boredom, but I do hope my services are beneficial. I do not want to create more work for you."

"You are most helpful, my lady. Forgive me. I did not mean to imply otherwise. I simply do not want you to feel overwhelmed. As you can see, the collection is large."

Catherine's eyes opened wide in surprise when she finally scanned the wall of books. She remarked, "Indeed it is. I suggest then, that you leave me to my work, so that I may accomplish something."

Alistair wanted to laugh at the serious face Catherine wore. He decided it best that he depart before he released a chuckle that would only embarrass and anger her. He turned, made his exit, and grinned when Catherine, finally comprehending the enormous job that laid before her, exclaimed, "Mercy!"

The mahogany book shelves spanned from floor to ceiling. Each shelf was filled with leather tomes that clearly made up sets of history, literature, and science. It was not uncommon for the aristocracy to fill their libraries with sets of books purchased by the yard. There were some books that seemed to stand out to Catherine, their size and color marking them unique. She wanted to pull out those aberrations to see what had interested the late viscount, but decided a planned approach would be more efficient and less distracting. After all, her job was to clean and not to read the books.

She decided, considering the dust and filth on the shelving, to start at the top level. It did not take a genius to know that gravity would bring the grit to the lower shelves when she removed the books, and while cleaning was a foreign concept to Catherine, she was far from a fool. She saw that a ladder was attached to the bookcase. It was a wooden stepladder, whose top rungs were attached to a rail at the top shelf, with rollers on its feet to allow the ladder to move across the shelves.

She took off her kid gloves, put them in her jacket pocket, and then untied the sheer scarf that secured her shako hat to her head. She carefully removed the stylish cover, so that the trailing sheer fabric would not touch the dirty floor. She looked about for a clean spot to place it and when she saw nothing but grime, she laughed at the absurdity over worrying about her hat getting dirty. She walked over to the weathered brocaded wing chair near the window and dropped her hat on it. Then, she put on the coarse apron that Alistair had given her to wear and constructed a neat bow with the ties. Happy with her progress, she cheerfully made her way to the ladder until she imagined her mother frowning at her.

She bit her bottom lip feeling guilty over knowing her mother would be displeased with her behavior, but quickly brushed off the emotion when she grabbed the ladder. She was determined to complete the task Alistair set before her. Carefully placing her foot on the first rung, she pulled herself up to rest both feet on the first step. Then, she advanced to the next rung, until she felt confident to take the steps with increasing speed. She felt quite proud and exhilarated when she was able to reach the top bookshelf and marveled at her accomplishment, since she did it with no servant or family member to watch over her. She expelled a nervous giggle over her reckless behavior.

Catherine reached for the first tome on the top shelf to pull it forward. She found the book's thickness too difficult to grasp with her hand, so with her fingertips, she decided to remove it from the shelf by tugging the volume from the top of its spine. The book tilted forward and she was sure, using her other hand that she could disengage it from its location. She pulled the spine further down to better grab the book and was scared witless when she saw a tumbling dark mass roll towards her. With all her might, she thrust the book as far away as she could from her body, screaming at a pitch that most likely set every dog in the area to barking. To her horror, the book flew in one direction and what was surely a dead mouse in the other. Both specimens produced a puff of dust when they hit the floor.

Catherine's whole body shook. She was afraid the corpse had touched her hands and with an urgency began to wipe them judiciously on her skirt. She gagged and mumbled, "Yuk, yuk, yuk!" She remembered placing her soft kid gloves in her jacket pocket, so they would not get soiled. They were her favorite pair and at the time, she did not want to have to relinquish them to the rag pile, but that was of little consequence now. She quickly withdrew them from her pocket and donned them. The image of the dead mouse she had just flung from her person, was enough for her to change her mind about soiling her fashionable gloves. Better the gloves than her hands, she professed.

She pushed each digit deep into its leather socket to make sure her fingers were tightly fitted in her gloves. Her heart raced and with nervous fervor, she laughed before exclaiming, “Fearless, indeed!" It took a few more cleansing breaths before she was able to master her fright and her nervous chuckles. After all, she rationalized, it wasn't a live mouse that scared her. The rodent was dead and could do her no harm. Her only worry would be that she would find more dead vermin. She hoped she had the fortitude to deal with them. Only time would tell, for Catherine was not yet ready to let fear defeat her. She cautiously reached for the next volume on the shelf and released the breath she was holding when she saw that no corpse plagued it. She continued with care to remove the next three books, always checking to see if anything lay on top, before placing her hands on the tome. She decided that four books was the safest amount she could carry down the ladder. Her focus on descending the ladder calmed her enough that she had her wits and nerves settled by the time her feet touched the floor. She was just about to congratulate herself on her fortitude, when to her dismay, she saw the wretched mouse lying nearby. Without thought, she threw her load to the wind and raced to exit the room. She stopped at the threshold, laughing so hard that she had to wrap her arms around her quivering belly. Once she stopped laughing and settled her nerves, she grabbed the straw broom that leaned against the wall and returned to face the dead mouse. With the broom, she pushed the offending corpse from the greatest distance she could make possible. Using the tip of her fingers, she grabbed the wooden rod and stretched her arm as far as she could, before she pushed the broom to where the vermin lay. She shoved the disgusting dead rodent, marking a trail free of dust, until the offal resided on the porch. She could only hope that the mouse would completely disappear, either by man or feline, before she left for the day. At a minimum, she wished to remember where she left it, so that she would not take fright of the rodent again or make a fool of herself in front of Alistair. Though she prayed that she would not need to repeat the process, the increasing pile of dead mice on the porch was proving she had more aplomb than she ever thought possible.

Alistair approached the front porch checking his pocket watch to make sure two full hours had passed before he collected Catherine for lunch. He snapped his timepiece closed and stopped at the scene before him. A number of guarded felines froze in their frenzy, watched and assessed him. Before he could chase them away from the pile of dead mice that they were scavenging, they raced away with a number of the vermin. He noticed the blazing trail through the dusty floor from which the mice were swept from the house and quickly looked for a laborer to rid the porch of the disgusting sight. He followed the path that led to the library and grinned when he saw Catherine, amid a pile of books, focused on her task completely unaware of his presence. He watched her. She wiped one of the leather tomes with a rag, blew a wisp of hair away from her face, then wiped her nose with her sleeve. He wanted to laugh at her grubbiness, but knew better than to embarrass her. By the pile of vermin he saw on the porch, he guessed that she came across more than dirt these past two hours. Her grit and diligence amazed him. Before he had a chance to make himself known to her, she sneezed.

"Bless you!" he exclaimed. Catherine jerked her head up to see Alistair smiling at her. With a grin, she replied, "Thank you."

He asked, "Are you ready for a respite or would you rather retire for the day?"

Catherine placed the book she was cleaning down, took off her apron, and answered, "I am having too much fun to end my day, but I am more than ready to eat. Is there some place I can freshen up?"

"I have placed some fresh linen in the first water closet on the upper floor," he answered. "When you are ready, please join me out front. I have set up a place for us to dine."

Catherine tidied herself as best as possible and then made her way to the front of the house, hoping that someone had removed the pile of dead mice. She was relieved to see the vermin gone and pleasantly surprised that Alistair had taken the time to concoct a rather fetching dining table under the canopy of a nearby ancient oak tree. A crisp white linen covered a plank of wood laying atop two barrels. The table was set with china plates and sterling service for two. She watched Alistair retrieve two goblets from a basket and set them on the table before she took her seat on a linen covered barrel. She continued to watch him pull out multiple small bundles from another basket. She earnestly smiled, her hunger heightening with each of the articles that Alistair unwrapped and placed on the table. There were mincemeat pies, assorted cheeses, fresh fruit, and cherry tarts. Alistair uncorked a bottle of burgundy wine and poured them each a glass. He raised his glass to offer her a toast, exclaiming, "To my Purveyor of Fine Decorating. May your talent always be at my disposal."

Catherine's good mood diminished. She knew it was very unlikely that she would ever be at Alistair's disposal again. More than likely, the duke would tire of her fickleness in choosing a suitor and force her to marry. This was her third season, and truth be told, she wasn't looking forward to a fourth, not when the man she wanted was unavailable. If she wasn't so highly coveted, the duke would have already settled her in wedlock, but he had too many offers for the *gossipmongers* to feed the rumor mill that Catherine did not take. Everyone knew it was her grandmother's influence over the duke that gave Catherine the time to find her "love match."

Alistair noticed immediately that his toast had turned Catherine sad. He soberly offered, "I do apologize, Catherine. I was only teasing. Do forgive me."

She answered, "I like it when you call me, Catherine, instead of, my lady."

He replied, "Do you? I mean, did I?"

"Yes," she answered.

Alistair was flummoxed and did not know what to say. Before he could apologize, again, Catherine took a sip of wine. She remarked, "I fear many of the Shakespeare volumes are damaged. The pages are glued together, probably from moisture and the bindings are warped. A master book binder may know how to fix them, but I think they are beyond repair." She continued, "Overall, it is a wonderful collection of the classics, history, philosophy, poetry, and literature. I have come across some first editions: Bunyan's, *Pilgrims Progress*; Defoe's, *Robinson Caruso;* and Swift's, *Gulliver's Travels.* Thankfully they are in good condition. I am sure there are others, but the Shakespeare volumes took up the majority of my time this morning. I am surprised, not to have recognized anything from this century, yet."

Alistair answered, "Not at all. The viscountcy has been dormant for over twenty years. There was no one around to add to the collection."

Catherine responded, "It is a pity they were left to wreck and ruin."

They continued to talk about the books Catherine inventoried and during a pause in the conversation, she elected to change the conversation. She asked, "Are you to improve the gardens, as well?"

Alistair sighed, "I wish I had Beaumont's talent for laying out a garden."

Catherine retorted, "Who said he has any? My grandmama asked the Duchess of Rutland to lend Beaumont her head gardener. You should talk to him about mapping out a proper garden."

Alistair's eyes widened and he cheerfully exclaimed, "That is an excellent idea, my lady! I believe I will do just that."

After their meal, Alistair suggested that Catherine retire for the day because he had to leave to do a final inspection on some tenant cottages. He would not return until late in the afternoon and he did not like to leave her alone. He would prefer that she took her leave when he did.

Catherine responded rather churlishly that she was more than capable of seeing herself off. She confessed that she was having too much fun to end her "treasure hunt." When Alistair asked what she meant. She explained how after finding a First Edition, she exclaimed, "'Oh, what a treasure!' I decided then and there that I was no longer cleaning books, but treasure hunting."

"Very well," he relented trying to keep his voice stern. "It is two o'clock now. You may stay half past the hour, but then you must make your way back to Aubry while the day is young."

Although Catherine thought he was arrogant to order her about like a guardian, she did not take offense. Truth be told, she thought his manner revealed that he cared for her more than he was willing to admit.

Before she left for the day, Catherine wanted to finish clearing the books from the shelf that she had worked on before taking her lunch. She had just removed a large volume when she was surprised to find a smaller book hidden behind it, owning a title that peaked her interest. She opened the book, but the diminishing light in the room made it hard for her to peruse it, so she made her way over to the window. She sat down in the weathered wing chair after pushing her shako hat aside, and began to read a couple pages of the novel. She was still reading the book when she heard Alistair bellow, "What the devil are you still doing here. I could not believe it when I saw your horse tied in the yard. Have you not noticed, woman, that you are alone in this house and completely vulnerable?"

Catherine had jumped out of the chair and dropped the book she was reading when Alistair's booming voice railed at her. Shaken, she retorted, "You don't have to yell, Mr. Chapman. You scared the wits out of me! To answer your question, I did not know I was alone. I am afraid I became quite enthralled reading."

She bent down and picked up the novel she dropped. Alistair walked over to where she stood and held out his hand for the book. He wanted to see what had captivated her. Catherine sheepishly handed over the book, blushing as she did so. Alistair thought her embarrassment duly deserved for putting the fear in him. When he returned and saw her mare, he thought something dire had happened to her. His fear quickly turned into anger, when he saw her comfortably situated in the wing chair by the window.

He read the title of the book and wanted to laugh out loud. He had never read *Evelina*, the novel by Francis Burney, now the famous Madame D"Arblay. He had once heard the book with the subtitle, *History of a Young Lady's*

Entrance into the World, appealed to feminine sensibilities, because its heroine is a young naïve girl thrown into London society. He wondered if Catherine recognized herself in any of the story.

Catherine saw Alistair grin and grabbed back the book from his hands, saying, "I have never read her work, so I started to flip through the pages. It is an epistolary work. I started reading and before I knew it, you were yelling at me."

"I am sorry to have startled you," he began softly, before exclaiming, "but you have put yourself at risk, Catherine, and I cannot abide it! Come. I will escort you home."

Catherine realized that he had called her by her name again and it warmed her soul. She started to place the novel down when Alistair ordered, "Keep and finish reading the novel at home. I will not see you do this again."

The sun disappeared below the horizon, bringing night upon them, before Alistair could return Catherine home. They both understood the whole household would be concerned over her absence. He knew his employment would most likely be terminated for allowing Catherine to engage herself in labor and he was stiffening his resolve to the outcome. They had each kept their own counsel riding abreast of one another as they made their way to Aubry. They had little to say, since their mind was filled with the confrontation that lay before them. Catherine pulled on her reins to stop and asked Alistair to check his horse when her Palladian home came into view.

"Alistair," she begged. "Please let me proceed from here. You can watch me reach my yard before you leave if you like. I prefer to deal with the consequences myself, since I am singularly to blame for everyone's worry. Besides, I must apologize to my grandmama and I would like to do so without an audience."

Alistair did not like her riding alone, but yielded to her request, thinking it served her better to deal with the dowager as she thought best. He said, "You must promise to send for me if I am needed."

Catherine agreed and then nudged her mare forward. He realized as he watched her depart that she had called him Alistair.

When Catherine approached the graveled courtyard, she could see the uncommon flurry of activity for an evening when her parents were not hosting a ball. She knew her grandmother must be beside herself with worry when the ostler, who came to collect her horse, exhaled a deep breath. Her grandmother must have put the fear into the grooms to locate her. Even Frenton who maintained a stoic expression, revealed his concern in his voice. "I believe her grace is in the Sun Room, my lady. She requests that you attend her as soon as you arrive."

She nodded and went directly to the large parlour, affectionately known as the Sun Room, where a profuse amount of sunshine flowed through the large arched white-framed windows to brighten the yellow painted walls during the day. It was the dowager's preferred room and when she was in residence, it smelled of her favorite flower, lilacs.

Normally, Catherine would have removed herself to her private suite to tidy her appearance before presenting herself, but she did not wish to worry her grandmother further, so she walked directly to the parlour where fragrant lilacs filled the room. Catherine hesitated at the parlour's threshold. Guilt washed over her when she saw the dowager seated in her favorite chair by the fireplace. Her head hung from her shoulders and her hands were clasped in her lap as if in prayer. Catherine called, "Grandmama! Forgive me for making you worry."

The dowager looked up and Catherine's dirty appearance caused her to exclaim, "Catherine! Were you assaulted?"

Catherine's eyes widened, she ran forward and dropped to her knees in front of the dowager, when she saw the fear alight in her frame. She exclaimed, "No! I am well, just sadly late in my return."

"But, Catherine," queried the dowager. "Look at you. You are in disarray and dirty. Did you take a tumble? Are you sure you are not injured?"

"Not at all," she replied."I was at the Atwood Home assisting Mr. Chapman in the library. I found a book and started reading it. Before I knew it, the time escaped and I stayed longer than I should have. I am sorry to put you to worry."

"Catherine! There is more to this story. Why are your clothes sooty and wrinkled? Your hair is out of sorts and dirt is on your face and hands. And if you were with Mr. Chapman, where is the man?"

"He did escort me home, Grandmama," she replied, "but I dismissed him. I saw no reason for him to be punished, since the blame is mine alone. He had taken his leave from the Atwood Home earlier in the day, after I promised to leave shortly after him. Through my own negligence and to Mr. Chapman's horror, I might add, I stayed longer than I expected. He found me upon his final inspection of the Atwood Home and then quickly dispatched me to Aubry."

The dowager scolded, "I have not remarked on your solitary journeys, Catherine, because I know you are a proficient rider and that you know our grounds well. But I would never have agreed to your leaving the estate or traipsing further than your regular rides without a guard or proper chaperone. I am disappointed, Catherine. You have taken advantage of my trust, therefore, I must insist that you not leave the house, until I have given this incident further consideration. I am exhausted and you are filthy. I suggest we both retire. I will convene with you tomorrow and will expect a thorough accounting of your activities these last days." The dowager rose and left without any show of affection for her granddaughter. Catherine felt bereft and duly chastised for her transgression. She followed in her grandmother's wake to return to her room.

Catherine was in the library engrossed in finishing *Evelina,* the novel that had led her to overstay at Atwood and cause so much concern for her grandmother. She marveled how society had not changed much from the last century. Family connections and status were of immense importance. The novel had plenty of charm, but the underlying message warned about the folly of inexperienced girls who did not observe the proper decorum in society, or who connected themselves with vulgar characters. It was obvious that Evelina's lack of familial protection is what placed her in so many mortifying adventures. She wondered how many rakes and scoundrels checked their behavior because they feared retribution from a debutante's father. No wonder the duke wanted her settled. He must worry over her constantly.

Frenton broke Catherine's reverie by clearing his throat. He informed her that her grace awaited her in the duke's study. This alarmed Catherine, for it suggested a stern interview. She would rather have had their *tête-à-tête* in her grandmother's private suite. Catherine closed her book and without thinking, carried it along with her to the study. She knocked softly and was bid, "enter." Catherine spied her grandmother seated behind her father's desk and asked, "Did you rest well, Grandmama?"

The dowager did not smile. She was not ready to dismiss Catherine's behavior so easily and simply stated with a stoic expression, "Yes, Catherine. I am well rested. Please sit down and explain how you have been spending your days and what motivates you to engage in such activity."

Catherine knew her grandmother was direct and that if she wanted her to understand how she felt then she needed to reciprocate in kind. She answered, "I met Mr. Chapman the other day while I was out riding our estate. He was visiting Baroness Litford and must have seen me. You may recall I met Mr. Chapman at Beaumont Manor when he was kind enough to escort me to see Mrs. Howard to deliver your letter. Upon our meeting, he spoke to me of the Atwood Home and all the renovations taking place. I was captivated by Mr. Chapman's enthusiasm for his project and invited myself over the next day to see the progress. I must admit to being a bit jealous of his industry, for my life at present has nothing of interest to engage me. I offered to inventory the books in Atwood's library. He denied the offer, but after much persistence on my part, he relented and agreed to let me help. I had no intention of staying late yesterday. I truly became engrossed in the novel."

The dowager looked at the book in Catherine's hand and asked, "Is that the novel you were reading?"

Catherine looked down and realized she was holding the culprit responsible for her fall from grace. She handed the tome to her grandmother, who to her surprise, laughed out loud.

"Well!" exclaimed the dowager. "I can understand your reluctance to put the book away. I believe I stayed up all night to finish the story when it was first published.

Now, explain to me why your visits to the Atwood Home were done secretly?"

Catherine dropped her mouth. She forgot her grandmother was keenly intuitive. She retorted, "They were not in secret!"

The dowager stared at Catherine and raised her brow. Catherine broke quickly and explained, "I did not want a chaperone to accompany me and if you knew what I was doing, you would have insisted. I am so tired of having my every single movement watched and remarked upon."

"And what did you not want remarked upon, Catherine. Speak plainly, Girl. Remember I was once young and am not foolish enough to believe a bunch of books led you to the Atwood Home. What circumstances are between you and this Mr. Chapman?"

She shouted, "There is nothing!"

Again, the dowager raised her brow. Catherine knew she revealed too much emotion. She softened her voice, and added, "There is nothing between us, Grandmama. I confess he affects me and if he were of my station, I would be plying my wares at him, but trust me, I know my duty to my family. If I did not, I assure you Mr. Chapman does, for he would not even kiss me when I asked him. He said he would not betray the trust that both Edward and Beaumont placed in him."

Catherine felt weary, her emotions were coming to a head and she needed to remove herself from her grandmother's scrutiny before that happened. "I am most tired, Grandmama," she admitted. "If you have no further questions, I would like to retire to my room."

The dowager handed the novel back to Catherine and said, "You are excused, Catherine. I will see you at supper."

"Yes, Grandmama."

Catherine left and the dowager pulled a piece of parchment from the duke's desk. She penned a note to her grandson, Edward, asking about the character of Mr. Chapman. She sent the missive by courier and demanded an immediate response. The dowager feared for her granddaughter who seemed on the verge of succumbing to an unrequited love.

That evening at supper, the dowager asked a gloomy Catherine, "How are the renovations at the Atwood Home progressing?"

Catherine hoped her grandmother's interest was a sign that she would allow her to return and finish her work in the Atwood Library, so after she described the progress, she asked, "May I return to complete the inventory of books?"

The dowager noticed that Catherine's mood improved once she started talking about the Atwood Home. She had already anticipated that Catherine would request to return. She wanted to hear from Edward before she made up her mind, so she responded, "I shall invite Mr. Chapman to dine with us and if I approve of him, I will consider it. I know Beaumont thinks highly of him, but it is my favor that he needs if I am to agree to let you visit the Atwood Home again.

The dowager cringed, remembering Catherine's filth. She added, "You know, Catherine, we have servants to do such tedious work. I know you say that you are engaged for your own amusement, but I would have thought you could have chosen something with less grime."

Catherine laughed and thanked her grandmother who promised to invite Mr. Chapman to dinner, two days from hence. Until then, Catherine was expected to remain at home. She could hardly wait to see him.

Chapter Nine

"Grandmama," called Catherine when she entered the Sun Room. "Do you know that every book that I have pulled from the library is a First Edition?"

"Your point, Catherine?" asked the dowager.

"Well, it is hard to call it 'treasure hunting' when there is nothing unique in the find," she retorted.

"What, my dear, are you babbling about?"

"Oh, nothing really," replied Catherine. "Have you heard from Mr. Chapman?"

"Yes, he will be happy to join us tomorrow evening."

Catherine smiled, turned on her heels and exited the parlour with such joy that the dowager became alarmed. She hoped the recently delivered and unopened missive, that she placed on her lap when Catherine entered, would assuage her concerns. She was pleased Edward had responded quickly, even though she knew that her request intruded on his honeymoon. Regardless, she expected nothing less than obedience from her grandchildren. He wrote.

Grandmother,

I am the most happy of men. Even your letter requesting my immediate attention could not disturb my cheerful countenance. If your inquiry were about any other man than Alistair, I would be most concerned and demand particulars. I can assuredly tell you, that aside from Westfield and of course, his grace, the Duke of Hartford, Mr. Chapman is the most honorable man I know. He has my complete trust.

I can only guess that my dear cousin is at the root of your concerns. I assure you that I learned after the fact, how much company she demanded of Alistair while at Beaumont Manor. I can relieve your fears and tell you that, as my man of business, Alistair, would never transgress against Catherine, nor insinuate himself in her life. I trust him to do what is in her best interests.

Yours to command,
Edward

The dowager thought Edward's message duplicitous, but it was clear he saw Mr. Chapman as no threat. While she was confident that Catherine would do her duty and marry the man the duke selected, she worried that Catherine had already given her heart to Mr.

Chapman. She saw how much her spirits rose talking about him and while the man may not take advantage of her infatuation, someone else might, someone ready to soothe her disappointment. An unrequited love could make Catherine an easy target. The villains of the world would see her wealth and despondency much too tempting to not pursue her. There were plenty of handsome lords who presented a noble front, but were indeed scoundrels. She would not wish Catherine to fall victim to their pretense.

Catherine's safety, above all else, was imperative. The dowager decided it was time for her son, the Duke of Aubry, to arrange a proper betrothal. It was not what her granddaughter wanted, but she knew that her son would consider Catherine's wishes. The duke would not force her into a union that repulsed her. The dowager went to the duke's study to write him the letter that she knew he would give his upmost attention.

Catherine had Mary lay out her pale-blue gauze evening dress. She hoped wearing the same dress she wore for the Spring Festival Dance at Beaumont Manor would remind Alistair of their special evening together. It was a glorious memory. She recalled seeing his eyes open wide when he first saw her and how attentive he was to her, monopolizing her company in a way that never put her reputation at risk. She never felt more euphoric than when he held her close during the waltz, whirling her across the dance floor.

They had shared glances and subtle touches, both when he escorted her around the ballroom and when they danced. The electricity that sparked between them brought a shudder of emotions. The current was palpable and she knew he felt it, too. His eyes were warm and inviting as she knew were her own. She cannot even remember if they talked, though they had conversed readily throughout the day. It seemed they were simply happy to be in each other's company. Catherine hoped the magic would show itself again.

The dowager made a point of receiving Mr. Chapman in a private interview before Catherine was scheduled to arrive. She was quite taken with his dress and manners. She knew he and Edward had made their acquaintance at Oxford where they became good friends. At first, the dowager deduced that Mr. Chapman earned a healthy salary for being able to afford clothes worthy of a nobleman, but it was his air of confidence that convinced the dowager that he was no visitor to her sphere. She wondered now if he was not some lord's *by-blow*. Regardless, whatever ran through his blood, he was still an unsuitable admirer for her granddaughter.

The dowager shuttered remembering how her son, Edward's father, left the sphere to which he was born to marry a woman in trade. The *ton* abjured him and his wife, and eventually their son. She would not see Catherine exiled from a lifestyle of which she knew no other.

"Good evening, Mr. Chapman," she greeted. "I am glad you accepted our invitation for dinner."

"Ah, an invitation!" he exclaimed. "Since your servant did not wait for an answer, I thought for sure I had been summoned."

The dowager raised a brow at Mr. Chapman's impertinence. Then, she saw his lips twitch and break into a smile. He bent at his waist and offered, "Your servant, your grace."

The dowager retorted, "I believe you are capricious and a charmer to boot. I see why Catherine admirers you."

Alistair's face lost its joviality and became serious. He answered, "I was unaware I was held in such high esteem by Lady Catherine. I am most honored and hope to always be fortunate to own her good opinion."

"I hope so, too, Mr. Chapman," she stated. "Tell me, how long do you have left at the Atwood Home?"

"A month, I expect," he answered.

She continued, "I am aware that Catherine is restless and seeks amusement at the Atwood Home. I am not pleased with her engaging in laborious and dirty tasks; however, I will allow her to visit again to see the improvements, as long as she is well chaperoned and safeguarded. Catherine does not know it yet, but the duke is contracting a betrothal for her. I prefer you not mention anything to her, for I will inform her in my own good time. I believe you are an intelligent man, Mr. Chapman, capable of understanding why I have confided this information with you."

Alistair stared at the dowager and wanted to assure her that he was no threat to Catherine, but he could not.

He knew that if he and Catherine did not check their feelings that heartbreak was inevitable. He replied, "I understand."

Catherine walked gracefully into the Sun Room to find the dowager and Alistair in a private interview. She worried, wondering why her grandmother looked so stern. She announced, "I did not know I was late. Forgive me for keeping you both waiting."

Alistair smiled upon seeing Catherine dressed in the same gown she wore at the Spring Festival. She looked radiant and surprisingly sophisticated. He had to remind himself that she was only twenty years old to his eight and twenty years, still too young to know her own heart. While most women are married at eighteen and thought to lose their bloom at one and twenty, Alistair always thought that when he married he would choose a woman in her mid-twenties to a jejune girl with little life experience. He wanted someone young enough to breed, yet old enough to have lived a life and formed some opinions. He wanted someone that would engage his mind and challenge his wit. Although Catherine was only twenty, he found in her someone with enough grit and spirit for him to question his pre-conceived notions. He checked his thoughts before they led him in a direction where only disappointment waited.

Catherine thought Alistair looked remarkably handsome, dressed in his formal black evening attire. She noticed his sorrowful expression until his eyes reached her own, then she saw his whole face brighten with gladness.

She responded in kind and in unison they grinned at one another. She did not know what transpired between her grandmother and Alistair, but she decided that she would not mark the little time between them with woe and weariness. As much as she liked to think that she could give up her position in society for Alistair, she was astute enough to know she would not do so without the duke's approval.

Unlike the romance novels that she privately enjoyed reading, she knew fairy tales rarely came true. She was brought up among the idle rich to be pampered and while she thought herself open-minded, more compassionate and headstrong than her peers, she knew she would be unhappy living among the serving class. She was not one to abide orders and was too used to have her own pleasures looked after to see to the wants of others. Besides all that, she could not affront her grandmother and father who had always supported her whims, nor could she tolerate being exiled from those she loved, or abjured by those who once called her friend. Even upon further reflection, she realized that Alistair had never professed his love to her and that it was ridiculous to jeopardize her future over a one-sided affection. He offered her friendship and Catherine would not toss it aside. She was determined to have no regrets. She would take whatever time she could get with him to make a lifetime of memories.

Catherine watched Alistair and her grandmother chat through dinner. He spoke of the time he spent with the late Mr. Howard and how Mrs. Howard continues to have him over for dinner at her cottage. Catherine noted his friendship with Mrs. Howard seemed to please the dowager. Alistair described Beaumont's tenants, the Spring Festival, and Catherine's attempts at weaving. As their chatter began to dwindle, Catherine interjected, "Grandmama, I told Mr. Chapman that he should speak with the Duchess of Rutland's gardener to help him map out the Atwood Gardens. What do you think?"

"I think that is a splendid idea," she answered. "His handiwork can be seen throughout the realm. He is sought after relentlessly for his knowledge on botany and landscape. I believe he even wrote a book. It is rare to gain an interview with him unless the duchess permits it. Would you like me to request a meeting on your behalf? I believe Elizabeth owes me a favor."

Alistair beamed and answered, "You are too kind. I would, as well as Atwood, be most grateful."

The dowager was pleased with his gratitude. She said that she would write to the Duchess of Rutland and send the missive first thing tomorrow morning.

Alistair asked, "Are you acquainted with Baroness Litford? She is one of your neighbors."

She replied, "No, we are not acquainted, though I am aware that her properties border one of Aubry's northern flanks. I understand she is Atwood's aunt and that her validation of his claim facilitated his receiving his inheritance sooner, rather than later."

"Indeed," he replied. "In fact, she was the one that informed him of it. If she had wanted, she could have done him great harm by not acknowledging him to keep the inheritance dormant. I do not think Atwood cared about such things, but through Felton's guidance, he is learning his duties to his title and his responsibilities to his tenants."

Catherine noticed Alistair's smile falter and his eyes grow angry. It did not last long, but it made her think that something troubled him. She wondered if someone had failed to do his or her duty to him.

He continued, "I am invited to tea tomorrow. I want to ask the baroness if there was anything of the old gardens that she particularly liked. I myself would like a knot garden with some sculptures; a place for meditation. I am hoping that she may have an old sampler of Alana's that may serve as a design. As you know, Beaumont's knot garden is based on a medieval tapestry that hangs in his state room. I know the baroness would be most pleased if you and her ladyship were to accompany me."

The dowager looked at her granddaughter who exuded so much anticipation, she looked ready to jump out of her skin like a pea from a pod. Her alacrity concerned her and she knew she had to inform her of her impending betrothal. She was quite put out that Mr. Chapman should suggest a meeting with the Litfords, it seemed obvious to her that if they had not met, it was of her choosing. She had no wish to associate with a family that ranked on the bottom rung of her social order. He was a smart man and she felt manipulated into forming an acquaintance with someone she had chosen not to cultivate. Yet, she would placate her granddaughter and not allow herself to become distressed over a trifling matter. She returned her gaze to Mr. Chapman and said, "We would be delighted to join you Mr. Chapman. Shall we remove ourselves to the parlour. Considering you are our only gentleman in attendance, perhaps you will take your port with us in the Sun Room, instead of alone."

"It would be my pleasure."

Alistair escorted the dowager into the Sun Room and placed her in her favorite winged chair near the crackling fire, while Catherine took a seat on a nearby settee. He placed the embroidered fire screen next to the dowager to temper the heat that could easily burn her skin if left unprotected. He looked at the available seats and wondered whether he should sit next to Catherine, take a singular seat or continue to stand. The dowager decided for him.

She said, "There is a decanter of port on the console. Please pour yourself a glass if you like. Regardless of your preference, I insist that you serve me a glass of sherry. Then, you must sit down, Mr. Chapman. I will get a crick in my neck, if you stand there all proud like our hearty English oak."

Alistair ignored the dowager's sassy remark and asked Catherine, "May I offer you anything, my lady?"

"No, thank you, Mr. Chapman," she answered.

Alistair walked over to the elegantly carved gilt wood eagle console where two crystal decanters holding port and sherry resided on its marble countertop. He served himself a splash of port in a short glass tumbler and then poured some sherry into a petite crystal goblet for the dowager. Upon handing the dowager her evening drink, she ordered, "Play something on the pianoforte, Catherine, to prove you have not been negligent in your study. I am sure Mr. Chapman will be discreet should you embarrass yourself from the lack of practice."

She asked, "Must I sing?"

The dowager replied, "I know not why you blush, Girl, when you know your voice is exceptional. You might as well offer us some amusement, as I expect your future husband will wish you to perform."

Catherine scowled at her grandmother, replying, "Very well, Grandmama. Do you have a request for me?"

She answered, "Play the Beethoven you have been practicing. When you finish you and Mr. Chapman may play a hand at cards before we bid him leave. I shall close my eyes, allowing your music as it always does, to lull me into that act of reflection, that in my dotage seems to entertain me profusely."

Alistair took a seat near the pianoforte and watched Catherine shuffle the music sheets. She settled herself and prepared to play, placing her fingers on the keyboard. He marveled at the array of talent this young woman owned and waited anxiously for her to begin.

Catherine had never performed in front of someone for whom she admired in a romantic fashion. She was nervous to perform Beethoven's Opus 75. No.2, "Neve Libe, Neus Leben, (New Love, New Life) for she was afraid that Alistair would think her immature for singing of love. She blushed with embarrassment realizing just how childish she was to religiously practice the sonata, since leaving Beaumont Manor. The music had soothed her grieving heart and become a favorite of her grandmother's. At least, she thought that was the reason she requested she perform the piece. Catherine took a deep breath, releasing it slowly. She closed her eyes for a moment and then when she opened them, her fingers began to dance across the keyboard. She let her mastery of the music lead her. She played the prelude and then opened her voice to the lyrics. She sang from her soul, carrying the heartfelt words to her listeners.

> *"Oh, my heart, what has come over you? Everything is changed and unrecognizable, I cannot break the little magic thread by which my sweet, yet, carefree loved one holds me in thrall. Oh, love! Love! Let me go."*

Catherine finished the piece to Alistair's resounding applause. His admiration thrilled her and she was compelled to look away from him, not wanting to reveal how much his praise meant to her. She was afraid her grandmother would read her sentiment as well, so she was glad when she sought her out, that she was dozing in her chair. She returned her gaze to Alistair and felt her heart quicken. He was making his way to her and the admiring look on his face had her heart pounding fiercely. He took her hands into his own and said, "You never cease to amaze me, my lady. You are indeed one of our realm's jewels."

Catherine blushed knowing that her uncommon timidity betrayed her sentimental feelings. She looked to see if her grandmother was a witness to her shy manner. When she saw that she still slept, she felt more confident to reply more sophisticatedly, "One of many, I am sure, Mr. Chapman. Thank you for your praise. Now, shall we follow grandmama's direction and have a hand at cards?"

He nodded and escorted her over to the card table where he helped her into her seat. He took the other chair and gathered the deck of cards on the table. While he shuffled the cards, he asked, "What is your pleasure, my lady? Vingt-et-un?"

Catherine nodded her approval. Alistair was happy she agreed to the card game that relied more on chance than strategy. Each player tries to get cards whose face value is one and twenty or as close to that number as possible without going over it. He was glad the game took little concentration, for he doubted he would be able to do anything but admire the young lady that sat across from him. He dealt the first hand and immediately became entranced with the passing and collecting of cards than with the actual winning of any set.

The dowager, whose body suggested she napped, was keenly aware of the subtle brushes of hands and lingering of fingers being held by the young couple. Not a word they vocalized, but much was said in their looks. Based on Edward's letter, she knew Mr. Chapman would not declare himself to Catherine, but she could tell that he wished he could. It was time to end the evening and she did so, without further hesitation.

Mr. Chapman took his leave, but not before promising to escort them tomorrow to Litford Hall.

Alistair was happy to see the English sky was clear of the blanketing grey clouds that so often released thrashing sheets of rain unto the countryside. The sun radiated down on him with its soothing warmth. Chirping and cooing birds proclaimed his party would have exceptional weather for the day's excursion. He was in good spirits traveling in his hired coach to pick up his guests until he approached the circular driveway. He saw the ducal carriage waiting to transport the dowager and Catherine and felt foolish to have forgotten the dowager's consequence. It would have been *beyond the pale* for her grace to arrive at Litford Hall in anything that did not announce her regal station. He had to subdue his embarrassment when he exited his coach. He quickly ordered his driver to return his carriage to the Atwood stable and then he requested for one of the ostlers to bring him his own steed. He explained he would travel with the dowager to the Litfords; and then after escorting their return to Aubry, he would ride his own stallion back to the Atwood Home.

He walked up the steps and was about to bang the door knocker, when Frenton opened the entrance to let Catherine exit with her maid in tow. Alistair caught his breath, surprised to meet Catherine on the portico. He did not exhale until he saw Catherine's eyes twinkle with mischief.

"Mischief, indeed," he thought, for Catherine was dressed in her riding habit, unlikely attire for a lady being transported in a carriage. He watched her nod to an attending ostler.

Then, she spoke to him, "You are right on time, Mr. Chapman. Grandmama has given me leave to ride my own mare over to the Litfords, as long as Mary attends me. I have taken the liberty to saddle one of our horses for you should you care to accompany me. Grandmama, as you see, will travel in her own carriage and meet us there."

He replied, "It would honor me to be of service to you, my lady." He then almost burst out laughing when he saw the sorry beast he was expected to ride. The black stallion was clearly pulled out of retirement for this particular excursion. He remarked, "Is the steed able to make the journey, or perhaps I am being asked to take him to his final resting place."

Catherine checked her grin, "Really, Mr. Chapman. Ulysses is a fine specimen and more than capable of carrying you to your destination. Granted, he is a bit mature, but his bloodline is regal. You should feel honored. The duke, once called him his own."

"Indeed, I am honored," he answered with a grin. He placed Catherine on her side saddle before mounting his own sad looking animal. They followed the gravel drive riding side by side, until they passed what could be considered the front lawns, before leaving the road to traverse across the Aubry Estate. They kept to a canter, not wanting to kick up any dirt or sod at Mary, who followed behind them as chaperone. They continued in an easy manner, sharing polite conversation until they reached a meadow, that part of the land that stretched flat and verdant. Catherine checked her mare and called Mary to come forward. Alistair watched Catherine speak to her maid and then he was surprised to see Mary leave.

Noticing Alistair's questioning expression, she explained, "Mary is not one to gallop, so I have sent her ahead to the Litfords."

"Gallop, my lady?"

"Indeed, sir. I fear I was badly represented at our last race. You, yourself, admitted to having the better horse. Well, the tables are turned and while you can see that my mare in terms of bloodline, may not be superior to yours, she is younger. I challenge you to the copse of trees. Do you accept, or is your ego too frail to pick up my gauntlet?"

Alistair grinned, "I am prepared to meet your challenge, my lady." He tried to take the advantage by jump-starting the race. He kicked his heels into the horse's flanks and urged Ulysses on. The old horse must have remembered better and more exciting days, for he responded to Alistair's command and sped off. But it was not long, before Ulysses recognized his folly and slowed down to a trot, then a sedate walk. Within seconds, Catherine passed him and reached the trees to claim her victory. She was laughing with gusto when Alistair reached her. He announced, "Well done, my lady. I am happy to call you victor and to give you much joy. I only hope I have not used what little life this poor steed has left."

"Nonsense," said Catherine. "Ulysses likes to exert himself every now and then. I should know, because I am the one to put him to the task. Come, let us continue to the Litfords, before Mary arrives before us and confesses my unladylike indiscretion to my grandmama."

They rode their mounts side by side, enjoying the serenity of the encompassing lush green landscape. He said, "I did not get a chance to remark on the duke's properties, my lady. They are quite pristine and as I look at the lush evergreen countryside about me, it is hard to tell what was natural around your estate and what was contrived. The Atwood Home does not enjoy Aubry's expansive lawns. I wonder if Capability Brown was the architect behind your beautiful landscape."

"Indeed, he was," she responded. "He was all the rage, as you know. I believe he is responsible for over one hundred seventy gardens in our realm. If my recollection is correct, he improved the Aubry Estate in 1750. The lawns that make their way to our house and the three ornamental lakes are all fashioned from his design. Even some of our trees were supplanted to enhance his vision."

Alistair replied, "I see why you ride whenever possible. This scenery soothes the soul."

She countered, "Very much." In a more somber tone, she confessed, "I will miss it when I marry."

"Do not fret, Catherine," he replied. "Your husband will wish to sojourn at Aubry, for who would not? You will not be absent for so long, that you will have time to miss this beautiful countryside. Come, let us hasten our canter or we will not arrive with Mary."

Chapter Ten

Baroness Litford was still in a state of astonishment when her butler announced the arrival of the Dowager Duchess of Aubry, her granddaughter, Lady Catherine Brentwood, and Mr. Alistair Chapman. She owed Mr. Chapman a debt of gratitude for introducing them to her. Just the fact that the dowager entered her home was enough to recommend the Litfords as good *ton* to the upper echelons of society.

The baroness could not do much for her daughters when they had made their *come-out,* for most of her friends were from the gentry. She hoped owning the acquaintance of a powerful family like the Brentwoods, would help her present her granddaughters to the *bon ton* when they came of age. She could not believe it all came about because her sister, Alana, had a grandson whom Lord Felton had taken under his wing and through his beneficence, she met Mr. Chapman.

"I am sorry that I could not present my daughters to you, your grace" expressed the baroness. "But they could not come on such short notice."

"Baron Litford, I expect, remains in Town with the House of Lords," she remarked.

"Indeed. He is a most dutiful subject of the realm," the baroness replied.

Mr. Chapman knew that Baroness Litford was uncomfortable in trying to converse with the dowager, especially since her grace was determined to exude a lofty manner. No doubt, the dowager knew her visit was the result of Alistair's shrewd handling, since she would never have availed herself to Lady Litford otherwise. Her grace's haughtiness made the baroness shy and that led the dowager to believe the lady owned little acquaintance with the *haute ton* and even more importantly, little fortitude. The dowager believed that only a debutante was allowed to be shy and that a matron should own backbone and grit to deserve admiration.

Before the visit became insupportable, Alistair interjected a topic that he hoped would leverage both of the ladies' personalities and asked, "Baroness, what do you recall of the Atwood Gardens?"

"Oh," she offered, "It has been years since my ancestral home was picturesque, but I remember the splotches of color and hanging vines. I particularly recollect the smell of freesia. Are you planning on installing a garden, in addition, to all the other home improvements?"

He answered, "As you know, the lawns are not extensive and I am not prepared to cut down trees to expand them. I shall leave any major alterations of the landscape to your nephew. I do wish to create those gardens that are an extension of the house, those areas that one comes across when they exit the first floors. I think it prudent to install an area for meditation. I am considering a knot and sculpture garden. What do you think?"

"I must say I have never been one that could stay quiet enough to meditate, but I think a knot and sculpture garden would be most appropriate for the Atwood Home," replied the baroness. "I do not have any of those type of gardens here because they require constant pruning and our gardeners do not excel in such delicate work. Do you have a master gardener?"

"Not as yet," he replied. He looked to the dowager, and asked, "Beaumont's knot garden is based on a family tapestry, is it not?"

"Yes," she answered. "It hangs at Beaumont Manor in the Green State Room. It was a favorite of my mama's. I had the same design copied at Aubry when I reigned as duchess."

"Ah," remarked Alistair. "Did you duplicate the secret garden at Aubry, as well?"

The dowager laughed, "You know about that?"

The baroness queried, "A secret garden? Do tell."

"Well, the secret is not in the garden, but in the location," retorted the dowager. "Only the head gardener and the marquis know of its location, though I expect Lord Felton as heir has been informed."

Catherine, who had sat quietly until now asked, "They never showed you, Grandmama?"

The dowager replied, "When I was a young girl, I overheard my parents say that they would meet up in the secret garden. Later, I asked my mama if she could take me to see it. She said that she could not because it would mean breaking a promise to my papa. I guess the refusal troubled her because the next day, my brother and I were summoned. My parents explained that the garden was their personal refuge and that no one, aside from the head gardener, entered it. They did not want us to be curious and make more of it than what it was, so they agreed to show it to us one time, on one condition."

The dowager laughed before she continued. "We were blindfolded. I will tell you that the flowers were in bloom on that day with plenty of butterflies fluttering about. My parents had Cook prepare a special repast for us and we spent the afternoon in picnic. My parents read to us. I remember lying on a woolen blanket next to my mother, trying to discern figures in the clouds. My brother wrecked havoc running around to catch butterflies. It was a memorable day that I will always treasure. I witnessed my parents in a state of relaxation that I had never noticed before. I guess that they left their burdens outside the garden walls and were able to do so because they knew they would not be disturbed. The solitude has served my brother well, granting him the occasional repose, as I expect it will do for Felton."

"That is amazing," replied the baroness. "Imagine a *Shambhala*, a place of peace, in your own backyard."

The dowager, Catherine, and Alistair looked at one another and then grinned at the baroness's sentimental reference to the ancient Tibetan myth that spoke of a magical land where people lived in peace and harmony. The esoteric remark dissipated the friction that had prevailed and the rest of the visit was spent discussing the realm's greatest gardens and the recent *on dits* among the *bon ton*.

As the visit came to a close, Alistair asked, "Is there a design your sister favored that I might use for the knot garden?"

Baroness Litford smiled. She said, "Alana was an exceptional embroiderer. I fancied one of her samplers that she left behind and had it mounted for display in my personal study. I remember her working on it. It is a simple geometric pattern that would easily lend itself to the layout of a knot garden. I am surprised I did not point it out to you when you last visited. You may borrow it if you like."

"I would like that very much," he replied. The baroness stood to summon her butler. Alistair checked her before she could pull her bell cord and said, "Do not bother your servant. I know my way and will collect the sampler myself."

Before he could leave, Catherine rose and asked, "May I go with you, Mr. Chapman?"

Alistair noted the dowager was not pleased, but he would not embarrass Catherine with a refusal and replied, "Of course." He then looked to the dowager and stated, "We will only be a moment."

Baroness Litford did not notice anything out of the ordinary and interjected, "Take her to the formal dining room and show her the baron's ancestral tapestry, as well. He would be pleased to learn that you have viewed it. Do not rush, for we still need to finish our tea."

Alistair proffered his arm to Catherine and watched her delicately and timorously place her hand on his arm. He could feel her heartbeat quicken, but did not remark upon it, nor did they speak to one another until they reached the baroness's study. The mounted and framed sampler hung prominently across on the wall from the baroness's writing table. Alistair realized he missed seeing it the day he visited because his focus was on the baroness's elegantly carved gilt wood escritoire. He thought the framed sampler would garner more attention if the baroness had hung it behind her desk, but upon further reflection, he understood the sampler was hung for her own pleasure and not to impress visitors. Lady Litford had the perfect view of it from her desk and Alistair, in that moment knew that the baroness had gravely mourned the loss of her sister.

He went over to the wall and carefully unhooked the framed sampler. Catherine watched him place the embroidered design on the desk, so they could both view it together. She carefully ran her fingers over the silken threads that formed the under and over design. She accidentally touched Alistair's hand and froze. She knew she should pull her hand away, but the contact, like the sun, warmed her body. She was embarrassed that she gave herself away so easily. She kept her head bent low, her eyes shut, and waited for him to speak, though he said nothing. Instead, she felt his finger gently stroke her own. It was a loving and delicate touch and drew her eyes to him. His eyes were expressive and seemed to communicate pity, but she demanded more. She asked, "Will you never profess to an admiration for me?"

Alistair grinned, but there was no light in his eyes. He asked, "For what purpose?"

Catherine was surprised that he asked her a question in return to her own and without thinking, blurted, "For our pleasure."

Alistair's features sobered. He disengaged their fingers that somehow had clasped upon one another and said, "There is no pleasure in a confession that will only bring heartbreak."

"How do you know that my heart is not already breaking," she chided. "Do you think I am not pained to know that the feelings I have belong only to me? If I am wrong, then give me the salve to heal my wound."

Alistair was surprised to hear such a passionate declaration and wondered at its sincerity. He released her hand that he unknowingly held and said, “May I ask, my lady, how many times your heart has been broken?”

Catherine crimsoned in anger as though she had been reprimanded like a child, someone who was too young to know their own feelings. She retorted, “You are the first to do so, Alistair, even though I have been charged with breaking many. I only hope that I had the grace not to affront my admirers as you have injured me.” She then turned and walked away, leaving behind an open mouthed Alistair.

Catherine was sorry she did not check her temper or take the time to allow her features to soothe before entering the parlour alone. She knew her error as soon as the dowager raised an eyebrow. To the baroness’s inquiry on the location of Mr. Chapman, Catherine lied. “Mr. Chapman stayed to admire the tapestry a bit longer. I returned in case grandmama was ready to take her leave.”

The dowager rose and said, “It is indeed getting late and time we bid adieu. Thank you, Lady Litford. We have enjoyed ourselves immensely.” She then asked her to call on her next week, so as custom dictated she could reciprocate her hospitality. The dowager looked at her granddaughter and said, “I wish you to ride with me in my carriage, Catherine. One of the footmen will see to transporting your mare home.”

“As you wish,” she answered stiffly. It was at that moment, Alistair entered the parlour carrying the framed sampler in his hands. His face gave away some of the remorse he owned, upon seeing them take their leave. The dowager gave him a nod to which Alistair bowed. Catherine said not a word and hastened quickly after her grandmother.

Baroness Litford rose and walked over to Alistair. She said, "I cannot thank you enough for the introduction, Mr. Chapman. It is more than I could ever have wished." She looked at the sampler that he held and asked, "What do you think? Will the design serve for your knot garden?"

He smiled and replied, "I think it will serve nicely and I believe Atwood will be most pleased." He then professed his gratitude and said goodbye. Upon which, the baroness invited him to return soon. When Alistair made his exit, he was happy to see that Catherine had left Ulysses to carry him back to the Aubry Estate where his own steed awaited him. He was sad to make the return jaunt alone. He missed Catherine's company and the silence of his ride plagued his conscious. He argued with himself, trying to decide whether he was a brute for his manner towards Catherine or merely a fool.

Two days passed since Catherine left Alistair at Litford Hall. Her emotions teetered between ire and sadness. On the one hand, her pride was offended that a commoner dared to abjure the admiration of a duke's daughter, not any debutante, but one considered *a diamond of the first water*, a lady of standing with more offers of marriage than anyone of her acquaintance. Was it not the *on dit* that her hand was impossible to claim? Yet, Alistair seemed unaffected by her charms.

The first day, she slept late, ate little and spent most of her day drifting in and out of sleep, while she laid in repose. On the second day, she was determined to be industrious, a position new to her, aside from the time she worked in the library at Atwood Home. She found herself in the duke's library, searching behind the books, hoping to find a tome that was known to only one. She pulled a volume forward and when she saw nothing behind it, she moved forward to pull out the next one. It was a tedious task, but it kept her hands busy even if her mind continued to trouble over Alistair. She wondered when she fell in love with the self-assured, arrogant man. Was it the first moment she saw him in Beaumont's study?

She remembered he had peaked her emotions that day with his ability to make her angry one moment and then amuse her in another. It seemed every time she was in his company, her emotions were constantly fluctuating, especially with his confusing behavior. Did he admire her or didn't he? He had a mesmerizing effect on her, yet she found herself powerless to charm him. He was a man whose will she could not bend. Coquettish ploys were useless on him, for he did not care if he pleased her. He treated her with respect, but not adulation. Even though he did not try to impress her, she was impressed with both his inner and physical strength. She might have thought him bookish when they first met, but she knew no other man could ever compare to him in looks or character.

Her thoughts took her into a dark mood, leaving her to feel unloved, unworthy, with no prospects for happiness. She envisioned her future bleak with no husband or children, but she could visualize Alistair happily ensconced with a lovely wife and child. She finally recognized the self-pity that she had indulged in when her visions began to resemble a Minerva Press novel that she had once read. She chastised herself for falling into a depression and proudly vowed that she would make her own happiness. Devil take the man for not appreciating what she freely gave.

Catherine gave up searching for a book that someone might have secreted away and selected a book of Shelly poems to read. Her thoughts of Alistair continued to distract her. She did not know how long she sat, staring onto the pages without thought to the prose on the page, when Frenton cleared his throat to get her attention. She looked up. He said, "Excuse me, my lady, but, her grace seeks an audience with you. She is in the Sun Room."

Catherine answered, "Thank you, Frenton. I will seek her out immediately."

The dowager stood by one of the tall arched windows and turned towards the entryway when she heard footsteps. Catherine thought she looked serious and the tightness she felt in her stomach made her chary. She asked, "You wished to see me, Grandmama?"

The dowager waved her arm to the two Queen Anne chairs that faced each other and said, "Sit down, Catherine. I have news from the duke."

Catherine took her seat and watched her grandmother take the seat across from her. She opened a letter and announced, "Your parents are to follow the Prince Regent to Brighton. Afterwards, the duchess will travel home to Aubry, while the duke will accept Lord Gracemoor's invitation to partake in the hunt at his manor. He will join us at the end of the summer to collect you and the duchess for the Little Season, at which time he will announce your betrothal."

Catherine's face lost all color when she gasped, "My betrothal? I do not understand. Papa said I was allowed to choose my own husband. He said I could take my time. What has changed? Who am I to wed?"

The dowager looked at Catherine and replied, "It is time, Catherine. Your heart is open for affection and you must make a suitable match before you find that you have closed yourself to any hope of happiness. I do not wish to see you suffer."

Catherine raged, "And you think forcing another man on me will not make me suffer!"

"Don't be ridiculous, Catherine," she chided. "No one is going to force you into a repulsive marriage. My own marriage was arranged to a man I did not even meet until my engagement was announced and I came to love him, dearly. It is not impossible to find love with your husband, if you are willing to open your heart to him. However, I warn you that if you allow this foolishness with Mr. Chapman to continue, you will turn into a shrew with no prospect for happiness."

Catherine sobered to her grandmother's words. She said, "I do understand. I just did not realize that papa was contracting a marriage. Who has he chosen for me?"

The dowager handed Catherine the duke's letter and said, "He has sent a list of offers that he finds acceptable. You are allowed to choose yourself or permit him to make the choice for you."

Catherine perused the list. Each gentleman held a title, land, and was undoubtedly wealthy. There was not one among them that was not highly eligible. She knew the duke would have delved into their background to ensure they were not lecherous or brutal. She futilely reviewed the list once more for the name she knew was not there. With a heavy heart, Catherine handed the letter back to her grandmother. She said, "Let him choose. I see no difference among them." She then rose from her chair and left to retire to her private suite.

Catherine reposed on her bed, rested her forearm across her eyes and tried to block the images of her future. She had known all along that her joining to another would be contracted, it was the way of the aristocracy after all, but never before had the thought accosted her in the way it currently did. Like every other debutante, Catherine had also thought an exceptional alliance would be all that she desired in a marriage. But now, the thought of an indifferent marriage where neither husband nor wife held those feelings that made their body stir, seemed abominable. She wondered how she was to live the rest of her life with a man that did not hold her heart.

At her most bleak moment, her mind chastised herself for once again letting her emotions overwhelm and misguide her, for as much as she thought she loved Alistair, there was no evidence aside from her intuition, that suggested he loved her. She wiped the tears that pooled in her eyes and cursed her feminine sensibility and the man who made her feel so wretched.

Mary entered Catherine's room and set the breakfast tray she was carrying on the table by her bed. Then, she walked over to the windows to pull and tie back the drapes to allow the midday light to bathe the room. The clatter of noise she made and the bright light streaming through the windows stirred Catherine awake. She scolded, "What is it, Mary, that you must disturb my sleep?"

Her maid answered, "I am worried about you, milady. Spending the days sleeping. I think it was unwise of you not to travel with her grace to Belvoir Castle."

"Oh, Mary," grumbled Catherine. "I was in no mood to visit the Duchess of Rutland. You know that grandmama felt she was obligated to accept her invitation because the duchess served her well in soliciting her head gardener to help Mr. Chapman, but I am too wearied for road travel. I am glad I remained home."

"I am surprised," continued Mary, "that she left you without a chaperone. His grace would not have allowed you to stay home without supervision. Remember when you wanted to come home and you had to wait until the dowager accompanied you?"

"Yes, Mary," she replied. "But this is quite different. I am already home, plus you and Frenton are with me. I am hardly alone with a house full of servants. Besides, you know very well that my brother, Jason, and his family are to arrive for their annual visit to see grandmama. Someone had to stay to formally greet them."

"Well," interjected Mary. "I don't think it's healthy, sleeping the day away. Why don't you get up and take a ride. It is a beautiful day outside."

"I don't think so, Mary," answered Catherine.

Mary pulled the covers back from her mistress, grabbed both of her hands, and started to yank her off her bed.

"Enough!" she shouted. "You forget yourself, Mary. I am no child that needs to be risen from her bed."

Mary returned, as loudly as her mistress, "Well, you are acting like a wee one, fretting over a toy they cannot have!"

Mary's remark sobered Catherine. She asked, "Is that what you think, Mary? That I am distraught because I only want something I cannot have?"

"Begging your pardon, milady," she whined. "I should not have said what I did, but please get up and have some food. You have me so worried that I am forgetting my place."

"Do not worry, Mary," Catherine replied. "I will rise and perhaps take that ride you suggested. Thank you for your concern." Catherine rose from her bed and grabbed Mary by the shoulders to ensure she had her full attention. She looked into her maid's eyes and said, "And Mary, your place is always with me, as long as you desire it."

Mary blushed and then went about her business, laying out her mistress's toilette and dress. As she worked, a knock sounded at Catherine's door. Mary answered the call to find Frenton holding a silver salver where a card was placed. Mary picked up the calling card while Frenton announced that Baroness Litford and her daughters were inquiring if the dowager was at home to receive visitors. Mary asked Frenton to wait, while she relayed the card and message to her mistress.

Catherine took the card and pondered over it for a moment. Then, she said, "Tell the baroness the dowager is away, but that I will receive her in the Sun Room. I will be there shortly. Please have Cook prepare a pot of tea and serve some cakes for our refreshment."

When Mary returned from relaying the command to Frenton, Catherine said to her, "Best to change that riding habit for a day dress. I doubt I will want to ride after their visit. I will wear my rose sarsnet and present myself the picture of color."

Mary smiled because she heard spunk in her mistress's voice and that spark of mischief was enough to ameliorate her worries.

Catherine walked into the Sun Room and found Baroness Litford and her daughters sitting on the edge of their chairs with their backs straight as a rod. She could feel the overwhelming excitement in the room when her guests spied her. She almost jumped with them, when they sprung up in unison from their seats. Catherine thought it was peculiar that her appearance could ignite such cheerfulness, but then she wondered if this was the first ducal estate they had ever visited. Compared to their property, the Aubry Estate rivaled any of the royal residences. Catherine thought they must be overwhelmed by its grandeur.

Honed into Catherine since her aristocratic birth, her social skills naturally rose to the surface when she became mistress of the manor. She immediately worked to put her guests at ease. With grace, she said, “Please sit down, ladies. I see the tea and cakes have arrived." Catherine took a seat across from her guests near the mahogany inlaid tea table. She waited for the ladies to retake their seat before she added, "I am glad you have brought your daughters, Baroness. Will you introduce them to me?”

The baroness beamed and said, “May I present my eldest, Mrs. Sarah Clayton, and my second born, Mrs. Anne Hodgson. Sarah and Anne nodded their heads in respect and replied, “Your ladyship. It is an honor to meet you.”

Catherine smiled and tried to ease their nerves by inquiring about their family. She reciprocated, “The honor of your acquaintance is mine, as well. Now, tell me about yourselves. Do you have children?”

Both Sarah's and Anne's face brightened at being asked to speak about their daughters. The only time their face sobered was when they confessed how terrible they felt in failing to produce a male heir for the Atwood title. They were glad that Mr. Cowper had claimed his birthright, relieving the encumbrance that weighed on them and then passed to their daughters, when they were unsuccessful in producing an heir.

Catherine understood the burden aristocrats carried having to secure their title, property, and wealth through marriage. Wasn't she commanded to marry a man of nobility? Yet when she looked at these women, one married to a vicar, the other to a solicitor, she could not help but feel prejudiced against the aristocratic edict. Before Mr. Cowper's claim, if they had produced a son, he would have become a viscount and elevated his common family into the aristocracy. However, Catherine, a duke's daughter, with more noblemen to call family than most, would lose all entitlement if she married a commoner. Her children with noble blood running through them would not be received at court, thereby abjured by the *bon ton*. She shivered at the thought and yet, looking at these matronly and amiable women across from her, she found it difficult to begrudge them their life.

Sara's remarks about the Atwood Home broke Catherine's reverie. She heard her say, "We have just returned from my mother's ancestral home. The house is near complete though the landscape is still under construction. Mr. Chapman was busy directing the laborers where to place the furniture and some items we brought to him that we held in trust. He has done a wonderful job. My mama was quite overcome."

"He will be leaving soon?" Catherine queried.

Baroness Litford replied, "Soon enough. He is interviewing stewards for Atwood. At present, I believe he plans to allow the new man to oversee the completion of the gardens."

Catherine noticed the baroness scrutinizing her interest into the affairs of Mr. Chapman, so she made an effort to check her emotions. She continued, "You will be happy to have your nephew situated so close to you."

"Indeed," she replied. His temperament reminds me of my dear sister, Alana, his grandmother. It gives me great satisfaction to be of service to him, since I could do nothing for my sister."

"You have given him family," remarked Catherine. "I am sure that pleases him well." She looked to the baroness's daughters and asked, "How old are your daughters?"

Sarah answered first, "My eldest, Jane, is three and ten years of age, and my youngest, Amelia, is nine years old." Anne then announced, "I own a set of twins, Marjorie and Meredith, who are eight years old."

Catherine laughed, "I have a pair of nephews. The eldest is eight years old and his younger brother owns two years less. They are expected to visit within the next sev'night. When they come, we always take the boats out on the lake. Perhaps, you would like your girls to join us and we could make a small party of it."

Astonished at the great compliment paid to them with Catherine's invitation, Sara and Anne looked to their mother for guidance. The baroness smiled. She saw that her daughters were too overwhelmed to answer, so she replied, "It would be our great honor to accept. I know my grandchildren will be thrilled to partake in such a special excursion."

Catherine grinned and thought it quite remarkable, that such a simple invitation could bring so much joy.

Chapter Eleven

After her visit with Baroness Litford and her daughters, Catherine realized that today might be her only opportunity to bid Alistair farewell and to wish him good fortune, so she rose and dressed to make her way to the Atwood Home. She hated that their last words to one another were said in anger. She could not believe that since her visit to Litford Hall, her pride had kept her sullen and indisposed. She cringed thinking how melodramatic she had behaved. She was not an injured party, aside from what she afflicted on herself. Alistair never suggested or aspired to anything more than friendship, a gift of amity that she carelessly discarded. If she was to be happy, then she would need to heed her grandmother's advice and not close her heart because of an unrequited love.

Catherine approached the Atwood Home and was amazed at the external changes that greeted her. First, fresh gravel marked the drive, the verdant lawns were scythed, the trees and yew hedges were trimmed and the house itself was freshly painted. An ostler met her and grasped her mare's bridle to guide her horse to the front of the house, where a mounting block was placed. He helped her to descend and before he could take her mare away, she asked him to retrieve a book from the pouch that hung from her saddle's pommel.

With the small tome in hand, she went forward to be announced, hoping someone would attend her. She balked when she saw Alistair standing at the threshold, waiting to greet her. He bowed and said, "My lady, you do me great honor. Have you come to see the house?"

Catherine answered, "I would like that very much, Mr. Chapman." He motioned Catherine to enter before him. She made her way down the hall, glancing from side to side to look at all the polished wood, gleaming brass, sparkling chandeliers, and other improvements. Alistair followed her and watched her inspect the refurbished home.

She remarked, "Baroness Litford and her daughters paid me a visit yesterday. She told me about Atwood Home's completion. She is quite pleased with the result. She also informed me that you would be leaving soon, so I wished to return the novel you loaned me and to thank you for your kindness."

Alistair moved around Catherine when they entered the library to better see her expression when she took in the room's transformation. Her approval was easy to read. With sincerity, she remarked, "You have done wonders, Mr. Chapman." The room was completely renovated with refurbished wood paneling and wall paper. The book collection was smaller than what she remembered, but looked impressive on the mahogany shelves. She noticed the new furniture, drapes, and rugs. The room boasted of somber hues, appropriate for a bachelor's residence, though Catherine thought a wife would be quick to add a splash of color.

He asked, "Do you like it?"

"Very much, so," she answered. Catherine walked over to the wall case to return the book, *Evelina,* to the shelf. She saw Alistair raise an eyebrow in inquiry and asked, "Do you think I should hide the novel as I found it, for someone else to find?"

"As you like," he replied, "or you may keep it. I do not think Atwood will care to read it."

"No, I could not keep it." she grumbled. "It is a treasure. If not for Atwood, then for his daughter."

Catherine waited for Alistair to speak.

Alistair thought she was a brave soul. It was obvious to him that she was keeping her emotions in check, her stiff posture and arms betrayed her. He noticed she was opening and clasping her fists to release some of the turmoil that was playing havoc with her. He wondered why it was so difficult to shirk these feelings that lay between them. The chemistry was tangible. At first, he excused his attraction to her, believing it came from the premise of *forbidden fruit*, a desire for the unattainable and held onto that rationalization to keep himself from acting on his burgeoning feelings, but Catherine had a way to break through his barriers. He could not help but respond to her. She made him believe that a bright future awaited him and he hadn't felt that way in a long time. He would never forget her and most likely she would always own his undeserving heart. He could not stop looking at her. He could see the silence was beginning to unnerve her, so he said, "Come, let me show you the new parlour."

Catherine did not take the arm Alistair proffered knowing it would only unsettle her more. She knew the way to the parlour and rushed ahead of him to make her way there. She thought he looked disappointed, but then chastised herself for her romantic notion. When she entered the parlour, the familiar design made her laugh.

He commented, "It is in tribute to your Sun Room."

The Atwood Parlour was not even half the size of the Aubry Sun Room, but Catherine found it owned a similar grandeur. In the fashion of her own ancestral home, Alistair had the walls painted yellow, divided by a white chair rail. White pinewood paneling decorated the bottom half of the wall. The old rectangular framed windows were replaced with arched framed windows that were painted white, similar to those at her own home. Like Aubry's Sun Room, gold-damasked curtains flanked the windows.

Catherine asked, "You have purchased new furniture?"

"Yes," he replied. "I have kept what was left of the Atwood estate and used it in the upper rooms. Since I redid this room completely, I thought it wise to furnish it with new pieces. I hope Atwood likes it."

"I can see Holland's influence with the Greek and Roman ornamentation," she remarked. Henry Holland was a gifted architect who influenced what would come to be known as the Regency style in England. Catherine walked over and let her hand run over the mahogany sideboard table whose supports were composed of a head and chest of a lion resting on an elongated leg that terminated into paw feet. She scanned the room and found, while the coloring mirrored her family's Sun Room, the Atwood Parlour distinctly exuded its own character.

A large portrait hung over the fireplace and caught her attention. She walked over to it and let her eyes take her fill. Without asking, Alistair joined her and said, "It is Alana, Lady Atwood, before she married. Her father had it commissioned when she made her *come-out*. It was never displayed for Alana had eloped before its completion. The viscount hid it in the attic where it would have been left to ruin if the baroness had not discovered and removed it to her own residence when she closed up the Atwood Home. She is quite pleased to return the portrait to its rightful place."

Catherine remarked, "She was beautiful. I can see why Beaumont fell in love with her. The artist captured her spirit in her eyes, even then, I think she wanted to laugh."

"Yes," he agreed. "Atwood said she was always in high spirit."

Catherine saw Alistair take her hand and thread it through his arm, drawing her closer to his body. She looked up and found him looking back at her, his eyes beseeching her not to pull away. Knowing that she might never have a private moment with him again, she decided not to disengage and to let herself enjoy being close to him. It amazed her how she trusted the man, never fearing for her reputation or safety.

She walked with him and listened to him speak of the completed work and about the gardens that would be designed. She offered her opinions, from a mistress's point of view, of all the things she would add to the house and how she would use each room. She noticed that Alistair had incorporated some of the ideas she suggested the first time she toured the house, regarding the placement of furniture and artwork.

Alistair saw Catherine smile when she spied the escritoire placed by the window. He knew she was happy that he had remembered her recommendation. He teased, "I, too, find that light is beneficial for reading."

Embarrassed, Catherine chided, "You mock me, sir, and take liberties with my remark. You know very well I made no ridiculous statement; however, I forgive you, since it appears you took my suggestions seriously."

The hour passed pleasantly and when Catherine walked out the front door into the sunshine, she was sad to see her visit come to an end. She said, "I understand you leave soon, Mr. Chapman."

He answered, "A few days still. I have some staff I need to hire."

Catherine mentioned, "My brother and his family are coming for their annual visit. I have invited Baroness Litford and her family to join us for a picnic. We will take the children on excursion to the lake. Perhaps, if you are still here, you would like to join us?"

He enthusiastically replied, "I would like that very much, my lady." He helped Catherine onto her mount and watched the fine wisps of her golden hair sparkle in the sunlight as she rode away.

Catherine favored Jason the best of her two brothers. She had disowned both of them for being mean to their cousin, Edward, when she was a child. Eventually, her anger diminished, though she never grew close to Marcus, who matured from a haughty boy to an arrogant man. Jason, through his apology to Edward, managed to rise in her esteem, especially when she saw him greet Edward with felicity at a ball.

Jason was the Duke of Aubry's second son. He did not have to worry about inheriting the dukedom, because that privilege and burden went to the duke's first-born son, Marcus. Having a fearless nature, Jason always yearned for adventure and travel. At three and ten years of age, his father fulfilled his greatest wish and purchased for him a midshipmen's commission in the British Navy. Over time, Jason earned the respect of his officers. He always considered himself lucky to have fought under Nelson's fleet against the Franco-Spanish fleets in the Battle of Trafalgar. He had distinguished himself during the sea battle that confirmed Britain's naval supremacy. His competency and bravery earned him many prizes, as well as his current rank of captain.

One of the things Catherine liked about Jason was that he was not so *high in the instep.* Having dealt with every class of man in the navy, Jason found that as he grew older, he judged a man on character, more so, than rank. Catherine was not worried what her brother would think of the picnic party she was organizing. She was only concerned how her grandmother would feel once she learned that she continued to cultivate the acquaintance of the Litfords and Alistair. Her worries eased when she received news that the dowager was to stay an additional sev'night at Belvoir and therefore, would not be home to receive Catherine's guests. It seemed the Duchess of Rutland could not bear to see her grandmother leave, and since she had no prevailing excuse to depart until Jason arrived at Aubry, the dowager agreed to remain.

Catherine planned to picnic at the largest of the ornamental lakes to take advantage of the row boats. She knew that Jason loved the water and reveled in playing with his sons, so she expected that he would help make the party a success with his general playful nature. His wife, Christina, was always good company and Catherine eagerly looked forward to a fun day.

Before Catherine's party arrived at Aubry House, the ducal footmen, dressed in their red and gold livery, departed in wagons to the largest ornamental lake, carrying the food and the other necessities for Catherine's picnic. They transported barrels and timber to set up into a long table that would be covered with a pristine white linen to serve the banquet. Cook, her staff, and several maids would follow in another wagon to help set the table with the multiple dishes she packed in baskets. Sweet meats, fruits, cheeses, nuts, breads, and other delicacies would be placed on the table for the party to feast at their leisure. The footmen and young maids assigned to serve at the picnic would be happy of the light duty that let them gambol about to enjoy the scenery and the fine weather, while working to clear the lawn of rocks and refuse where the rugs for the party's repose would lay. The site was prepared by the time the ducal carriage arrived, and the servants stood proudly in a line like soldiers ready for inspection. They made an impressive and regal sight.

Jason and his wife received the Litford family and Alistair with alacrity. Catherine knew Jason adored children and would warmly welcome her guests if only because they offered their daughters as companions for his boys.

The servants snapped into industry the minute they saw their mistress disembark from her carriage. The footmen brought forth refreshments, while the maids followed with trays of appetizers to offer Catherine's guests, who had become enthralled with the majestic scene before them. The Litfords stood mesmerized and gazed at the panoramic picture, full of vibrant colors and textures, as if viewing a master's painting.

Shimmering and refracting like a faceted diamond, the crystal blue lake sparkled from the bright sunlight that bounced of its smooth plane, where no wind had prevailed to break its serenity. Reflecting in the calm water was the small island at the lake's center, the dock with rowboats tied to it, and the bordering lush evergreen foliage.

"It reminds me of the painting Gainsborough did of Holywells Park, my lady," remarked Baroness Litford. "I do not believe I have ever seen a more beautiful landscape than what I am beholding at this minute. Thank you for inviting us to enjoy it with you."

Catherine responded, "The pleasure is mine, baroness. Your company has turned what would have been a dull day into an entertaining one. Trust me, the gratitude is all mine." She added, "You will be interested to know the late duke commissioned Gainsborough, not long after Capability Brown proclaimed the landscape finished, to capture this view for his personal pleasure. The painting resides in our London town home, though few have seen the masterpiece rich in color and texture. My papa did not move it to a public room when he came into the title, but left it in his ducal suite like his papa before him, to enjoy privately.

The party made its way to where the rugs were placed. Catherine noticed that the women convened like a gaggle of geese on one large rug searching out their goslings who had made their escape the minute they left the carriage. With drinks in their hand, the gentlemen continued walking until they reached the dock, where they engaged in their own private discourse. Catherine followed where the matrons were looking and found the children at play, running about the lawn without purpose.

Drawn by their laughter, Catherine decided to put some order into their fun rather than join the ladies who most likely were speaking of the trials of motherhood. She no sooner made her way to the children, than they flocked around her, squawking with excitement. She laughed at their antics and immediately put them to task by lining them up to race to a nearby tree and back. She hoped the run would calm them down enough for her to garner some control over them. The boys returned first to cross the finish line, their chests heaving from exertion. She cheered and encouraged the children to applaud when another runner completed their lope. Once they all caught their breath, she set them to scavenge the area for round smooth rocks, dandelions, and twigs. She announced that the first person to bring back the best of each item would win a prize. Catherine was used to carrying peppermint sticks with her whenever her nephews visited and today, she brought enough for all the children to enjoy. She decided to use them as the prize for the tasks she set them to do, and would ensure that each child won one. Their enthusiasm for her silly events made Catherine laugh.

Alistair wearied quickly over the gentlemen's conversation. Ordinarily, he would be engaged with the common topic of the realm's trials and tribulations, but Catherine's laughter beckoned him to no end. He found himself drawn to that special world she had created for the children. He excused himself from the group and joined her right when she was presenting the youngest of Sarah's daughters with a peppermint stick. He grinned. Catherine was declaring Amelia's dandelion the most perfect of all and made the announcement with so much pomp and circumstance that Amelia blushed. Catherine's nephews look dumbfounded. Alistair was sure the boys did not see any difference between their weeds and Amelia's, but he was glad to see that they did not take exception to losing. It seemed they were more interested in the quest than the prize and were quick to inquire about the next item they needed to find. Catherine set them to look for an oak leaf. Alistair waited until they each ran off before he remarked, "You are very good with children, my lady."

"They help brighten my world," she commented.

He asked, "Is your world not bright then, Catherine?"

Catherine smiled at his use of her Christian name. It was as intimate as they would ever get and she would not chastise his use of it. She answered, "Oh, I do not mean to sound bleak. I only mean that as we get older, I think we tend to take things for granted and often let our experiences jade us. Children are forgiving and they tend to marvel at everything around them. Would either of us gleam satisfaction in searching for nature's debris? No, I think not. When I am around them, I am able to see the simple joys that life has to offer, and in that moment my life becomes brighter."

Once again, Catherine enchanted him. He thought she would brighten anyone's world and so he remarked, "I think, these young urchins would argue that you are the beacon in their world right now. It is your energy and cheer that brings pleasure to this game, not theirs."

She smiled and retorted, "Then, we are both well served for I am truly pleasured. And what of you, Mr. Chapman? Are you finding amusement in the day?"

He smiled. Before he could answer, Jason was calling the children forward to eat. He announced that after the children fortified themselves, then to the boats they would go. He asked who wanted to partake in the excursion. To Catherine's dismay, she was the only female, aside from the children, who wanted to join in the fun.

Baroness Litford preferred her repose and Jason's wife said she knew better than to get in a boat with her husband at play. She was in no mood for getting wet. This comment sealed Sara's and Anne's decision to decline.

Each father took his own two children in a boat leaving Alistair to accompany Catherine. The plan was to cruise around the island at a sedate pace; however, before long, Catherine heard the men start to bark rants back and forth. The splashing of oars set the children to giggle in earnest, while the men taunted each other on their skills. A competition soon ensued. Catherine noticed that

Alistair ignored the childish attempts to engage him in competition; even Jason's heckling did not employ him to join the race. As the other boats cruised ahead of them, Catherine thought Alistair looked pleased to be left in their wake. She could distantly hear her brother singing some sea chanty to bolster his sons and Catherine laughed. She saw Alistair smiling back at her with inquiring eyes, so she explained, "My brother learned many a tune in his youth as a midshipmen, most of the lyrics unsuitable for female ears. But there were a few songs he taught me that his captain had taught him. I am happy to hear he has educated his sons on them, as well."

Alistair interrupted her to profess, "I did not get the chance to answer you earlier when you asked if I was finding amusement, my lady. I must thank you, for I am enjoying myself. I must confess to you, Catherine, that I always feel good when I am in your company."

"You are not quite honest, Mr. Chapman," she chided. "Our interlude at Litford Hall did not find us either in good spirits."

Alistair stopped rowing and soberly said, "I am sorry that my behavior grieved you, Catherine, but I stand by my remark, I always feel good when I am in your company."

"I do not know what you insinuate by using my Christian name and making dubious remarks," she berated. "I will not embarrass myself again with any declaration that I know is not welcomed, so why do you insist on stirring up my kettle of emotions? I am resigned that an alliance between us will never happen. I have accepted that all you desire is friendship, though my vanity and intuition believes otherwise. For even now, I find it hard to understand that you do not have feelings for me. If you only want me as a friend, then why do you look at me in a romantic fashion and make remarks that make me feel, that you want to call me more than friend?"

Alistair grimaced and retorted, "You are very bold, Lady Catherine."

"And you, Mr. Chapman, are a conundrum. One I am afraid I will never solve, for my time as a maiden is nearly at an end. I am to be betrothed and soon will be unable to receive you, friend or not."

With anger in his voice, he asked, "And which lord is to be the luckiest of men?"

"I do not know," she shouted. "The duke chooses for me. I am to be engaged for the Little Season. Papa comes for me at the end of the summer."

Shocked, Alistair gasped, "What do you mean, you do not know? Are you to have no say?"

"I have had my say, Mr. Chapman, to no avail," she confessed. "It matters not whom I call husband, if that man cannot be the one for whom my heart is already engaged." With glistening eyes, and doing her best to cheer up their discourse, she said, "You must come about, Mr. Chapman, and make some headway, or else I fear my brother will mock your incompetence in returning me to our party."

Alistair was not amused, but heeded her advice and put his muscle into rowing and returning them to the dock. His mood did not improve. It bothered him to see that Catherine's temperament had rebounded quicker than his own. It was clear that she would not pursue him or try again to seek his good opinion. She was to be married. He would continue to live his life as he had chosen. A life that pleased him, so why he asked, was he not pleased?

Chapter Twelve

Alistair felt his muscles flex with each pull of the oars that brought him and Catherine closer to the landing dock. He was glad for the exercise that was helping him to expend the fury churning inside him and glad that Catherine was mesmerized by the undulating waves his oars were making. From the moment she declared, "It matters not whom I call husband," her eyes had veered from his own and remained focused on the rippling water.

In the silence, he was able to reflect on his astonishing anger. The dowager had already informed him that the duke was to contract a marriage for Catherine and after the initial shock, he had reconciled himself to the idea, but that was when he imagined Catherine settled in a loving relationship with someone more deserving than himself. It never occurred to him that she would suffer a *marriage of convenience* and end up with a man unlikely to appreciate her independent nature. When she said that she did not care whom she married, his outrage was so keen, that had his overwhelming anger not been diminished through exertion, he very likely would have planted a *facer* on the first poor bloke to have looked at him oddly. He was bloody mad and seeing the men waiting on the pier to greet them, no doubt to make him the brunt of their joke, did little to ameliorate him.

Jason held a goblet of wine in his hand, which he raised to toast to Alistair when the boat docked. Alistair could see Jason's lips trembling, ready to burst with laughter. He gritted his teeth to control his temper and took a calming breath while he placed the oars on the bottom of the boat. He took the rope to secure the vessel to the landing and then helped Catherine to debark. No sooner did he step on the dock, than he heard Jason taunt, "I say, Chapman, you should have given the oars to Catherine. I think she could have made better time than you."

The other men chuckled before Alistair could offer a retort. Baron Litford came forward and handed him a wine goblet. He watched the men raise their glasses to him and cheer, "Hurrah, to our inept coxswain!"

To his embarrassment, Catherine laughed. He turned to her and scowled, but her cheerful smile disarmed him. His grimace turned into a grin and he fell into laughter with the others.

Warren, Jason's youngest son, interrupted their revelry, "Father, when will we get to visit the island?"

Jason patted his son's shoulder and looked to his wife who shook her head with a distinctive negative motion. He said to his son, "I fear the day has passed and that it is time for us to return to the house." Jason, hating to see his son's disappointment, looked to his party and queried, "Let us come back tomorrow and have tea on the island. We will have an authentic treasure hunt for the children, the same adventure that the duke and his father before him organized for their own family."

In her excitement, Catherine gave a little hop in delight, much to Alistair's surprise and mirth. She asked, "Oh, Jason, could we? I had forgot all about the treasure hunts."

Before Alistair could ask about the excursion, Baron Litford, knowing his sons by marriage could not take the time away from their work, extended their regrets. "I am sorry to disappoint you, Captain, but I am afraid we must decline. You see, we have taken our holiday from our industry and must return to our businesses tomorrow."

Sarah's eldest daughter, Jane, whispered to her father, Mr. Clayton, "Please, Papa, can you not take one more day?"

Mr. Clayton, looked down upon his daughter and replied, "I am sorry to say, no, Sarah."

This exchange did not go without notice and Jason inquired, "May I not act in your stead, Gentlemen? I promise you that if you entrust me with your daughters, I will guard them with my life."

All four girls exclaimed in unison, "Oh, please, Papa!"

Both Mr. Clayton and Mr. Hodgson looked to their wives who gave their approval. Then, they looked to the baron as the head of the household to respond. The baron had seen the exchange between his daughters and their husbands and answered on their behalf, "Very well, Captain. It seems that you have mesmerized our children with your adventure. I think we will never be forgiven should we decline. You do us great honor with your invitation and we are in your debt."

"Indeed," chimed Mr. Clayton and Mr. Hodgson.

"Nonsense," replied Jason, "you have thoughtfully yielded in order to please my sons. It is I, who is grateful. Alex and Warren would not find the excursion much fun if it only included them. I will send the ducal carriage to pick up your daughters tomorrow."

Catherine marveled at her brother's kindness and turned to Alistair. He had an inquiring face and in a soft voice she began to explain how her grandfather was the first to organize a treasure hunt as a strategy to keep his three energetic boys busy, so that he and his wife could enjoy their tea in peace on the island. He had a chest filled with various toys, sweets, ribbons, and even some pieces of coin, hidden on the island. The boys were given a map and while he and his wife enjoyed their repast, the boys traipsed the island, following the map for buried treasure. Over the years, Catherine learned there were five locations marked with an "X" on the island and five corresponding maps to lead treasure seekers to the loot.

Each map looked remarkably authentic, aging over the years from wear; the parchment depicted the island and a route for the treasure seekers to follow. There was a definitive start point and an "X" to mark the spot where the treasure was hidden. In addition, there were notes instructing the treasure seekers on how many steps to walk or jump; and showed other landmark clues, like an arrow on a tree or a rock to show the way. The treasure hunt made an impression on her father who kept the tradition with his own children. No doubt Jason intended to initiate his own sons into treasure hunting and continue the ritual with them.

As the party made their way to the ducal carriage, Alistair took Catherine's arm in escort. He wanted her to continue to describe her youthful memories of treasure hunting. He loved watching her face animate while she described her recollections. She explained, "I am a decade younger than my brothers, so by the time I was at an age to join in the fun, my brothers had nearly made their majority. The duke would not see me disappointed, so he commanded their participation in order to add to my amusement. Until now, I had forgotten how animated and excited they were in the hunt, considering they knew exactly where the treasure was located. They always let me lead the way and acted as surprised as I was in finding the clues. I see now that it was all for my enjoyment." She reflected, "They used to scare the dickens out of me, by telling me that we had to be chary of the pirates that buried the loot. They told me the swashbucklers would run us through with their swords, if they found us trying to steal their treasure." Catherine laughed. She then realized her reminiscing had distracted her from her companion, so when she looked up to see if Alistair had found humor in her story, she was taken aback by the warmth she saw in his eyes. She asked, "You will come tomorrow?"

"I will."

The next day, Alistair watched Jason pass out wooden swords to his sons and wooden pistols to the girls before they prepared to board the rowboats. He grinned hearing the girls each inhale a sharp breath after Jason told them that the weapons were to protect them, from the scurvy pirates who might return to claim their loot. Both boys swung their swords, slashing through the air in preparation for battle, while their counterparts simply looked at the toy weapons, unsure what to do with them.

Catherine walked over to Jane, took the wooden gun from her hand, and said, "Do not look into their eyes, Jane, for they will fool you into believing that they are worthy. They are the scum of the earth. They have maimed and killed for greed. You must protect yourself. Be steady, point, and shoot!" Catherine extended her arm and then bellowed a shout of "kaboom" from her lips. She then returned the wooden pistol to Jane who smiled at her. Jane marveled at how a lady, even in battle, could look elegant. Before long, the four girls were running around making sounds to imitate guns discharging.

Alistair grinned at Catherine and remarked, "You are a brave soul, my lady. I have remarked on it before. You must have warrior blood in you to take on such ghastly foes with no thought to injury."

She replied, "You give me too much credit, Mr. Chapman. I am sure if I was faced with real danger, I would not act so decisively; however, I do believe I would act. My greatest fear is in having regrets. I hope that when I am old and look back on the life I led, I will have too few to mention." Catherine sobered and added, "I would hate to have missed out on happiness, because I failed to act for fear of being rebuked."

Alistair once again was confounded and awed by Catherine's directness. As much as he liked that she spoke her mind, it also angered him. Her honesty showed an inner strength he felt lacking in himself. He thought himself gallant abjuring her admiration of him, so as not to trespass upon the trust bestowed upon him by Beaumont and Felton, yet instead he felt cowardly. He wondered how a woman just two years past her majority, could know her heart so well, and a man almost decade older, had no understanding of his own.

His reflection was interrupted when he heard Jason assign duties. Catherine was assigned to ride with his sons, Alex and Warren. Alistair would transport the Clayton girls in another boat and Jason would convey the Hodgson twins to the island. Before they left, Jason unfolded the ancient pirate map and laid it on the lawn. He smoothed out its creases and asked the children to look at the map and the island. Then, he asked them to determine where they should beach their boats. It was instantly clear, even to the youngest of the brood, that the start point was on the southeast point of the small island. From their vantage point, they could see the outline of a rock formation that matched the map. A circle, the symbol for start was drawn near the depicted landmark. Their hunt was to begin and the excited children practically jumped into their assigned boats.

Catherine let her fingers glide over the cool crystal blue lake water while she watched her nephews pull the oars towards their chests. They sat next to each other, each responsible for the industry of one oar. She looked over her shoulder to see Alistair's boat follow her wake and she noticed his eyes were on her. She smiled, waved, and was pleased to see Jane and Amelia return her wave. Alistair, she noted, merely nodded, for his hands were busy rowing. She turned to watch her nephews row and heard her brother, the captain, bellow a *sea chanty*.

"Come all you young sailormen, listen to me
I'll sing you a song of the fish in the sea,
And its..."

To her amusement, Alex and Warren joined in the chorus.

Windy weather boys, stormy weather, boys
When the wind blows we're all together, boys

Blow ye winds westerly, blow ye winds, blow
Jolly sou'wester, boys, steady she goes.
Then Alex bellowed,
"Up jumps the eel with his slippery tail,
Climbs up aloft and reefs the topsail,
And it's...

Catherine could hear Alistair and the girls join in the chorus and could not resist adding her own soprano voice to the mix. They continued to sing the sea ditty, each boy adding another verse at the end of each chorus; she was nearly hoarse by the time she reached the island.

They grounded their dinghies on the east bank of the island at a small sandy beach inlet, planting a stake in their mooring line to ensure the lapping water would not pull them free to float out onto the lake. Catherine watched her brother march to the edge of the inlet that marked the boundary between coarse sand and thick green foliage. He placed the map on a large boulder and beckoned the children to gather around him. Catherine followed in their wake, keenly aware that Alistair hesitated in his steps, so as to follow last. She watched Jason ask his eldest boy, Alex, to determine which way they needed to set off. She smiled remembering her own father asking her a similar question.

She could not see Alistair with her peripheral vision, so she turned to see where he might have went. She almost ran into him when she swung her body around to scope the beach, only to learn that he stood behind her.

She was so surprised to see him that Alistair had to check her balance by placing his hands on her shoulder. He grinned seeing she was happy to find him so close at hand. She said not a word, letting her smile communicate her pleasure and turned back around to watch the children.

Catherine refocused her attention on her brother who was in charge of this expedition. She could tell he was pleased with his son's analytical mind. The boy located the key landforms that marked their position and direction. When Alex was sure of his bearings, he pointed and said to his father, "That way, Captain. We need to mark twenty paces."

It thrilled Catherine that Alistair was seeking her company. Try as she might to pay attention to the children, she found herself totally distracted by him. She felt him step to her side and was surprised when he bumped into her shoulder. She knew it was no accident. His shove reminded her of one of the duke's hounds seeking attention by pushing his snout into her body. She wanted to laugh at Alistair's jejune playfulness, but immediately checked her assumption, just in case his light shove was the result of being clumsy and not flirty. Any doubt she had left her mind when she looked up into his face and saw his mischievous grin.

She checked her laughter and returned her attention to the children who began their trek to follow the map's direction. Alex led the party to a well-used path that cut through the island shrubbery. He counted off each step; his followers echoing his count. Catherine waited for Alistair to precede her, but he waved his arm in a fashion that directed her to go first. She followed the children, slowing her pace to create a gap between her and the rest of the party. Then, she sprinted as if to catch up to them before stopping abruptly. Matching her quick steps, Alistair did not have time to check his gait when she unexpectedly stopped and he bumped into her.

He apologized, "I do beg your pardon, my lady."

Catherine giggled and continued upon the path the children had taken without looking back. Had she taken a glance back, she would have seen a bemused grin on his face.

Alistair had felt foolish shoving Catherine's shoulder when they were watching Alex read the map. Aside from a moment of tomfoolery, he knew not why he did it, but he gained great pleasure from it, especially, when Catherine made no complaint about the contact. He thought their collision was her response to his playfulness and he was enjoying their childish game. He hastened his steps to catch up to her.

At the end of twenty paces, Jason next called Jane forward to deduce their next clue on the map. She studied the drawing to try and decipher the symbol on the map. She took a moment to investigate her surroundings and then ran over to a massive tree trunk. She moved aside some leafy foliage that climbed its bark, and shouted, "Look!" The children ran over and found an arrow that was deeply cut into the pulp of the tree. Jason called Amelia over to ask her to look at the map. He pointed out how there were no markings from the arrow to the next point on the map. He asked her where they thought they should go. There was not much to the clue, a simple stake with a flower on it. Amelia spied the landscape before her and then ran off without saying a word. The crew followed her into a nearby patch of wild flowers.

Alistair and Catherine caught up with everyone after being held back with another collision. While the children looked for their next clue among the flowers, Alistair picked one of the yellow daffodils at his feet and pressed it into Catherine's palm. He was happy she took it and did not let it drop to the ground. She did not look at the flower, but surreptitiously proffered him a warm smile. He saw that she pocketed the flower in her spencer and when no one watched, he brushed the back of her hand.

It did not take long for Amelia to find a stake with markings on it. The stake had an arrow pointing in a northern direction and had ten tick marks below it. Jason asked the twins and his youngest son, Warren, what they thought the message meant. Warren was quick to point in the direction of the arrow and shout, "That way!"

Jason looked to Marjorie and Meredith, and asked, "How far do we go?"

The twins looked at each other to confer and then raised both their palms and wiggled their fingers. Jason cheered, "That is correct. We need to count off ten paces."

The youngsters led the way, screaming when they finished off their pacing. They saw a skull and crossbones flag draped over a thick evergreen shrub. Alex, as the eldest boy, drew his sword and cautioned the other children to keep back until he checked for pirates. He probed the bushes about him with his weapon, sticking the wooden blade here and there. After what he deemed a satisfactory period he summoned his crew. The children advanced and searched the shrub where the pirate flag lay to find an ancient chest. Jason pulled and dragged the wooden trunk from the bush unto a grassy spot. He then retreated to allow the children to open the treasure chest. He was pleased to see his eldest son, Alex, though only eight years old, the same age as the youngest girls, step aside to let the other children have the honor of opening the chest. Reluctantly, six-year-old Warren copied his brother's behavior, though his big eyes and restless body revealed his impatience and excitement.

The girls gasped when they saw what filled the treasure chest. There were miniature painted military soldiers, various colored silk ribbons, assorted marbles, oriental fans, peppermint sticks, and other delights that amuse children. Jason announced that each child could select one prize and then the chest would be taken back to Aubry for distribution. Jane began to pick up an oriental fan when she spied a shilling. She hesitated before she could choose, Jason saw her dilemma and remarked to the children, "You may choose any item aside from coin, for those will be evenly distributed among you all later."

Jane looked up at the captain and thanked him. Then, she quickly grabbed the exotic fan. Each child followed suit in selecting a prize. They all began to prance around in play. Alex fell into character immediately, raising his sword in the air. "Beware!" he shouted. "There are vermin nearby. Quick, follow me!"

Jason waved an arm to Catherine and Alistair, suggesting, "Go ahead and climb to the crow's nest to have your tea. I will watch the monsters and when we begin to make our ascent, then I will call to you, Mr. Chapman, to help me get the girls up the stairs."

Catherine looked to her brother and mouthed, "thank you," wondering if her feelings for Alistair were so blatantly obvious. She realized she did not care and would simply enjoy Alistair's company.

Alistair queried, "Crow's nest?"

Catherine smiled and replied, "It is meant to be an old classic ruin, but my grandfather had it built to use as a tea house. It rests at the top of this island's peak. There is a stone staircase that takes us to the top. My brothers in their infancy named it the crow's nest for it gives a bird's eye view of the lake and its surroundings."

Alistair followed Catherine allowing her to precede him up the stone steps that snaked up the side of the hill. He protectively watched her take each step and after awhile, he relaxed his guard for she was adept at managing the steps. It was in that tranquil state that he saw Catherine flounder and start to lose her balance. His hands reflexively went to grab her waist to prevent her fall, but accidently fell onto her derriere. Like hands on a bed of hot coals, he instinctively removed them, before they could get singed. His gesture had been enough for

Catherine to regain her balance. He was about to apologize for manhandling her, when Catherine turned her head to look over her shoulder at him. She remarked sternly, "Well, Mr. Chapman, I fear you have compromised me beyond redemption and must make an honest woman of me."

His eyes widened. Catherine took advantage of his stunned countenance. She bunched up her skirts with one hand and raced up the rest of the steps. Without thinking, Alistair chased her and caught her when they reached the top. Grabbing her shoulders and turning her to face him, he was pleased to see her eyes twinkling with mirth. They both laughed and then sobered, seeing the panoramic view that encircled them. It was a beautiful day, clear and sunny. They found they could spy the green lush countryside in all directions for a mile.

Catherine directed Alistair to take a seat. She dismissed the serving maid, choosing to pour the tea herself. Alistair watched a very elegant woman play hostess for him. After taking a sip of his tea, he asked, "What will you do, Catherine, after you marry?"

"What a strange question, Mr. Chapman," she remarked. "Most women of my acquaintance would say 'getting married' is the doing part."

She could tell that Alistair was trying to sort and organize his thoughts, so she added, "I will remove the perplexity from your question and answer that I will do what wives before me have done. I will be my husband's advocate, supporting him and fighting alongside his causes." Catherine paused and then with a mischievous grin added, "Let me qualify that statement. I will fight his causes if I believe in them, for if I do not, then I will enlighten my misguided husband, so that we are of one mind."

"Perhaps," he retorted, "it is you who will need to be enlightened."

Catherine smirked, responding, "I doubt that, but for theoretical purposes, I will tell you that I will keep an open mind and always weigh my husband's opinion against my own."

"What if it is his will that you follow his direction, whether or not you believe in it?" he asked.

"I will be an obedient wife, Mr. Chapman, and trust in my husband to know what is best, be it begrudgingly or not. I hope to have a union that is based upon a partnership nature rather than a subservient one. I pray that over time, there will be enough respect earned between us that we will find a happy medium."

"What of love?" he probed.

"As you know, there are not many love matches in the sphere to which I was born. The aristocracy is a contracted affair. I can only hope that the duke chooses wisely for me. At a minimum, I hope to have children who will love me."

Catherine surprised herself by answering all of Alistair's questions. She marveled at how easy it was to share her deepest thoughts with him. She asked, "And what of you, Mr. Chapman? Who will you marry when your time comes?"

Alistair was dumbfounded and made no reply. Catherine probed, "Come now. All is fair. I answered your questions. Now you must answer mine."

He replied, "I have no answer, Catherine. Perhaps, I will not marry."

"That would be a tragedy, Alistair," she replied, forgetting decorum and using his Christian name. "You have so much to give if you will only open your heart to someone."

"How do you know?" he queried.

"Because I know you," she answered confidently, before adding, "I wish you a bright future, Alistair, and I hope that one day you will find your love match. I wish nothing less for you."

"Ahoy in the crow's nest!" bellowed Jason. Alistair sprang from his seat, remembering his duty to help bring the children up the steps. He was glad for the interruption, for the affection he saw in Catherine's eyes, nearly crushed his gentlemanly resolve.

Chapter Thirteen

Catherine had retired to her bed with a heavy heart after spending a wonderful day in Alistair's company, but like all good things, the day ended. She found his departure distressing, especially knowing that she was unlikely to ever see him again. Even if she was to visit Beaumont Manor, she was sure that he would make himself scarce. As much as he tried to act indifferent to her, Catherine knew that her elevated sphere is what kept Alistair from declaring himself to her.

She rose early and rang for Mary to help her dress as soon as she opened her eyes. She was not about to lull in bed, fall back into slumber and drift into sadness. She was determined not to let her mood decline and decided a brisk ride would help her to rid her mind of Alistair and what could not be between them.

When she entered the breakfast parlour, she balked at seeing Alistair in conversation with her brother,

Jason, who upon seeing her, asked, "Why are you up so early, Catherine?"

"You need not be surprised, Jason," she reproved, disappointed that he did not greet her warmly. "I routinely rise early to ride our estate. I have come to snatch a scone or two to take with me to break my fast halfway through my jaunt. I did not mean to interrupt you." Remembering her manners, she greeted Alistair, "I bid you good morning, Mr. Chapman."

Alistair had stood when Catherine entered the dining room and responded to her salutation, with a nod of his head. Jason remarked into the silence, "We have just returned from the Atwood Home. Chapman invited me yesterday to visit and inspect the property. Marvelous improvements. I insisted he return with me to break his fast." He paused, wiped his mouth with his linen, and continued, "I was just inviting him to return later this afternoon to join me and my boys for some fishing at our pond. Frenton informed me it was recently stocked. Grandmother doing so, no doubt, for our benefit. What say you, Catherine, you were always chasing after Marcus and me when we went fishing. Do you wish to join us men?"

She smirked, "I am no longer a child, Jason, and have no need to chase after men." She then mischievously added, "I find the tables have turned, Brother. It seems that nowadays the gentlemen chase after me."

Catherine's bold remark embarrassed Jason. He offered, "No doubt, no doubt. I did not mean to offend. I just remembered that you actually liked to fish. I recall that you were more patient than either Marcus or me in waiting for the fish to bite."

She replied, "You are right, Jason. I do like to fish and thank you for the invitation. I will accept, but ask that you not wait upon my arrival to set off to the small lake. I will meet you there when I am able. Wishing to divert their attention back to their own conversation, she turned her back on them and made her way to the sideboard. She folded two scones into a piece of linen and placed the repast into her coat pocket. She then bid her brother and Alistair, "Good day," before leaving.

Catherine knew the reason she reacted strongly to Jason's invitation was because she had felt her heart flutter upon seeing Alistair. She had expected never to see him again and then, there he was, looking remarkably handsome. She knew he would be difficult to forget and that she would suffer for loving him. She also knew that until she was betrothed she would not forsake his company.

Later that morning, she made her way on foot to the smallest of the ornamental lakes. She found Jason and her nephews easy enough, for they were making a lot of racket. She came upon the willow tree that flanked the bank of the lake, offering a canopy of shade with its crown of arching branches thick with long narrow leaves. She remembered the many naps she awoke from under its guard. The tree was a favorite spot of hers for midday reposes and recreation. More than once, she hid as a child within the thick leafy foliage to escape her governess. She spied the extra rod that Jason had brought for her to use laying on the thick grass that bordered this side of the pond. A rolled woolen blanket tied with a rope lay next to the rod. She felt a warmth of affection for her brother's thoughtfulness when she saw he had brought a blanket for her comfort. Since becoming a husband and father, Jason had changed much from the boy that could not be bothered with her, to a man full of consideration for the female gender. She saw her brother was instructing Alex and Warren on how to fish, while Alistair stood watching nearby. As she approached them, she inquired, "Any fish, yet?"

Jason shook his head, reminding her, "Instructions first, application second, Catherine."

Looking at Alistair, she asked, "Are you a student as well then, Mr. Chapman, or have you fished before?"

Alistair smiled, answering, "I have fished before, my lady."

Catherine grabbed a large oak leaf that rested near her foot and helped herself to some bait that Jason had nicely collected. She called to Alistair, "Come with me, Mr. Chapman, if you want to fish. My brother is making too much noise. I fear my nephews will not fare well for instructions or not, his rants will scare the fish away."

Jason waved his impertinent sister off and returned to teaching his sons on how to cast a line. Alistair shrugged his shoulders and followed in Catherine's wake. He noticed she never once looked back to see if he trailed her. She walked a good distance from where Jason stood with his sons. The trees and shrubbery that bordered the lake shielded them from their view. Alistair realized Catherine walked until she could no longer hear Jason's booming voice. He watched her untie and roll out the worsted blanked, smoothing out its folds near the water's edge. She sat herself down and beseeched Alistair to sit down next to her. She said, "I am happy to share my blanket so your trousers, pardon my indelicacy, do not stain with the dewy grass." Catherine laughed at Alistair's raised brow. She knew a lady did not refer to a man's pant, but Catherine was a bit of a hoyden and rarely refrained from being direct. She added, "Come now, Mr. Chapman. Do not tell me, I suffered your senses with my frankness."

He responded, "Even though we are not far from your brother, I am concerned that our location may be too private for propriety's sake."

"Nonsense," she said. "There is not a party in residence to feed the *gossipmongers* and I trust I am in no danger of being forced with unwanted attentions. Now, if you wish to stand and cast your line, do so, but I warn you, you will tire soon enough, for I have never known for the fish in our lake to take the bait very quickly."

Alistair heeded Catherine's advice and took a seat next to her on the blanket, being careful not to touch her person. He watched her skillfully bait her hook. It amazed him that she showed no squeamishness in stabbing the worm unto the sharp point. To his recollection, he knew of no other female acquaintance who would not swoon at the sight of an earthworm. Catherine positioned a piece of cork on the line to a certain length above the hook. The cork acted as a floating device to allow the hook to sink to whatever desired depth she wished. She raised her arm to a high noon position and with a flick of her wrist cast her line out onto the serene lake where a discriminative plunking sound broke the still water, forcing ripples to reverberate on its surface. She situated herself onto the blanket, adjusting her legs and smoothing her skirt, until she settled herself into a comfortable position. Alistair followed her lead and soon sat contentedly next to her.

He waited for Catherine to begin a dialogue with him, for he did not know any woman that was able to remain silent for long. The minutes passed and the quiet that ensued amazed him. He enjoyed feeling the cool brush of the afternoon's breeze across his face and listening to the whistling reeds along the lake's edge. He guessed Catherine liked the peace that resonated as well, for not one iota of discourse left her lips.

A quarter of an hour must have passed before Catherine's line tugged. She jumped up and pulled her fishing pole up to garner enough slack to reel in her line. The trout fought gallantly against being pulled out of the water, flapping its tail vigorously from side to side, trying to disengage its mouth from the hook, all the time causing great splashes of water. Over and again, Catherine jerked her rod up and then brought it down while she turned the crank to reel in her line. Alistair laid down his rod on the grassy bank and watched Catherine's tug of war with the trout. He readied himself to grab the end of her line once the fish was free of the water. When Catherine finally prevailed and the trout hung in the air, Alistair grabbed and removed the fish from the hook. He then hit the head of the fish on a rock to end its misery and with a piece of thin rope, threaded the trout through its gill and mouth. He set the fish in the cool lake water to keep it fresh, anchoring the line to the water's edge.

Alistair watched Catherine bait her hook and cast her line again, before settling herself back onto the blanket. She looked at him grinning from ear to ear and smugly reported, "One."

He laughed, apparently the gauntlet was thrown. He wondered what the prize was if he should win. The quiet continued, but Alistair was far from relaxed. Catherine kept distracting him. He was highly sensitive to every move she made. He even noticed when she jiggled her line to attract her quarry. He could have easily staked his rod on the bank for all the attention he gave it and realized he cared little if he caught a fish. He would rather covertly look at Catherine. He wondered when her eyes gleamed with amusement, whether she knew he was watching her or simply found pleasure in fishing.

Alistair saw a slip of Catherine's golden hair fly over her lips and stick to them. He wished he could gently brush it away, then take her in his arms and kiss her, but he was not so unfeeling to prey on her admiration of him, simply to satisfy his own desire. He was not so callous to hurt her inexperienced and delicate heart.

While he pondered what he wished he could do with Catherine, he saw her once again stand to pull up her rod and reel in her line. He rose to help her remove the trout from its hook and add it to the thin rope where her first catch was being kept fresh, marveling the whole time at how adept she was at fishing. He watched her bait her hook with another earthworm, cast her line into the water, and then lower herself again onto the blanket. He followed and sat himself next to her. He was still watching her when she turned her head to look at him. With a cheeky delivery, she declared, "two," before returning her attention back to the lake.

Alistair had to check his laughter from bubbling forth. He blatantly shook his rod to wiggle his line in the water as evidence that he was indeed in the competition. When Catherine caught her fourth trout, he conceded her the winner, declaring, "I hail you the greatest of fishermen, Catherine. You truly are master over my untested skills."

Catherine laughed with gusto and laid her rod on the bank. She turned to Alistair and remarked, "I know not what occupied your mind, Mr. Chapman, but it was not fishing. Look to your hook, I expect you lost your worm when you first cast your line. I noted earlier, that you only pierced the bait once when you hooked it, making it easy for the fish to grab at its end to tear it off. With nothing to lure the trout, you were bound to lose."

"And yet," reproved Alistair. "You did not bring my handicap to my attention!"

"I am no fool, Mr. Chapman," she retorted. "Do not forget it was a competition. As a woman, it would be imprudent of me to alert you of anything that gives me an advantage."

"Do not imply you think women are meek creatures for I have seen your warrior spirit, Catherine, and your own stubbornness to know otherwise. We were equals in this endeavor and you must own to winning unfairly."

She argued, "I will do no such thing, Mr. Chapman. Fishing is not the luck of the draw; just like in hunting, a skilled and knowledgeable sportsman will be the victor. It is your own folly in *woolgathering* that put you at a disadvantage."

Alistair smiled at her temper and with sobriety admitted, "I stand corrected, Catherine, and concede that you are indeed the victor. What is your prize?" He hoped it was the kiss she once requested and became excited.

Catherine pondered over naming a prize and then surprised him by asking, "I would like to know what is your greatest wish, the only thing that will make you happy?"

He did not hesitate to respond, "That is easy. I want peace, Catherine. I want the anger that has washed over me these last years to dissipate." Alistair could not believe he exposed his inner thoughts to her. He tried to minimize what he said by laughing, hoping to distract her. He added, "Yes, truly, peace for all mankind, that is my wish."

Catherine was not fooled. She took Alistair's hand with her own. She felt him flinch and try to disengage, but she held on to his hand tightly. Then, she looked into his weary eyes and said, "I will offer you the wisdom my grandmama gave to me when I became angry that my papa was contracting a marriage for me. She reminded me that she herself did not meet her husband until they became betrothed. Though she knew not this stranger, she opened her heart to him and found not only love, but happiness in their union. She warned me that if I closed my heart, I would be stuck in a loveless and unhappy marriage. I am too stubborn to subscribe to such a fate, Mr. Chapman, so I am heeding my grandmama's advice. I am choosing to open my heart to possibilities. No matter what, I will make the best of my lot for I would rather be happy than sad. I say to you, Mr. Chapman, that you are in charge of your being. If you want peace, than the power is yours to open your heart to forgiveness and resolve those burdens that weigh heavily on your soul." Catherine gave his hand another squeeze before releasing it. She ended her sermon with, "You are a good man, Mr. Chapman. You deserve the peace you seek."

Alistair had to remind himself to breathe, for Catherine's words touched his troubled heart. How he wanted to believe in what she said. He marveled at her wisdom for such a young woman and asked, "How did you become so wise, Catherine?"

She grinned, "I am far from wise, Mr. Chapman. I am only a student willing to accept and share the wisdom of others." She added, "Come, let us see how well my nephews fared."

The walk back to her palatial home was full of chatter as Alex and Warren plagued their father with questions regarding their cache. Alex asked him, "How is it that Aunt Catherine was able to catch four fish when all you could catch was one? Did you not say that you thought the lake was not well stocked?"

Jason gave Catherine an accusing stare and answered his beseeching son, "There is no rhyme or reason to Catherine's luck. I guess she took the fattest worms from our supply and reaped the reward of them."

Catherine was ready to rebuke her brother's statement until she saw him glare at her. She stopped in her tracks and from the corner of her eye she could see Alistair grin. He took her elbow and pushed her along, pacifying her by whispering, "Come now, Catherine. You must allow a father to remain his son's hero. Imagine his disgrace should his baby sister prove worthier than himself. Will not your ego be satisfied knowing that I conceded you are the master of all fishermen?"

She smiled and said, "Yes, your praise satisfies me greatly. I only wish I had arrived earlier in the day to meet you. Then, perhaps, I would have had more than one prize to remember you by."

He asked, "Will you then forget me that quickly after you marry?"

Catherine earnestly replied, "I hope so."

Her answer shocked him and then he realized that upon her marriage, she must forsake any feelings she had for him. They walked up the steps to the Aubry portico and found that Frenton awaited to greet and open the door for them. He watched Catherine enter before him into the dimmed entryway, leaving daylight behind her. The day was so bright that his eyes had not adjusted to the reduced lighting when he reached the threshold. Alistair shivered watching Catherine disappear into the darkened hallway. He was reminded of Persephone who left behind her the chill of winter when she returned to Hades. In that moment, Alistair knew that without Catherine around to brighten his days, his future looked bleak.

He had agreed to take his midday meal with Jason and his family before leaving. Jason's wife joined the party and before the food was served, Frenton presented a silver salver to Jason upon which a letter rested. Jason quickly broke the ducal seal and announced upon reading the missive, "Ah, our grandmother arrives tomorrow, Catherine. She sent the message ahead to alert us. We are to expect her for our midday meal."

Alistair turned to see that Catherine was watching him. He deduced that the dowager would not be pleased to learn that he had occupied so much of her time and that these visits were at an end. He suddenly felt sad. He did his best to mask his mood, by adding to the conversation when a lull appeared, but even he could tell his contributions lacked wit. He saw that Catherine's cheery disposition also diminished upon hearing of the dowager's arrival, noticing how she quietly picked at her meal, sliding a morsel to and fro on her plate. Looking down at his own full plate of food, it was clear she was not the only one who had little appetite.

Jason ordered the attending footman that stood behind him to fill Alistair's goblet with wine. He remarked to his guest, "You must have needs of more wine to wash down your meal, Chapman, for you have barely eaten a morsel. Eat hearty, for when we are through, we will have a go at a game of billiards before you leave."

"Nay," interrupted his wife. "You have neglected me enough this day, Husband. You may leave Catherine to entertain Mr. Chapman while you attend to me."

Catherine saw her brother make a face at his wife. He did not look pleased until she said, "Come now, Jason. I will let you tell me about the big fish that got away this afternoon and I will be as enamored by your story as if we have just met."

Jason laughed, saying, "Very well, Christina. I am at your service." He then looked to Alistair to say, "I leave Catherine as my second to secure my victory."

Alistair grinned, replying, "I will not abuse the advantage you have bestowed upon me."

"Oh, ho!" Jason bellowed. "Do not underestimate my little sister. She is quite the hoyden when it comes to competing. She has probably logged as many hours as myself honing her skills."

Catherine blushed and barked, "Jason! I am far from being a hoyden." She looked at Alistair who was checking his laughter and said to him, "However, my brother has given you fair warning, Mr. Chapman. If there is an advantage, I am bold enough to say it is mine. Do not think me a coy debutante who will flatter your ego by playing badly. I am too competitive to submit to being coquettish."

Jason crooned, "Good girl, Catherine." To Alistair he said, "Seek me out before you leave, so that I may bid you farewell."

"Of course."

Alistair followed Catherine into the billiards room and watched as she went directly to the rack of cue sticks and picked one out. She turned and said, "This is my personal cue, crafted and weighted for my needs. You may select from any of the others."

His visible surprise made Catherine chuckle and before she could tease him for his astonishment, he made his way to make his selection. He pulled a cue from the rack and studied it, looking to see that it was not warped, owned a comfortable weight, and was of the right size. Then, he tested to see if the pole could easily slide through his fingers. After inspecting a number of the sticks, he decided they were all superior and settled on using the first one that he had tested. He turned and saw that Catherine was already racking the balls to start the game.

She said, "Would you like to break, Mr. Chapman?"

He grinned and replied, "No, I believe the honor is yours, my lady. My manners keep me from preceding before you."

"Ah!" exclaimed Catherine. "Most gallant, but trust me, I am no damsel in distress. I am, however, too cut-throat to refuse your offer, so I will simply say, thank you."

Alistair watched Catherine take her cue stick in her hands and bend over to scrutinize her shot. She was quite a sight. While she focused on her strategy, Alistair enjoyed looking at the fine curves and lines of her body she so conveniently displayed. He stood to her side and had a pleasing view of her protruding derriere as she bent over the table to shoot. He was surprised Jason was not present to chaperone them. Granted, the door was open, but still, propriety dictated a chaperone. He felt quite honored to be entrusted with Catherine's virtue, even if the lady was far from defenseless. He expected she could put up quite a ruckus if anyone attempted to sully her innocence. True, she was not strong enough to prevail, but her attacker would definitely know pain for trifling with her.

Alistair heard the break of the cue balls and looked to see that Catherine had made a superior hit. A solid colored ball made its way into a pocket and he watched as she surveyed the table like a fey animal stalking its prey. She moved with stealth seeking the best approach for her attack.

Alistair thought he might never get a hand at the game for Catherine was pocketing ball after ball.

Eventually, she failed to execute and she begrudgingly relinquished the table to him. He found her competitive nature charming and he was glad to be adept enough at the sport not to humiliate himself. Providence was his friend and he reaped the rewards of Catherine's earlier success. She had cleared the table of most of her balls that could have blocked his shots. He heard Catherine groan each time he successfully sunk another one of his balls into a pocket. He considered he might actually win the game until he failed to make a difficult angle shot and had no choice but to give the table back to Catherine. She radiated with joy, knowing the game was hers to win. She only had two shots left. She needed to pocket her last solid colored ball and then sink the black ball to win.

Alistair exclaimed, "Bravo!" when she sank the last of her set. Catherine took a slight bow, knowing all she had to do to win was sink the black ball. She called out where she would pocket the black ball, taunting Alistair enough for him to engage in some mischief. She set her stance, but before she could take her shot, she saw Alastair make his way to stand behind her. Her nerves breached, wondering what he was doing. She hesitated and asked, "Mr. Chapman, why are you standing behind me?"

She did not realize that he had made his way to her blind side, brushing her arm as he passed. Catherine reflexively jerked her cue stick. Her ire rose knowing the movement counted as her stroke, forfeiting her from taking the winning shot. She turned to rail at him for being underhanded, but froze when she saw him bent over in laughter.

When he had calmed himself, he remarked, "This is the second time I have caught you unawares, Catherine. You really need to hone your concentration skills."

"Unfair," she chided. She was ready to argue with him to regain her turn when she decided to let Alistair take his final shot. She deferred, "You are right, Mr. Chapman, the err is mine. The game is yours to win, *if* you can sink the ball."

Alistair had not intended to win the game by such nefarious means, but Catherine's taunt had pushed him into devilry. He knew she was going to retaliate when he saw her eyes twinkle with delight. He did not want to derail her plans, so he picked up his cue stick to survey his shot. He thought he could sink the ball with no problem. His conscious nagged at him enough that he considered banking the ball to ensure he would miss the pocket. As he pulled back on his cue stick, he heard Catherine approach him from behind. Her steps were loud as if to announce her arrival. Alistair tensed, preparing for her to brush his arm as he had done to her. The seconds were excruciating long. He waited, using all his concentration to hold onto his cue stick. He did not want to lose his turn with a jerk as Catherine had done, but nothing prepared him for the warm breath that brushed his ear. The sensation so unnerved him, that he threw his cue stick onto the table.

Catherine stepped back, teasing, "I see I am not the only one in need of honing my concentration skills."

"Touché," he replied, grinning. "We will call it a draw, agreed?"

"Agreed," she answered.

They studied one another as if trying to read each other's mind. The act quickly diminished their cheerful moods. Alistair broke the silence, saying, "It is time I bid you good evening, my lady."

"You will not stay to dine with us?" she asked.

"No," he replied. "I have trespassed enough on your family. I want to thank you for your hospitality, Catherine. I have enjoyed our time together and wish you felicitation in your coming marriage."

Alistair's reference to Catherine's nuptials chilled her to the bone. Seriously, she replied, "Thank you, Mr. Chapman. I wish you happiness, also." To her own surprise, she tiptoed and brushed a kiss on Alistair's cheek, whispering, "I will cherish the time we spent together." Before he could reply, she turned and left.

Alistair found Jason in the Sun Room with his wife. When he entered, Jason rose and asked, "Pray, tell me, who is the victor?"

Alistair grinned and replied, "It was a draw, Captain."

"Then," Jason retorted, "Catherine must have a soft spot for you if she did not secure the win."

Alistair did not reply to Jason's glib remark. Instead, he said, "I have come to take my leave of you and to thank you very much for your generosity in sharing your family with me. I have enjoyed myself immensely and feel most privileged to be able to have made your acquaintance."

"I feel the same," he replied. "Come, let me see you to the door." As they walked, Jason said, "I have not made my sympathies on the loss of your brother, Chapman. Please accept my condolence at this late date."

Alistair was shocked that Jason knew of his brother. He asked, "You knew Erik?"

"Of course," he answered. "You do not think I would have allowed anyone but a gentleman, to flirt with my sister, did you?"

Dropping Jason's title, he replied using his surname, "I am guilty, Brentwood. I would be lying to say she does not affect me, but I have not trespassed upon her virtue. We are only friends. You see, I lost everything when Erik died and I am in no position to declare myself to anyone of Catherine's stature. I beg that you not betray my history to her for it will only injure her."

"I see," Jason stated. "Then, we will see no more of you for Catherine will be betrothed soon."

"It is for the best," Alistair replied. "Thank you again, Brentwood."

Jason proffered his hand to Alistair who took it and gave it a hearty shake. They bid their goodbyes and Alistair took his leave.

Chapter Fourteen

Alistair left early the next morning to return to Beaumont Manor. He had hired a competent steward to oversee the garden improvements to completion and to continue management of Atwood's properties, including the hiring of the household staff. He could have extended his stay to finish the work himself, but he decided the sooner he left Catherine's realm, the sooner he could try to forget her.

He felt alone at Beaumont Manor, since the marquis and Atwood were still on their Grand Tour. Edward and his bride of nearly two months were rarely seen and when he was in their company, their newfound love unsettled him. They were affectionate with one another and witnessing their playfulness reminded him of the time he spent with Catherine. The recollections tugged at his heart. He did not know when he realized he carried a *tendress* for Catherine, but the memory of her plagued him. His mind never rested, contemplating what she was doing, how she was feeling and most of all, whom she would marry. It bothered him that someone other than himself would own her esteem and he envisioned another gentleman being the recipient of her smiles. It irked him that she was not smiling at him or that he would not be the man to enjoy her wit, her mischief, or her opinions. It especially troubled him since it was by his choice that Catherine would not call him husband. He began to think about the decision he made five years ago that altered his life, making it impossible for him to pay his addresses to Catherine.

There were so many emotions that led him down a path that made him reinvent himself: grief, anger, spite. Grief over the loss of his elder brother and his betrothed; anger over his father's interference; spite that made him forsake his inheritance and title. For five years, he abjured his father, his position and to what purpose? He doubted very much if his father had changed his overbearing nature or that he regretted pressing him to marry Laurie. His father had argued that his brother's betrothed, Laurie, was pregnant and for that reason alone Alistair had to marry her. He ranted that the child might be a boy, the future heir, and without a marriage to validate him, Erik's baby would be nothing more than a *by-blow*.

Alistair agreed with his father that it was his responsibility to marry Laurie and legitimize his brother's child, but he wanted to wait until Laurie's grief had eased. He had grown up with Laurie and loved her as a friend. He was thrilled when he learned that he would soon call her sister, but his brother's death changed everything. Fearing that Laurie's condition would soon be visible, his father pressured Alistair and Laurie to marry expediently. Her overwhelming grief and the stress of marrying someone other than Erik diminished her health. She could not rally the strength she needed to carry her child to term. With no desire to live, she gave in to her wish to join her beloved.

Alistair blamed his father for Laurie's and her baby's death. He lashed out at him for his interference. Reason, had he considered it, might have tempered his ire, for then he would have known that his father was driven by what he thought was best. With a compassionate mind, Alistair would have understood that his father was also grieving over the loss of Erik, Laurie, and their baby. He would have comprehended that it was his father's fear and sorrow that compelled him, without giving thought to a respectful mourning period, to harangue his only surviving son to immediately wed and produce the heir needed to secure the title. Without duress, Alistair might even have checked his anger before it drove him to curse his father and forsake his birthright.

For five years, Alistair lived anonymously, never seeking to reconnect with his father, but in heeding Catherine's advice, he decided to open his heart to forgiveness and come to terms with his shame. As much as he was angry with his father, he accepted he was more so with himself, for not shielding Laurie from the pressure of his father's demands. He had felt an overwhelming remorse in failing to protect his brother's family. He realized that before he could forgive his father, he had to forgive himself for being so consumed in grief, that he had lacked the fortitude to check his father's interference.

It took Alistair a long time to understand his guilt had more to do with the relief he felt in not having to marry his brother's betrothed. He did not wish Laurie dead, but he saw little happiness with a woman who would cringe at intimacy with her lover's brother. He had difficulty with the idea of joining himself to someone he had always looked upon like a sister, regardless, he would have married Laurie to legitimize Erik's son and to do his best to care for his brother's family.

Lord Felton entered his study to see Alistair at his desk deep in thought. A week had passed since Alistair returned from the Atwood Home and Edward had noticed a marked change in the man. He wondered if his cousin Catherine was the cause for his uncommon solitude and introspection. He never learned any more details regarding why his grandmother inquired about Alistair's character. He had been too distracted with his lovely wife to care, but now that Alistair was here, he could see that his friend was troubled and he wanted to help him.

Not until Edward stood by his side and touched his shoulder did Alistair realize he was no longer alone. He looked up and found Lord Felton asking him, "How can I help?"

Alistair replied, "The burden is mine, Felton. It is time I went home and made peace with my father. I fear I was impetuous in my actions."

"You are too hard on yourself, Alistair," he replied. "I do not know what made you break from your father, but I know your character. You are not impulsive and would not have acted without thought."

"Thank you, Felton," he replied. "I am sorry, but you need to hire a new man of business. It is time I tended to my own affairs."

Alistair walked into his father's study and saw him with his head bent over a pile of papers sitting behind his imposing mahogany pedestal writing table. The mammoth desk had a kneehole and was flanked by tiers of drawers supported by lion paws and had owned that particular space at Gracemoor for as long as he could remember. As Alistair approached him, he noticed his father's hair sported more gray than from the last time he saw him, but overall he looked the same. He was glad to see things had not changed so much from when he had left. His father, a creature of habit, could always be found in his study at this time of day reviewing his ledgers and reconciling his bills. He realized that he was a lot like his father for he also kept to a schedule when he worked for Beaumont. He was glad his father had not yet noticed him. It gave him a chance to collect himself before he greeted, "Hello, Father."

The Marquis of Gracemoor looked up and was astonished to see his son. Surprise and glee alighted his face. He pushed his chair back to rise from it and exclaimed with joy, "Alistair!"

He expediently made his way around his desk and grabbed Alistair roughly by the shoulders, confessing, "It pleases me that you have come home, Son. I have missed you." His father then embraced him in a bear hug and it took more than a second before he released him. Alistair was awed by his father's affection and was so overcome that he became discombobulated. He was prepared to be abused, harangued for walking out five years ago and never looking back. At a minimum, he expected to be slighted and asked to leave, learning that his father had disinherited him and that one of his cousins was now his heir. He was prepared to do battle; he was not prepared to receive such ardor.

His father drew him over to a chair and told him to sit down. Then, he went over to a console where he kept a decanter of port and glasses. He poured out two draughts; he handed one glass to Alistair and kept one for himself, commanding, "Drink, Son."

Alistair needed no coaxing; he swallowed his liquor in one gulp, placed the glass on his father's desk and inquired, "You are not angry with me?"

Gracemoor swallowed his own portion, following Alistair's lead and placed his own empty glass next to his son's. He replied, "No, but I know that you are angry with me and blame me for Laurie's death. You may not be wrong to place the fault at my door, but as God is my witness, I meant the girl no harm. I thought I was acting responsibly in securing your marriage to her. I believed I was honoring your brother, Erik, by taking care of his loved ones."

Alistair heard the croak in his father's voice. He stood and placed his hand on his father's shoulder, consoling, "We have grieved enough over what we cannot change. I am as much to blame as you in not seeing to Laurie's needs. I have thought of nothing else these past five years. I have come to believe that Laurie would not have thrived as my wife. She loved my brother too much to join with another even for the protection of their child. She was so overwhelmed with grief that she could not even garner the will to live for the sake of her own baby. I now believe there was nothing that we could have done to prevent her fate. She willingly left this world to be with Erik."

He continued, "During that time, I have been angry with you, Father, but recently I have accepted that I was more upset with myself. I never told you how uncomfortable I was to marry Laurie. She was like a sister to me and an intimacy with her seemed unbearably wrong. I believe she felt it, too. When she died, I blamed you for not giving us the time to come to terms with what seemed an unthinkable alliance and betrayal against Erik. I left this house in a rage over your interference, but looking back, it was the relief in knowing I did not have to marry Laurie, that shamed me and forced me to leave. I was not worthy to replace Erik as your heir. I felt guilty in somehow not saving Laurie and his baby. I finally accepted that neither you nor I were responsible for Laurie's death. Her connection to Erik was too great for us to break. I accept that it is not necessary for me to understand God's will, but only to accept it. I have come home to make amends, Father. If I am to be happy, I must reconcile with you and accept my birthright. Will you forgive me?"

Gracemoor answered, "You need not ask, Son, but yes, I forgive you. Can you find it in your heart to forgive my meddling?"

"Yes," he sincerely replied.

Gracemoor exhaled the breath he was holding and a long sigh echoed. He felt lighter, reborn, like the rain that cleanses the London sky free of smoke and contaminants. Gracemoor felt as though his slate had been washed clean. He was happy and he hoped his son would stay to visit for awhile. He inquired, "Are you home for good or do you return to Beaumont?"

Alistair scrutinized his father and asked, "How long have you known that I have worked for the Marquis of Beaumont?"

A sparkle alit from Gracemoor's eyes, he answered, "You are my son, Alistair. I have known of your whereabouts and actions since the day you were born. You have served Beaumont well and prided me in your stewardship of his properties."

"The accolades are yours to own, Father. If I was good at my job it is because you taught me well. I have enjoyed working for Beaumont, especially the privacy. It was quite novel not having my every move communicated through the *ton's* grapevine, but I cannot live the life I want or make the changes to better our society as a commoner. I was born into nobility and have an obligation to that position that I do not wish to shirk."

Gracemoor noted, "You have matured, Alistair. I am proud to see that you have come to terms with your responsibility to our realm. What are your plans then?"

He answered, "I want to take my seat in the House of Lords and craft legislature to guard our commonwealth. I want to focus on laws that protect women and children from being worked to death in our industries and revoke those edicts that keep the common man from being able to afford a loaf of bread."

His father remarked, "You are most passionate, Alistair. You have never before desired to take a seat in Parliament."

Alistair had a true peerage that gave him the right to sit in Parliament, unlike many sons of the aristocracy who only used one of their father's inferior titles to distinguish themselves from the common. He became the Earl of Mercer upon his brother's death and could vote in the House of Lords if he wished. He replied, "I have seen much these last five years, Father, that in the past my youthful indulgences kept me from noticing. I always understood my obligation to the realm, though until recently, I did not understand the privilege of it. I am determined to use my influence to improve our commonwealth."

"Then, no doubt, you will," he responded. "You will solicit my support in your endeavors, Alistair? I am not indifferent to our nation's tribulations."

He answered, "I would be most grateful for your support and wisdom, Father."

"You must be hungry, Alistair," stated Gracemoor. "I was so happy to see you that I forgot to see to your needs. Have you had your trunks sent to your room?"

Alistair asked, "You kept my room?"

He remarked, "No matter what grievances we have, you can always find shelter and protection here. Yes, I have kept your room intact. Come, let us get you settled before my guests begin to arrive."

Alistair queried, "You are expecting guests?"

With surprise, Gracemoor admonished, "Do not tell me, you forgot about my annual hunt, Alistair?"

He laughed and said, "Forgive me, Father, but my mind weighed with other thoughts. May I ask if you are expecting a large party?"

Gracemoor reciprocated his son's mirth and answered, "Of course; however, in case you do not remember, ever since your mother died my party is made up of men, their wives preferring not to accompany them without a mistress to greet them. I am sorry to inform you that there will be no young maidens to amuse you, but perhaps you will find the time well served in persuading your peers to advocate for your political aspirations."

Alistair liked the idea of generating some interest for the causes that were close to his heart and commented, "Thank you, Father. That is an exceptional idea that I shall make good use."

Alistair had just finished enjoying his midday meal with his father when Gracemoor's butler entered and announced that the marquis's guests were beginning to arrive. Alistair felt a measure of peace that he had not felt in over five years. He should have returned home sooner and discussed his feelings with his father, but he knew it was not until Catherine entered his life that he began to reconcile himself to what he felt. He would not regret his exile. He had needed time to grieve and to grow to become a man capable of forgiveness, both to himself and his father. Plus, he thought with a grin, he would never regret his time spent with Catherine. Their chance meeting and recurring interludes allowed them to know one another in a casual way that was rare for members of the aristocracy, where courtship was strictly governed.

Alistair thought his father looked more relaxed, even younger. He had to admit that he felt invigorated himself, acknowledging his tension was gone. He was at ease and wanted to enjoy the feeling. He was not ready to disrupt his good humor with chatty discourse among his father's guests, so he asked his father to be released from greeting them, assuring him that he would join his party later for the evening meal.

Gracemoor inquired, "Will you join the hunt tomorrow, Alistair?"

He replied, "If you will excuse me, sir, I have a lot to contemplate and would prefer to spend the next few days walking the grounds, visiting our tenants and looking to my future. I believe I may make you happy for I have been thinking of securing a wife of late."

Gracemoor smiled and exclaimed, "And a nursery too! Capital! Do all the meditating you need for nothing would please me more than to bring some life into this old manor with children. It is moments like this when I miss your dear mother. She would be much pleased to see you happy and settled."

He smiled and replied, "Until dinner, sir." He then made his exit and left his father to greet his arriving guests.

There were at least a dozen gentlemen in the drawing room engaged in small chatter waiting for the announcement that dinner was served when Alistair entered. Many were old cronies of his father. Some men were unknown to him. He remembered that his father said that he expected a large party, so either the others had not descended from their suites or had yet to arrive. As soon as his father spied him, he exclaimed, "Ah, Alistair! Gentlemen, may I introduce my son and heir."

Alistair watched as each man acknowledged him. He was surprised to meet Lord Crane for whom he did not know was an intimate of his father. He had never met the man, so he gathered that he was a recent acquaintance made in the last five years. Crane looked like a dandy in his bold and bright pink waistcoat. He was loud, boisterous, and Alistair thought he held too high of an opinion of himself. He knew that Crane held interests in one of the textile factories that he toured. It was still his hope to build a factory with Lord Felton that would provide the extra income needed for Beaumont's tenants to keep their family and farms intact.

His thoughts were interrupted by the butler who announced that dinner was served. Alistair wished he had been seated next to Crane for the gentleman had managed to hold the attention of those around him with his discourse. He wondered what sermon awed them to remain uncommonly quiet. His own neighbors spoke nothing but horseflesh and the coming hunt, subjects that in Alistair's state of mind held little interest for him. He was happy to see his father rise and beckon his party to the drawing room for a glass of port and a hand at cards. Without a mistress in the house, there was no need for them to seclude themselves in the study or censure their dialogue. It would be a gentlemen's club that reigned the manor for the next sev'night.

Alistair made the round to greet the gentlemen and then positioned himself close to Lord Crane to hear what the man was saying that still captured his dining audience. Alistair's own dinner partners had already sat down to a game of faro and were not even aware of the solicitation being sought. He heard Crane say, "I tell you, Gentlemen, this industrial revolution of ours will fatten our coffers to the breaking point. I am in the process of building another factory in the north and am looking for investors. The profits are incredible, the costs minimal, and the risk non-existent. Clothing our own troops keeps a high demand on wool."

Alistair became distracted when he noticed a very stately nobleman enter the room. He saw his father rise to cheerfully greet the regal lord and then walk with the gentleman towards the group with which he was engaged. He returned his attention to Crane and inquired, "How many women and children laborers does your factory hire, Crane?"

"Excuse me?" he rebuffed.

Alistair repeated, "I asked you what is your labor ratio?"

Lord Crane pulled from his pocket a quizzing glass, a single magnifying lens with a handle, and raised it to his eye to peer through the lens at Alistair. The act is meant as an insult, to demonstrate a superiority over someone. He thought to embarrass Alistair for questioning him, but Alistair was made of sterner mettle and owned too much of his own arrogance to allow such flummery to affect him. He prodded, "Do you need me to rephrase the question, Crane?"

Alistair saw the man crimson from anger. The man's neck began to color first, then spread upwards toward his face. He thought Crane might call him out, especially since the subtle slur to his intellect did not go unnoticed by the other gentlemen. A number of chuckles at Crane's expense filled the room before Alistair could try to soothe the man's ego. He placated, "I am all in jest, Crane, but really, did you expect a look through your monocle to deter my questions. England's factories are a serious business and if you are an owner, then I hold you accountable for the welfare of your laborers. I ask you again, how many women and children do you have working for you?"

Crane curtly replied, "It is not against the law to hire women and children. I do not know the exact number or ratio to men for that matter."

Alistair countered, "But yet you are clear on demand, costs, and profits. When was the last time you toured your factory?"

Crane balked before answering. He did not like the tone Alistair used and began to feel defensive. He confessed, "I have not. I keep a man of business to oversee such drudgery." He laughed and exclaimed, "Can you imagine me, in my finery, in such a filthy environment?"

The gentlemen around Crane laughed and the tense atmosphere dissipated, everyone appearing cheerful. He saw his father shift his weight from one foot to the other, concern written on his face. He probably worried that his son was about to upset his hunting party. Alistair knew he should abandon the controversial subject, but he also knew that this scene encapsulated the views he would find in Parliament. If he could garner support among a few, then he could be hopeful of affecting change in a bigger arena.

He persisted, "I have toured your factory, Crane. I found it a deplorable environment not fit for human industry. I will tell you that your workforce is made up of only women and children who look so emaciated from lack of food and rest, that I could not understand how they were able to stand, much less work."

Crane countered, "No one forces them to take these jobs, if they are unhappy they are free to quit."

Alistair argued, "You are wrong, Crane. The moment we implemented the factory system to replace our domestic system, we forced our proud and earnest countrymen to relinquish their tenant farms. They could no longer afford to keep them without the supplemental income they earned from the spinning and weaving of wool. We have forced them to move to the cities to take these industrial jobs. I say, we are responsible for their welfare."

Crane rebutted, "I am no master craftsman, nor do I own any apprentices. I am a businessman who hires labor. My responsibility to them is in payment of their wage and I pay what is equitable for their skill. I meet my obligation, SIR!"

Alistair countered, "I am sure you do, Crane. I am sure you pay the lowest wage for your unskilled workers. Now that we have machines to do the work that once took experienced craftsman to complete, it is the women and children, the obedient and submissive, that are hired as the cheapest of labor to do the work."

The Marquis of Gracemoor thought enough had transpired and took the moment of silence to introduce his guest. He said, "Aubry, may I present my son, Lord Mercer, to you. Alistair, meet the Duke of Aubry."

Alistair nearly fell over. Never in his wildest dreams did he think that providence would have aided him in his quest for happiness. Surely, he thought, this was a sign that Catherine and he were meant to join in matrimony.

The duke said, "Mercer, your father has spoken highly of you. I am interested in what you have to say. Perhaps, we can take a private corner and continue this conversation. Amazingly enough, my daughter Catherine recently wrote to me about the plight of laborers in the textile industry. You will think I am very lenient in allowing her to voice her opinion regarding gentlemanly concerns, but anyone that knows Catherine does not even bother to comment."

Alistair walked away with the Duke of Aubry. It brought him joy to know that Catherine had championed his cause to her father. He remarked, "Your daughter sounds delightful."

Chapter Fifteen

The Duchess of Aubry entered her daughter's private suite to find her sitting at her toilette table. Her abigail, Mary, was putting the finishing touches to her coif, pinning a tendril here and there. She waved her hand to dismiss her and Catherine's ire rose to see her personal maid released from her service with not so much as a "by-your-leave."

Catherine abruptly asked, "What is it, Mama?" In her mirror's reflection, she saw that her mother carried a letter. They had been waiting for the duke to arrive at Aubry to escort them back to London for the Little Season. Since he had yet to arrive, Catherine supposed the missive was from him. She turned in her seat to face her mother and waited for her to reveal her news.

"It seems the duke is enjoying himself too much at Gracemoor. He commands us to precede him to Town where he will meet us in another fortnight. I have *carte blanche* to purchase your bridal clothes." The duchess smiled at this revelation and remarked to her daughter, "You are to have everything you desire, Catherine."

"Not everything," Catherine glumly retorted.

The duchess was unaware of her daughter's heartbreak, so she cheerfully exclaimed, "Oh, yes, Catherine, everything! I shall alert the staff. You might as well have your abigail pack your trunks, though you need not bring much, since we will purchase a new wardrobe for you." She grabbed her daughter's hands and helped her to rise to her feet. She affectionately remarked, "You must be getting excited, Catherine. Imagine, soon you will be married and most exceptionally matched, too, for the duke has chosen wisely for you." She turned and left her daughter to ponder her private thoughts.

Catherine chanted, "I will choose to be happy." Ever since Alistair left her company, she had owned the mantra. She hoped that through sheer will, her pledge would prevail. Her mother told her that the duke favored Lord Rushton for her betrothed. He was a gentleman in his thirties with title and property. His family's ancestry dated back to Norman times and his coffers and inheritance were substantial. She would be a countess and perhaps, one day a duchess like her mother. Her future husband was third in line to a dukedom. He was one of the *ton's* most eligible bachelors.

Catherine had seen him only once. He had attended a ball to see his cousin make her *come-out*. He did not patronize Almack's or those affairs that the young debutantes attended, so she had never made his acquaintance. He was a man of advanced years, compared to the young men that usually made up her admirers. He spent his time in his own amusements, reposing at his gentlemen's club, purchasing horseflesh at Tattersall's, practicing his pugilistic skills at Gentleman Jackson's and cavorting in the houses of the demimonde. It was a normal life for a wealthy aristocrat, so she could not prejudice herself against him for it, nor think less of him just because she knew little about him to admire. She would keep herself open to the alliance and discover why the duke found this man worthy of her hand.

It was fortuitous for Catherine that upon her first excursion in Town she came across Lord Rushton and his friend on Bond Street. She and her mother were just exiting a shop when his lordship tipped his beaver hat to the duchess. Catherine's mother acknowledged him with a nod. Apparently, the duchess had met his lordship at one of his mother's soirees and approved of him. The nod gave Rushton permission to speak to her.

"Duchess! I had no idea you had returned to Town." For years, Rushton had been harangued to marry. At five and thirty, even he agreed it was time to start his nursery. He knew he had a duty to secure the title with an heir and with a pragmatic approach he looked to the *marriage mart* for a lady of consequence to wed. Catherine's beauty and lineage were acclaimed, so when his mother suggested her name as a candidate, he did not hesitate to petition for her hand to the Duke of Aubry. The duke informed him that his offer was one of many and that he would not settle Catherine's betrothal, until his daughter had the opportunity to meet her admirers, which she would do during the Little Season. Rushton wanted to win Catherine's hand, so after a summer retreat to his estate, he returned to London to charm the young debutante into accepting his addresses.

While the duchess made polite conversation, Rushton took in Catherine's countenance and he noted she was no timorous maiden. It amused him that she matched his look, never wavering under his scrutiny. If anything, her eyes burned with a fire that betrayed her anger at being judged. He had to check his laughter and in that moment, he thought that the spirited Lady Catherine might be the perfect wife for him.

The duchess added, "We will be receiving guests tomorrow if you would like to present yourself."

Rushton grinned, replying, "I would indeed." He then looked to his acquaintance and said, "Please allow me to introduce, Lord Brenner, to you."

In her parlour, Catherine found herself, once again, the center of attention with young admirers panting for her favor. This was her third Season regulating the advances of her suitors. She was always careful not to offend them and was diplomatic in expressing both her gratitude and indifference to their admiration. She had become quite adept in moderating a friendly atmosphere, reducing rivalry, and sharing equal consideration to each man that flocked to her side. She wondered if once she was married whether anyone would be interested in her company for the sake of friendship. She may not have wanted to marry any of these jejune noblemen that flattered her with their attentions, but she did enjoy their company.

She was in the middle of listening to Lord Brenner, a gentleman whom was recently introduced to her, tell a story about a highway robbery when Lord Rushton was announced. Catherine thought he looked quite elegant in his superfine midnight blue riding coat. He sported a colored print cravat that could have marked him a dandy. She realized that Mr. Rushton had worn it to illustrate to her that he was beyond ridicule when all the young gentlemen sprang to attention to ape about him, remarking, "It is quite the thing, Rushton." Apparently, Lord Rushton was an arbiter of fashion and whatever he chose to wear was deemed stylish. Catherine wanted to laugh when the earl smirked at how Catherine's admirers easily transferred their attentions to him. They looked like a bunch of fireflies trying to get near the light. She thought it was generous of his lordship to allow them their excitement, but apparently enough was enough. He quickly put an end to their questions and flattery.

He stepped away from the fanfare and greeted the Duchess of Aubry, before turning his attention to Catherine. He said, "I bid you good day, Lady Catherine. I see I have arrived early and that you are still engaged with company. I am happy to wait, but request that you do not keep my cattle waiting too long."

Catherine looked to her mother for clarification, but the duchess had no response, only perplexity graced her features. Catherine queried, "Forgive me, My Lord Rushton, are you suggesting I have an engagement with you?" She instantly bit her lower lip and wished she could retract her inquiry for it brought attention to her coming nuptials.

Rushton saw her discomposure and jumped to confirm that he understood the reason behind it. He replied with a grin, "Indeed, you do. My phaeton awaits us as soon as you bid your guests farewell."

Catherine was ready to give the arrogant man that stood before her a proper set down. She thought him quite confident to think she would dance to his tune. If she had not wanted an excuse to escape the exhausting company she was currently engaged, she would have done just that, but instead she extended her apologies to her guests and summoned a servant to collect her pelisse and hat. Apparently, she thought with chagrin, *"I am dancing to this man's tune."* Stiffly, she inquired, "Our destination, my lord?"

"Hyde Park, my lady. I thought we could give my cattle their legs, since we will make our jaunt before the proclaimed social hour when the *ton* arrives to promenade along *Rotten Row*."

The duchess quickly exclaimed, "Lord Rushton! You will be careful."

Before he could respond, his friend, Lord Brenner announced, "No need to worry, Duchess, Rushton is a capital whip. His membership in the Four-in-Hand Club is proof of his skill."

Rushton smiled, took Catherine's arm and escorted her out the front door to his high perch phaeton. He was happy to see that her ladyship was indeed impressed with the sporting vehicle that gentlemen drove mostly when they wanted to drive fast or show off their driving skills. The seat was open on all sides perched high on a light well-sprung four wheel carriage. Rushton was pleased that Catherine did not balk at ascending to the high elevated bench. After settling Catherine, Rushton made his way around to the driver's side of the carriage to hop up and take his seat next to her. He quickly took the reins from the attending Aubry groom, before directing his team onto the avenue.

Catherine scolded, "That was very mischievous of you, my lord, and if I wasn't in need of escape, I would have chastised you accordingly for your underhandedness. Instead, since it is a glorious day and your phaeton is entertaining me immensely, I shall compliment your cleverness in securing my company in private."

"You are not afraid to be direct, my lady," he amused. "Well," he added, "I am not afraid to use the whip."

Catherine's eyes opened in fear and Rushton laughed when he cracked his whip over his cattle's hindquarters. They responded and sprang into a canter. Catherine jolted forward in her seat, believing she was about to meet her maker when she flew from her seat, but Rushton grabbed her and secured her safely. Amazed at his dexterity in managing her and his cattle, Catherine turned to him and queried, "It is true then, that you are a member of the Four-in-Hand Club?"

"Yes," he answered. "We are a small and arrogant group, even though it is all for folly. Still, being recognized by one's peers for superior horsemanship is humbling and I wear the title honorably."

Catherine was smiling when his lordship returned her to her front porch of her town home. She had enjoyed herself and was surprised that she could find delight in another man's company. Her thoughts were still consumed by Alistair, but Rushton had proven that he could make her laugh and lift her spirits. He was good company and not difficult to look at with his thick dark chocolate hair and light brown eyes. He had a strong chin, a straight nose and breathed an air of confidence that reminded her of Alistair. He was very eligible and she wondered when her father would announce her betrothal to him.

Rushton watched Catherine exit her town home with her abigail trailing her. He waited at the bottom of the steps to greet her and saw Catherine's eyes widen in surprise when she saw him. Days had passed since their jaunt to Hyde Park and Catherine thought his absence meant that did not wish to further an alliance with her, especially when he did not bother to call on her the next day. The rules that govern polite society dictated some form of acknowledgement when a gentleman paid particular attention to a lady. Catherine always received a visit or flowers from those gentlemen that kept her company, so she had expected a serious suitor, as Lord Rushton declared to be, to present himself the next day. She had waited at home to receive him and was disappointed when he only sent a bouquet of primroses along with his calling card to her. The flowers arrived without a personal message to mark them exceptional, so she interpreted his gesture as nothing more than good manners.

At first she felt slighted that the man had lost interest in her, but within the next day she discovered she was not truly bothered at all, except for wasting a day that she could have spent in a more entertaining way. Today, with Mary in tow, she was on her way to retrieve a special order in Piccadilly when she saw Lord Rushton waiting at the bottom of the steps for her with his beaver hat in his hand. He bent slightly at the waist to greet her.

Smiling, he said, "I am glad I have arrived in time to bid you good day, my lady. Where do you hasten?"

"I am on an errand of purchase, My Lord Rushton. What brings you to my doorstep?" she queried.

"I should think that is obvious," he smirked.

Catherine's eyes widened at his bold flirtation. She thought he was an awfully clever and experienced charmer. She wondered how many maidens had lost their heart to one so gallant. She acknowledged his wit amused her, but sadly he did not move her and Catherine could tell she did little to stir his feelings. His indifferent eyes betrayed him. There was no passion or wanting in them. She found herself thinking of Alistair and all the emotion that exuded from his eyes when he looked at her. She chastised herself for holding onto memories that served only to sadden her. She collected her wits and said, "I am sorry to disappoint you, my lord, but as you can see I was on my way out. Perhaps, you could return on Wednesday when we are home to receive guests." Catherine squinted her eyes at him to see how he would take her set down. She was amused to see him grin.

He replied, "I shall be sure to remember that Wednesdays you are thoroughly engaged and be joyful that providence nudged me to your doorstep on a day that grants me your singular attention."

Catherine laughed and replied, "Touché, my lord. I will have to remember that your tongue is clever and equal to anything I have to offer."

Rushton held his retort, for as intelligent as her ladyship was, he doubted that she had given him license to take their conversation to a more intimate level. He simply raised a brow in inquiry. It did not take long for Catherine to blush. She knew she was too inexperienced to volley flagrant remarks with him and bit her lower lip in frustration.

His lordship thought it quite charming to see Lady Catherine discomposed, but immediately sought to put her at ease. He said, "I do hope you will allow me to accompany you. I am at your disposal since I had planned to spend my day with you. Do not put me out of sorts trying to determine what else to do."

Catherine retorted, "You are pure fustian, my lord, for I know better than to think that a man of your consequence would be put out of sorts by a young woman like myself; but as you are good company and have a way about you that makes me cheerful, I grant you permission to accompany me."

"I am all gratitude," he replied with good humor.

It surprised Rushton to see that Catherine's errand took her to Hatchards, the esteemed bookshop in Piccadilly. The crowded bookstore frequented by many literary-minded people was a common meeting place for socializing. He asked, "Are you a great reader, my lady?"

"Not until of late," she replied. "I confess I am not one to sit idle to improve my mind. I am often too distracted to engage myself in reposing pursuits, but over the summer I was most industrious in inventorying the duke's esteemed collection. Somehow, I engrossed myself with the pleasure of it. I am far from a *bluestocking*, but am taking pride in completing whatever book I have started to read."

"May I ask what you have read this summer?"

"You may ask, my lord," she teased, "but I will only confess that it was of interest to the feminine line and would not be to your taste."

He retorted, "You may be wrong to censure me, my lady. I am of the mindset that reading all styles of literature is beneficial. I myself have even read Byron, not because I think it stellar, but because our society so enjoys the cant. How could I hold any opinion, unless I have subscribed at least once to it."

"You are most wise, my lord."

"And you are a flatterer, my lady, so, tell me, are you browsing or are you here to pick up an order?"

"A special order. If you will excuse me, I will conclude my business and then if you are still in a mind to accompany me, you may take me for a spot of tea before escorting me home."

Rushton admired that Catherine knew what she liked and did not seem to ask permission for those things she wanted. Nothing annoyed him more than a lady who could not make up her mind or needed to be informed on what preferences she owned. He watched Catherine from a distance wondering what the name of the book was that she had ordered. Unfortunately, the brown paper that wrapped the book concealed its identity. He expected it was one of Mrs. Radcliffe's gothic romance stories that were all the rage and wondered if she would eventually reveal the title to him.

They settled next door at the popular Fortnum and Mason's. The shop was renowned for their teas and gourmet food. Most everyone in the aristocracy, especially since the store was patronized by the royals, stopped to socialize and enjoy a midday meal after they shopped. During their repast of tea and cakes, Catherine noticed his lordship's eyes kept darting to the brown parcel she had placed on their table. She raised a brow to him and he responded, "Oh, come now, my lady. You must know by not revealing the title, you have made more of it than necessary. Why not tell me? Perhaps, I should add the tome to my own collection."

Catherine shook her head at Lord Rushton. She said, "My lord, I have already remarked that it is of a feminine interest and that I do not want to identify it to you. Pray, desist with your inquiries."

He countered, "If you will not reveal the title, then allow me to guess. Provide me with one clue, one character name, and if my guess is incorrect, I will bother you no more. However, if I guess correctly, then you shall read me your favorite passage from it. What do you say?"

Catherine grinned at his boyish ardor. She felt like a matron whose son was asking for a second helping of pudding. Lord Rushton only needed to exclaim, "please," to complete the comparison. Her grin widened to a smile and she relented, "Very well, my lord. I will name a character and if you guess the title of the book incorrectly, you will desist, agreed?"

"Agreed," he responded. He was reminded of the fable *Rumpelstiltskin* except, that old coot gave the queen three days to guess his name. He had only one guess, so he hoped the clue Catherine revealed was a good one. He should have asked for more guesses, but it was too late to renegotiate. He waited impatiently and could tell that Catherine was enjoying herself over his quandary.

She said, "Lord Orville is the name of a major character in the story."

"Lord Orville," repeated Rushton. He pondered the name and came up blank. After a few moments, he picked up his cup, drank the final drop of his tea and returned his cup to its saucer. He inquired, "Are you ready to take your leave?"

Catherine blinked her eyes in astonishment. She gasped, "What of your guess, my lord?"

He said, "I am not prepared to answer, as yet. Perhaps, you would like to give me another clue?"

"That was not part of our agreement," she chided.

"Alas," he retorted. "I disagree. I said I would desist if I guessed incorrectly. I have not yet guessed, so I am under no obligation to desist."

Catherine ground her lips together in disapproval and shook her head from side to side. She could not help but admire the gentleman's cleverness. She exclaimed with laughter, "You are nothing more than an imp, my lord. I am sorry I engaged in your folly for I see that your inquiries will not relent, will they?"

Rushton smiled. He proffered his arm to escort her home. He whispered, "I would not think of ending anything between us, my lady, that clearly adds to our amusement."

Chapter Sixteen

When Catherine returned home, the Town butler summoned, "Excuse me, milady, but his grace has arrived and commands you to attend him immediately."

It was moments like this when Catherine missed her family butler, Frenton. He would have assured her with the wink of an eye, that the duke was not about to berate her for some unknown indiscretion. The loyal servant had remained at Aubry with her grandmother because the lady refused to travel after her recent fatiguing journey. The dowager told Catherine that she would see her and her betrothed when they returned to Aubry for the holidays. Catherine knew her grandmother owned a sterner constitution to believe she could not make the trip. Instead, she guessed the dowager felt guilty about pushing Catherine into a contracted marriage and did not have the wherewithal to see it to completion.

After visiting the Duchess of Rutland at Belvoir, the dowager returned home to learn that Mr. Chapman and the Litfords had been guests at Aubry. She listened while Jason recalled the picnic and treasure hunt. The dowager was surprised when her grandson spoke respectfully of Mr. Chapman as though he was a peer. The information explained Catherine's lackluster persona and she felt wretchedly guilty for her part in her granddaughter's heartbreak. It saddened her that she could not support an alliance between Catherine and Mr. Chapman, no matter how genuine the ardor, especially when the chasm of class was so great.

Catherine removed her hat and pelisse, handing them to an attending maid, before making her way to the duke's study. She knocked and waited to be bid "enter." She was happy to see that a smile graced her father's face and felt her nervousness dissipate. She walked over to where the duke sat behind his imposing writing desk and when he motioned her to take a seat, she lowered herself onto the wing chair that faced him,.

The duke exclaimed, "Ah, good, Catherine! I see you are home. The duchess tells me that your bridal clothes are near completion and that you have spent time with Lord Rushton."

"Yes, Papa, that is correct," she answered.

"Well then, are you content with Mr. Rushton for your betrothed?" he asked.

"My heart is not engaged, Papa," she responded. "I believe I mentioned that to grandmama when you asked her to review the list of candidates with me. I will abide by your decision. Lord Rushton has proven himself to be amiable."

The duke was disturbed by his daughter's lack of feeling. "Amiable" was not a word to describe a man you wanted to marry. It was not a bad word, simply not an amorous one. He had allied himself to his best advantage when he married, but he owned he never obtained the level of satisfaction in his marriage that he had witnessed in his parents. Their marriage was full of emotion that teetered from angst to sheer pleasure, unlike his marriage where emotions rarely flared. He had a pleasant and comfortable alliance. He had an amiable marriage, yet he had hoped more for his daughter.

Catherine's birth came late in his life and because she was a girl he held a tender heart for her. He knew he was more lenient towards her than he was with his sons, for whom he demanded much. Her lackluster persona regarding her betrothal alarmed him.

He proceeded, "Well, Catherine, if you are not set on Lord Rushton, then I have recently received an offer for you of whom I would like you to consider. The choice is yours, but I have just spent the last fortnight in the gentleman's company and I must say I found him most impressive. He was also very interested in learning about your person which I found favorable. Most offers made for your hand are interested in your dowry; he seemed not to care of your wealth, but of your interests. He is aware of your hoyden tendencies: riding, hunting, fishing and he did not balk at them. I think you will find him to be the most accommodating of husbands which pleases me for I would not like to see your spirit broken. He is extremely eligible, owning both title and fortune. You met his father the Marquis of Gracemoor at the DeRos Ball this past season."

She shrieked, "Oh, Papa! Do not tell me it was that lord who was so gauche as to contract for me in my presence. Surely, his son is of the same mind. How can you be tricked into believing he is interested in me as a person and not an asset?"

"Do not be churlish, Catherine," he chided. "My Lord Gracemoor may be candid, but he is far from gauche. It was not him who promoted the match but his own son, Lord Mercer. He is a friend of your favorite cousin, Edward, whose opinion I solicited. Edward hails Lord Mercer to be the best of men and believes you would be agreeable to the match. I have invited Mercer to dine with us this evening. I expect that you will be the gracious daughter that I know you are capable of being. Remember Catherine, that you placed your trust in me to make you the best alliance."

She apologized, "Oh, Papa, I do trust you. Please forgive me. I will be the best of daughters and will give Lord Mercer the same opportunity to advance his offer as I gave Lord Rushton."

The duke replied, "Very good and Catherine you may be pleased to know that Mercer is an advocate for improving the industry conditions for textile workers. I know the cause is dear to you."

"Really," remarked Catherine. "Thank you, Papa. I am now even more intrigued to make the acquaintance of Lord Mercer."

Catherine entered the parlour to see the duke engaged with a gentleman she assumed was Lord Mercer, for his back was to her. The duchess sat near her favorite mahogany side table that owned the space between the parlour windows. A candelabrum on the marble tabletop gave off enough light for her mother to work on her embroidery. The Duchess of Aubry had never been a great hostess and she preferred, when offered, to remain in anonymity rather than be the auspicious center of attention. She gratefully relinquished the task of entertaining Lord Mercer to her husband. Catherine knew her mother was not well esteemed among the *bon ton* for her timorous ways. They thought her a meek duchess and disliked her for it. The duchess cared little for what was said of her in the parlour rooms. The duke had assured her it mattered not, whether she was liked or not. Only her opinion as one of the highest ranking peers of the aristocracy, aside from royalty, mattered. He reminded her that her silver salver always overflowed with invitations and that truism always comforted her.

"Catherine," called the duke. "Let me introduce you to our guest."

Catherine made her way to where the duke stood with Lord Mercer. As he began the introduction, Lord Mercer turned to greet her. Familiar bright eyes and a warm smile overwhelmed Catherine. The duke continued, "Mercer, may I present my daughter, Lady Catherine. Daughter, meet the Earl of Mercer."

Catherine balked when she saw Alistair introduced as the Earl of Mercer. She worried that he would be hung for impersonating a nobleman and then she remembered that her father had spent the last fortnight at Gracemoor where he was introduced to the marquis's son. Then, Catherine's temper began to rise when she remembered her father had consulted Edward, who knew enough of her feelings to proclaim that she would be "agreeable" to the Earl of Mercer's offer for her hand.

The duke noted Catherine's lack of speech and said, "I have never known you with nothing to say, Catherine, are you well?"

She gasped out a reply, "Actually Papa. I am afraid I have contracted a terrible headache. I only came down to make Lord Mercer's acquaintance. If you will forgive me, I shall retire."

"Yes, of course," he replied.

Alistair took Catherine's hand and placed a kiss on its backside. She gaped at his boldness. A part of her was shocked that such a simple gesture could bring forth an abundance of emotions. She did not know if the reason for her heightened feelings were because it was the first kiss he ever bestowed on her or because she remembered all the times he had refused to kiss her.

She heard him say, “I will call on you tomorrow to see how you fare, my lady. If you are better, perhaps you will allow me to convey you to Hyde Park where we may become better acquainted on the jaunt. I am sure you have a lot of questions for me.”

Catherine made a simple nod, retrieved her hand, curtsied and retired to her room. She fell to her bed, chastising herself for not tugging her bell cord to summon her abigail. The make-believe headache she conveniently used as an excuse to leave the parlour, now debilitated her. Her head relentlessly throbbed. She had no will to rise and ring for her maid, so she turned over and draped her arm over her eyes, not knowing whether to cry or laugh. What did it all mean? While her mind tried to organize her feelings and thoughts, Catherine was relieved to hear Mary enter and say, “Here, milady. I have made a tisane for you. Try to sit up and drink it. It will relieve your head pain.”

She whispered, “How did you know I needed this?”

Mary answered, “The duchess may be quiet, milady, but she sees all. She ordered the remedy for you to drink and commanded me to attend to your needs.”

Catherine managed a smile and said, “Ah! Thank heavens for mothers who love their daughters.” Catherine swallowed the bitter drink and then started to lie down again.

Mary begged, " Wait, milady! Let us get you in your night clothes and then you may go to bed."

Catherine did not argue. She allowed Mary to remove her clothes and make her ready for bed. Then she laid her head down and bid her maid to leave. Mary refused and Catherine found she was happy to have someone near, who promised that all would be well again soon.

Catherine's night was not restful. Her mind was filled with Alistair. From their first meeting he had intrigued her and every meeting thereafter, affecting her both emotionally and physically. There was as much comfort as angst when she was in his company. One moment she could feel at peace and safe; another had her ire rising enough that she wanted to plant him a *facer*, though it seemed she was always happy to be in his company. She was pretty sure she loved him, for no one else could hold her thoughts or affection as he did. Even though he had rejected her advances, she knew the reason he did not pursue her was because he believed she was incapable of quitting the sphere to which she was born. Yet now, with the revelation of his status, it was clear that he owned equal responsibility for their unrequited love, since he was always in a position to court her. His refusal to do so proved how inconsequential she was to him. Now he had offered for her. It was more than she could comprehend.

When Alistair presented his calling card to the Aubry butler the next day, he feared he might not be received. He had made a grievous error to surprise Catherine with his noble lineage. He thought she would be ecstatic to learn that he was indeed worthy of her affection. Instead, he had caused her to be ill, out of shock or disgust, he did not know. He had let his heart guide him to kiss her hand and when she did not repel from his attentions, he felt lighthearted. Her hand had trembled slightly, so he was sure that she was not indifferent to him. He hoped to make everything well between them today with his explanation, but first he needed to be received.

Catherine watched the butler enter and present Lord Mercer's calling card to her mother. The Duchess of Aubry asked her, "Are we at home for Lord Mercer?"

"Yes, Mama. I have accepted his invitation for a jaunt through Hyde Park. I promised papa I would receive him with alacrity."

The duchess returned the card to the silver salver the butler held and commanded him to bid Lord Mercer entrance. Then, she spoke to her daughter. "If you promised the duke to receive Lord Mercer with cheerful readiness, then I fear daughter that you are failing miserably. Are you sure you wish to see him? I am happy to make your regrets and spend the required quarter of the hour with him."

Catherine knew how her mother hated to singularly receive unknown guests and was warmed at her generous offer. She smiled and said, "Thank you, Mama, but I am well. I believe the brisk air will do my countenance good. I will meet my obligation."

"Very well, Catherine. It will be as you wish."

Alistair followed the butler into the parlour where he made his greetings first to the duchess and then to Catherine. "I am happy that you have recovered, my lady," he remarked, "for I would have been sorely disappointed to have been refused your company."

Catherine nodded her head and rose. She graced her mother's cheek with a kiss. She realized she could not remember the last time she had done so, for the blush that rose up her mother's face and the pleasure she witnessed in her mother's eyes, gave evidence that she was negligent in showing her mother affection.

As they crossed the Aubry threshold to exit her town home, she saw out of the corner of her eye Lord Rushton approaching. By the time they reached the bottom of the steps they had joined each other's company. He spoke first, "I see I am too late to secure your company, my lady." Lord Rushton surveyed Alistair with an air of arrogance. Catherine could see that both men were assessing each other and she wanted to avoid any unseemly behavior, so she remarked, "I am sorry, my lord, did we have a prior engagement that my memory has failed to remember?"

He replied, "No, I am here only because it delights me so to be in your company." Rushton noticed that the gentleman tightened his grip on the hand that Catherine rested on his arm in escort and his protective instincts surfaced. He became aware of Catherine's weary demeanor. He wondered if she was under duress, being forced to accompany the man that was unknown to him. He queried, “Are you well, my lady? Perhaps, you should defer your outing for another time. I would be happy to escort you back to the sanctity of your home.”

Catherine smiled at Rushton's concern and his lordship's face brightened from her benevolence. She thought that he was awfully gallant to be worried over her welfare, noting his manner was a desirable trait for a husband. She responded, “You are very kind, my lord, but I am quite well, aside from a restless night’s sleep. Forgive me, I have been negligent. Allow me to introduce his lordship, the Earl of Mercer to you. Lord Mercer, this is his lordship, the Earl of Rushton.” Both gentlemen made their nod in greeting. Alistair did not wait on ceremony to excuse themselves, he pushed Catherine on and helped her into his phaeton.

Rushton was quick to remark to the departing Catherine, “I will pick you up this evening, my lady, as promised. You are still to attend the Cleveland Ball?”

“Yes, thank you, my lord,” she replied.

On her last word, Alistair cracked the reins to leave Rushton in his own company. He was not feeling generous at the moment, allowing his temper to get the better of him. With no sense of decorum, he chided, “Who was that gentleman, Catherine?”

She answered, “I thought he was my betrothed.”

“You have accepted him?” he gasped.

"No, but the duke favors him," she answered curtly, her own ire beginning to rise. She turned to rail at Alistair, "I once told you that it did not matter who I married, since the man I wanted was not available."

Alistair bellowed, "Well, I am available now!"

"Well," she countered. "Maybe, I have changed my mind. Maybe, I am not interested in a man that could cause me injury on a whim. It is obvious that you lied when you said our stations made an alliance between us impossible. I misjudged your character, my lord. You are not worthy of me."

"I may not be worthy of you, Catherine, but I did not lie. I had forsaken my title and wealth. I indeed prospered only as Beaumont's man of business. As such, I was not an eligible suitor, no matter how much I wanted to be. I cared too much for you to place you in a position that would never make you happy."

She asked, "Yet, how is it that you are eligible now?"

"I took your advice," he replied. "I returned home to resolve the issues with my father that caused me in anger to relinquish my title and inheritance."

"I am happy that you are at peace, my lord, for that was your greatest desire," she responded, "but, I do not see how that is of consequence to me. I offered you my heart and you chose to refuse it. You did not honor me with your trust, confide in me your situation, or have any faith that together we could find a resolution. These truths alone, show me that you never loved me. I do not know why you have come, other than to provoke me further for your amusement."

"You will allow me to explain, Catherine. It was because of you that I am finally at peace and can look to my future. Did you know I was born second son? My brother Erik was the rightful heir. From birth he was groomed to take my father's place and he would have made a magnificent marquis. He was everything that a lord should be and he was betrothed to a girl name Laurie, someone I loved like a sister."

Alistair was happy that Catherine was listening to him. She had not interrupted him and he could feel her compassion. She knew he was about to reveal an unhappy tale and while recalling the tragedy of Erik's and Laurie's death was difficult, Alistair found the confession uplifting.

"When Erik died, my father and I learned that both Erik and Laurie had precipitated their wedding vows. She was nearly three months with child and beginning to exhibit symptoms that would have the staff speculating. My father immediately confined her to her room under the pretense of grief, which was indeed truthful. He pressed us both to wed to legitimize Erik's child. While my mind agreed with my father's assessment, I balked. I claimed it was too soon after Erik's death and fought for time. Laurie seemed to appreciate my efforts to stall the wedding, though I am not now sure that she knew her own mind. She was so wrapped in her grief that I doubt she even remembered she was with child. She slept most of the day and when she did receive me, her eyes held so much pain that I never kept her company for long. Looking back, I believe my own sorrow was mirrored in her eyes. I did not want to replace Erik. I never craved what was his. I was glad to be second son. You see, I admired my brother and loved him very much. His death was insurmountable."

"I will not recall Laurie's demise. It is too tragic to describe, but I will tell you that both my father and I grieved and reacted strongly. He accused me of neglecting my duty to marry and care for Laurie. I accused him of pressing Laurie to the point that she chose death over an alliance with me. Our guilt over her loss shamed us into acting horridly to one another, at a time when we could have offered each other comfort. I left and I thought I had secreted myself away as Beaumont's man of business. Recently, I learned that my father kept track of me. I am grateful he never contacted me for it would have been ruinous. It took you, Catherine, to help heal me. Your compassion, wisdom and love helped me overcome my grief and guilt. Although it was unspoken, I felt your love. I know you felt my ardor, even though I never professed it. My father and I have reconciled and in doing so, I have secured my inheritance. I would not offer for you unless I could provide for you in a style you are accustom. I can do that now, Catherine, and I want to marry you."

Catherine clenched her fists that lay in her lap. Her eyes filled with tears. Her heart ached for the pain he suffered, but what of her anguish? He claimed he loved her, but how could that be when he did not trust her enough to share his burdens with her. It was too much to comprehend. She felt overwhelmed. With her head hung, she said, "Please take me home, Alistair. I am not well."

Extremely frustrated, Alistair turned his phaeton around and replied, "As you wish, Catherine, but this conversation is not over. You know we belong together."

Chapter Seventeen

Alistair did not like to see Catherine miserable and accepted his fault in making her feel ill-used. He would find a way to prove to her that he loved her, but would not push her now. He heeded the silence, not breaking it until he relinquished her to the Aubry butler. Alistair bid Catherine farewell, saying, "I will call on you tomorrow, my lady."

Without thinking, Catherine nodded her head and entered her home. She never looked back or else she would have seen Alistair's bleak and downtrodden face. Had she snatched a glance, then all her doubts regarding his feelings for her would have been assuaged. Instead, her mind battled her heart in trying to discern Alistair's motives for wanting to marry her. Did he love her or was he fulfilling his father's wishes in order to receive his inheritance. He had wanted peace, but at what cost? Was a contracted marriage to her his only solution to mend the breach with his father?

She started to climb the stairs to her private suite when she realized she could not come to any conclusions on her own. She retreated to the lower floor and asked an attending footman if the duke was home. He replied that he thought his grace was in his study, so Catherine made her way there. His door was shut and she hesitated before knocking on what he considered his sanctuary. She wished she had asked the footman if he had a visitor, for she remembered the duke did not like to be interrupted. However, upon further reflection, she knew she could not wait and rapped a loud tattoo on his door. She heard the duke bid, "Come," and she entered.

"Ah, Catherine," he greeted. "How did you enjoy your ride with Lord Mercer?"

Catherine came forward after shutting the door behind her. She took the wing chair that resided in front of the duke's imposing and ornamentally carved writing desk. She felt weary and her father remarked on it. He asked, "Catherine, have you another migraine? You do not look well. Should I call for our Town physician?"

"I do not need a physician, Papa. I am merely weary, not ill. Actually, I am troubled and beg your counsel."

"What is it, Catherine?"

"Did you know that Lord Mercer masqueraded as Beaumont's man of business and that I knew him as a Mr. Alistair Chapman?"

"The simple answer is, yes, but I do not think Mercer masqueraded. I believe he was quite competent in his duties to Beaumont and he did not assume an alias. If you studied *Debrett's,* our esteemed guide to our peerage, as you are expected, then you would know that Chapman is Gracemoor's family name."

In her chagrin, Catherine nodded and agreed, "You are right, Papa, but I do not understand why he has offered for me, when he refused any advance I made to him." She blushed at her candidness and bent her head in shame. "Did Edward tell you that he misled me to believe he was common?"

The duke answered, "Yes, but I heard it first from Mercer."

The Duke of Aubry saw that his daughter was quite overcome. An overwhelming emotion pushed him to rise from his seat and walk around his desk to console her. He grabbed her by her shoulders and roughly pulled her up to a standing position. Out of character for his normally stiff manner, he enfolded her in a tight hug. Catherine began to cry and the duke bellowed, "There now, Catherine! Do not become a watering pot, or else I will have to summon the duchess and excuse myself, even though I am sure she is no better qualified than I am to soothe you."

Catherine laughed. She quickly collected herself, took a large breath, exhaled, and then backed herself away from her father. The duke offered, "I admit I like Mercer, especially for placing your happiness before his own. I spent quite a bit of time with him at Gracemoor. I believe he holds you in the highest regard and will do all in his power to make you happy. I do not think he meant to confess to me how very highly he esteems you, but it was clear he admires both your beauty and spirit. I was moved by how well he understands your need to contribute in both body and mind. I felt that as your husband, he would grant you liberties uncommon for ladies in our society. You have opinions, Catherine, that are hard to regulate. I feared your willfulness would never bode you well in a conventional marriage; but, Mercer seems to delight in your wit, intelligence, and fortitude. He is a man I trust to appreciate your special qualities, versus despise those assets that I have always found endearing. It takes a special man to concede defeat in gentlemanly sports, without finding fault in the victor, especially a woman."

"He told you of our competitions?"

The duke laughed and said, "Yes. I think you were hard-pressed to own a victory, for I can think of no other reason for engaging poor Ulysses in your folly. Mercer assured me he came to no harm."

Catherine grinned and concurred, "He came to no harm, Papa, but I wish you could have seen Lord Mercer's face when he was presented with your trusted and retired steed. That in itself, made me feel the victor."

The duke interjected, "Your face alights when you speak of him, Catherine. I wish to see you happy, so choose wisely. I will tell you Gracemoor spoke highly of him even when they were estranged. The marquis blames himself for their separation, though I know not the reasons for their break. I have thoroughly investigated him and found him a worthy candidate for your hand. Even

Beaumont and your cousin, Edward, praise him. It was your cousin, Edward, who informed me that he thought you favored him and for those reasons, I allowed him to present himself to you. However, Lord Rushton is a superior man and a most eligible suitor, as well. You could do no wrong in selecting him. I should tell you that Rushton approached me this afternoon, asking if he could declare himself to you. I believe your jaunt with Mercer may have provoked him to do so, but I told him that you had requested for me to settle your betrothal and that at present, I had more than one offer to consider. He was not happy when he left. The choice is yours, Catherine."

"I am not sure whether to trust my heart or my head, Papa." She confessed, "I think I will rest before I leave for the ball." She gave a bleak smile and added, "Lord Rushton is to escort me."

Catherine's station dictated that she marry a titled lord of distinction. She decided that only an honest assessment would help her to choose the right man to marry, since Lord Rushton and Lord Mercer were both very eligible suitors.

Rushton offered her a *marriage of convenience*. He wanted a marriage to set up his nursery and contracted for an alliance that would increase his connections and wealth. She would reap the same benefit as he, obtaining a marriage of stature. Catherine thought him a gallant man, a handsome man, and was confident that he would be respectful of her needs and do his best not to put her out of sorts. They were amiable with one another and based on the attention he gave her, she expected that they could probably continue to live their own lives without much interference, only meeting for the occasional tryst to grow their family and for the intermittent public appearance that showed they were indeed married.

Mercer's offer of marriage, on the other hand, was not easily discernable. She wasn't sure how they would manage, for one moment she adored him and the next instant she wanted to throttle him. He had hurt her with his lies and indifference to her ardor. She questioned whether his admiration would be constant. She felt vulnerable with him and she was not sure it was a good thing. While she could succinctly explain why she should marry Lord Rushton, she found herself adverse to the alliance, simply because of her feelings for Alistair; emotions that had already caused her too much suffering. Rushton had not made her suffer. She realized that she did not own those tender feelings for him that made her feel defenseless. She could almost say she was indifferent to him, even though she liked him and enjoyed his company.

Catherine stood before her full length gilt wood mirror. She wore one of her new ball gowns that made up her bridal clothes. As she saw her mirror image, she was not surprised to notice a remarkable change in her countenance. Not too long ago, she would have been prancing and twirling her skirts, feeling pretty, thinking about all the admirers that would flock to her and wonder which one, if any, she would favor with her attentions. At present, she spied herself bedecked in an off the shoulder short sleeve sapphire net dress over a matching satin slip that complimented her blue eyes and décolletage. The low cut square bodice was decorated with sapphire beads that trailed onto her sleeves, its border trimmed in puckered satin. Her single flounced skirt gave her figure a trim and regal stature. She looked aristocratic and sophisticated. No one would mistake her for a green girl out of the schoolroom, especially since she was not wearing the pastel colors that marked a young debutante. A year ago, Catherine did not know what she wanted out of life. The woman upon whose reflection Catherine studied, knew exactly what she wanted. Catherine turned to bid whoever knocked on her door to enter. It was time to leave. Lord Rushton had arrived. It was time to settle her future.

The Cleveland Ball was well attended for the Little Season. Anyone of any consequence that was residing in Town was present. Lady Cleveland only needed some type of scandal to make her ball a complete success. The ballroom glowed from the crystal chandeliers and brass sconces that lined the wall. Her ladyship had instructed her servants to festoon evergreen and cream colored ribbons over the windows and doorways. She placed classic Greek stone sculptures between the windows and strategically decorated the rest of the room with pots of verdant plants and miniature sculptured shrubbery.

The music from a string quartet floated through the room. Catherine stood with Lord Rushton near a secluded alcove enjoying a glass of lemonade, in lieu of partnering him in a dance. As usual, her card was full and even though she was distracted with her coming betrothal, she found her adeptness allowed her to dance in rote with each of her partners. She nodded and smiled at her admirers who attempted to converse with her, so skilled was she that no one aside from Lord Rushton was aware of her indifference.

She was watching the brouhaha over Lord Mercer, whose presence was creating quite a stir, assuring Lady Cleveland that her ball would indeed create the *on dits* necessary to call it a success. Being absent for five years, Mercer was new to the scene and the *marriage mart mamas* were hovering around him to introduce their young unmarried daughters. No sooner did Mercer break free from an interview than Lady Cleveland brought someone else to be introduced. Catherine watched from afar, forgetting her escort, Lord Rushton, was at her side. His lordship was keenly aware of Catherine's changed disposition. He saw that she was captivated by Mercer's popularity. Only a fool would ignore that she had a *tendress* for him.

He asked, "Who is he, my lady?"

"Who is who, my lord?" she queried.

Rushton discerned, "Lord Mercer. Does he rival me for your favor?"

Catherine was prepared to make a coquettish remark, but was too weary. She simply responded, "Yes."

Rushton besmirched a grin, and remarked, "I always forget how candid you are, my lady." He assessed her before continuing. "Is he the reason behind your changed mood? You seem distracted."

"Yes," she answered again. She looked into Rushton's eyes and said, "He has offered for me in earnest, my lord. I fear that if I refuse him that it will cause him great injury." Catherine's uncensored remarked helped her to realize that she no longer doubted the sincerity of Alistair's offer of marriage. She had no doubt that he loved her. She sincerely looked at Lord Rushton to try and discern what was in his heart. After a momentary reflection, she admitted, "I know that an alliance between us would be most exceptional, my lord, but I am sure that if I refused your very respectable offer that you would not be injured. I think you would rebound quite nicely."

Rushton laughed, professing, "You give my admiration little credit, my lady. I think we would do very well together. Do not think I am indifferent to you."

Catherine retorted, "You are kind, my lord, and I believe you would do all to make our marriage amiable, but I do not think you love me."

Rushton was speechless. One did not contract a marriage for love. He replied, "We are recently met, my lady. My feelings are not engaged, but over time I would expect our affections to naturally grow."

"I would hope so," she continued. "In honesty, I was determined to open myself to that possibility."

He prodded, "But now, you are not?"

"You will, I think forgive me, my lord, for being fickle?"

"You need not ask. Does he know you have chosen him?"

Catherine confessed, "No, my lord. In fact, I was so out of temper with him this afternoon that I refused to listen to his declaration."

Rushton laughed. He then asked, "Do you not know your own heart, my lady?"

Catherine grinned. She had struggled with her feelings, analyzing every word and action that Alistair had ever made towards her. She had questioned whether she could trust him to make her happy, but by being honest with Rushton, she accepted what her heart long ago knew. She replied, "Yes, I do know my own heart. Thank you, my lord, for helping me to listen to it."

She added, "You know, my lord. I am very weary. Would you mind summoning my maid and escorting me home. I think I am to have a busy day tomorrow and would like to retire early."

"I am at your service, my lady." Rushton proffered his arm and escorted Catherine into the great hall to await his carriage.

Alistair did not sleep well. He realized it was a mistake to attend the Cleveland Ball. He had arrived too late to secure a dance on Catherine's card and found himself the whole evening surrounded by a plethora of fawning debutantes. It seemed he was a novelty having been absent for five years. Everyone wanted to know where he had been hiding himself. As much as he tried, he could not break free from the hoards of females that kept him from seeking Catherine out. He had to settle for the few glimpses he caught of her dancing or promenading to and from the dance floor.

He remembered seeing her and Lord Rushton in what seemed to be a serious interview. He was not concerned until they left together. Then, he felt as though the floor had fallen from beneath his feet. He guessed that she had made her decision. At first, he was surprised and then he was not. Catherine had accused him of not trusting her and had argued that love could not flourish without it. He had said he would call on her today, but for what purpose? He was no fool, or was he?

Early that morning, Catherine had sought an interview with the duke to inform him that she had decided upon Lord Mercer for her betrothed. She had spent the whole night examining her feelings and knew she could not overcome the love she felt for Alistair. She told the duke that although Lord Rushton was a most exceptional and thoughtful admirer, she saw little hope of happiness with him when her heart was already engaged to Lord Mercer; and although she was sure that Alistair would test her patience and countenance, she would rather be irked in love than comfortable in friendship.

The duke smiled and said, “As you wish, Catherine. I will allow him to pay his addresses to you when he calls upon me."

Three o’clock passed without interruption while Catherine waited for Alistair to call. At half past the hour, she entered her father’s study and asked, “Papa, I am sorry to disturb you. I know it is quite bold of me to ask, but has Lord Mercer come and gone without my knowledge?”

He answered, "I have not been alerted to any visitors, Catherine."

She remarked, “I expected him to call on me today. His absence concerns me.”

“Then I will send him a reminder that he is expected,” replied the duke.

The Duke of Aubry remained home to wait for Lord Mercer and thought his daughter’s suitor finally arrived when Catherine once again entered his study. He was thoroughly put out to learn that not only was the man absent, but that his daughter was overly concerned with worry. She then astounded him with a request to visit his lodgings.

"No, Catherine. I will not have you visiting a bachelor's residence. I will send two stout footmen and they shall bring him to me."

"You must not, Papa," she begged. "I will not create fodder for the *gossipmongers*. As you know, the footmen, no matter how loyal, would comment on their errand. I have enough pride to keep me from making a public spectacle, though I would easily humble myself to him in private. If you will not allow me to go to him, then will you seek him out for me?"

Catherine's wretched face persuaded him. "Very well, Catherine, but you will remain at home until I return."

"Yes, thank you, Papa. Did you suffer this much trouble in securing your marriage to mama?"

The duke ground his lips together before replying, "No, Catherine, I did not. However, had I had to overcome the tribulations that seem to have marked your courtship, then perhaps, I might have appreciated gaining your mother's hand in marriage more."

"It is not too late, Papa," she replied.

The duke queried, "Too late, for what?"

"To appreciate your wife," replied Catherine. Then, she curtsied and retreated to her bedroom suite, but not before alerting her butler that she was not receiving callers.

Catherine felt enough time had passed for her father to have sought out Alistair to learn of his intentions towards her, so she could not understand why the duke had not returned home and summoned her with news. She decided to see if he was in his study. She descended the main staircase and entered the main hall where she heard the voice of Lord Rushton. Her butler was informing him that Lady Catherine was not receiving callers. Catherine had issued the order because she did not wish to be engaged in company when her father returned. She was now sorry that her concerns over Alistair had kept her from being thoughtful towards any guests that presented themselves. She hastened her steps towards Lord Rushton and exclaimed, "Thank you, but I will receive his lordship."

"Very good, my lady," replied the butler.

"My lady," regarded Rushton. "I would not impose upon you. I come not only because protocol demanded it, but because my curiosity needed to be put to rest."

Catherine understood that etiquette required Rushton to call on her or send her flowers, since he had escorted her the night before to the Cleveland Ball, but she did not understand his curiosity, unless it had to do with her betrothal to Alistair. She thought it churlish and out of character for a man of Rushton's consequence. She asked, "Pray, my lord, enlighten me. What are you curious about?"

Rushton thought it odd that Catherine had not asked him into the parlour. He was happy that at least the butler had shut the door behind him and had taken his greatcoat and hat. He noted Catherine's frigid demeanor and wondered why she looked so put out. Then, he started to laugh, understanding how he had offended her. He said, "Do not think so ill of me, my lady. Do you think I have come to learn of your affairs? No, no, I came to discover the name of the novel where Lord Orville plays your hero. I own I did not use much industry to uncover the title. Alas, I only consulted a few of my peers who knew nothing of your hero. I had hoped you would enlighten me before our company desisted."

Catherine's countenance relaxed. She replied, "I told you it was of a feminine sensibility. I do not know why you would think to ask your peers. You would have been better served to ask you mama."

"Indeed," grinned Rushton. "Well, tell me now, since the answer awaits me, if not here than with dear mama."

"You are very incorrigible, my lord," she replied, "but, since I am no longer a debutante who is easily embarrassed to reveal her romantic tendencies, I will tell you that *Evelina*, written by Francis Burney, is the tome you seek."

"Ah," replied Rushton. "The esteemed Madame D'Arblay."

"You know her?"

"I met her once when I was a boy attending court with my mother. You know she was "Second Keeper of the Robes" to our dear queen for a number of years. She was declared a "wit" by most, but I remember her warm smile and the wink she graced upon me." He prodded, "So, tell me, my lady. What was your favorite passage? Since I did not guess the title, you need not read it to me, but surely you can describe it to me."

Catherine answered, "You will be most disappointed that it was not a duel or adventure of some kind. My favorite part of the story was where Lord Orville confesses to Miss Anville, 'My heart is yours and I swear to you an attachment eternal.' You see, my lord. I am a true romantic, no different from any other female."

Rushton argued, "I disagree, my lady. Your passion and boldness to seek what you want, makes you very different from other ladies of our society. You are a jewel and I consider it my great loss that I cannot claim you as my own." He took her hand and gently kissed the back of it.

At that moment, Lord Mercer brushed past the butler to enter through the front door. Embarrassed at interrupting a tender moment between Rushton and Catherine, he exclaimed, "I beg your pardon. I did not mean to impose upon you. I came to see the duke."

The butler began to close the door when he saw his master approach. He reopened the door to welcome his grace, then took the duke's beaver hat and greatcoat. The duke exclaimed, "Ah, Mercer, good. You have come."

Rushton bellowed a guffaw. He looked at Mercer and then looked back to Catherine and said, "Lord Orville, I presume."

Before Catherine could speak, the duke escorted Mercer down the hall and out of her sight.

She looked back at Rushton who smiled at her discomfiture, he said, "I see you are engaged, my lady, and will take my leave. I wish you all felicitation and hope that you will honor me with your friendship for I give mine freely."

Catherine smiled and replied, "Thank you, My Lord Rushton. You do me great honor. You have my friendship and my greatest esteem. I bid you good fortune in all you seek." Rushton made his bow and he surprisingly left in good humor.

Alistair emerged a happy man from the duke's study. He quickly looked for Catherine. He found her in the library ensconced on a gilt painted green velveteen sofa reading a novel. He approached her in high spirit. She heard him enter and said, "Well, my lord, for one that is most capable managing the affairs of others, why is it that I find it is I, that own all industry in securing our union."

Alistair laughed. He grabbed her by the shoulders and pulled her to her feet. Looking into her eyes, he said, "Forgive me. I know we have had an uncommon affair and that I have been remiss in declaring that 'my heart is yours and I swear to you an attachment eternal.'"

Catherine gawked, "You read *Evelina*?"

"The moment you returned it," he answered. "I wanted to share in your amusements and when Rushton declared I was Lord Orville, it reminded me of how terribly I failed in professing my love to you. I may not have declared it openly to you, Catherine, but I owned the sentiment since the day you arrogantly strolled into Beaumont's study. I am, according to the duke, a most eligible gentleman, one I must add who would like to be removed from the *marriage mart*. So, tell me, Catherine, will you marry me?"

She retorted, "Will you kiss me?"

He smiled and asked, "Is it contingent to my proposal?"

Smirking, Catherine answered, "Most definitely."

Alistair pressed Catherine's body against his own with one hand and with the other he gently raised her chin to bring her lips to meet his. He lightly brushed his mouth against hers before embracing her in both arms and kissing her fully. He was overcome with emotion and before he lost all sense of decorum, he stepped back. He saw that Catherine's eyes were still closed. He asked, "Well, Catherine, will that do?"

She opened her eyes and responded, "Most definitely."

He prompted her again, "So, you will marry me, Catherine?"

She wrapped her arms around Alistair's neck to secure another kiss. Before their lips met, she replied, "Most definitely."

Acknowledgements

Thank you Alicia Floyd, my amazing editor for your astute corrections and insightful advice. I appreciate every happy face, correction and criticism you make.

Thank you Christina Brusaca for photographing the cover, Debby Ring for always answering my equine queries and my readers for giving my manuscripts your upmost attention.

I want to thank my friends and family, especially my husband Larry, my children, and my parents for whose support and encouragement I very much appreciate.

About the Author

Teresa Sweeney is a wife and mother of four adult children. She loves to read, write, and a myriad of other pursuits where she can use her creativity and imagination. She takes great pleasure penning historical romance novels that focus on the charm, wit, and banter of courtship. Visit her website www.teresa-sweeney.com for the latest information on her novels.

www.ingramcontent.com/pod-product-compliance
Lightning Source LLC
Chambersburg PA
CBHW030526310726
48979CB00010B/1818/J
* 9 7 8 1 9 4 0 3 1 9 0 2 5 *